"I'm not another one of your wounded chicks that you can cluck over and mother,"

Matt warned. "I'm a man, with a man's appetites."

His gaze dropped to her chest, and his eyes darkened. Maude Ann was about to protest, but instead a downward glance made her gasp. The front of her gown and robe were still sopping wet, and the thin fabric clung to her body like a second skin.

"Right now I'm not in any shape to do anything about those appetites, but I will be soon," he said. "Remember that the next time you come waltzing in here uninvited. You may get more than you bargained for."

Blushing from her hairline to her toes, Maude Ann stammered, "I—I was only trying to help."

"Oh? Is that what you were doing just now? *Helping* me…?"

Dear Reader,

Welcome to a spectacular month of great romances as we continue to celebrate Silhouette's 20ᵗʰ Anniversary all year long!

Beloved bestselling author Nora Roberts returns with *Irish Rebel,* a passionate sequel to her very first book, *Irish Thoroughbred.* Revisit the spirited Grant family as tempers flare, sparks fly and love ignites between the newest generation of Irish rebels!

Also featured this month is Christine Flynn's poignant THAT'S MY BABY! story, *The Baby Quilt,* in which a disillusioned, high-powered attorney finds love and meaning in the arms of an innocent young mother.

Silhouette reader favorite Joan Elliott Pickart delights us with her secret baby story, *To a MacAllister Born,* adding to her heartwarming cross-line miniseries, THE BABY BET. And acclaimed author Ginna Gray delivers the first compelling story in her series, A FAMILY BOND, with *A Man Apart,* in which a wounded loner lawman is healed heart, body and soul by the nurturing touch of a beautiful, compassionate woman.

Rounding off the month are two more exciting ongoing miniseries. From longtime author Susan Mallery, we have a sizzling marriage-of-convenience story, *The Sheik's Secret Bride,* the third book in her DESERT ROGUES series. And Janis Reams Hudson once again shows her flair for Western themes and Native American heroes with *The Price of Honor,* a part of her miniseries, WILDERS OF WYATT COUNTY.

It's a terrific month of page-turning reading from Special Edition. Enjoy!

All the best,

Karen Taylor Richman
Senior Editor

Please address questions and book requests to:
Silhouette Reader Service
U.S.: 3010 Walden Ave., P.O. Box 1325, Buffalo, NY 14269
Canadian: P.O. Box 609, Fort Erie, Ont. L2A 5X3

GINNA GRAY
A MAN APART

Silhouette®

SPECIAL EDITION®

Published by Silhouette Books
America's Publisher of Contemporary Romance

SILHOUETTE BOOKS

ISBN 0-373-24330-8

A MAN APART

This edition published by arrangement with Harlequin Books S.A.

® and TM are trademarks of Harlequin Books S.A., used under license. Trademarks indicated with ® are registered in the United States Patent and Trademark Office, the Canadian Trade Marks Office and in other countries.

Visit Silhouette at www.eHarlequin.com

Printed in U.S.A.

GINNA GRAY

A native Houstonian, Ginna Gray admits that, since childhood, she has been a compulsive reader as well as a head-in-the-clouds dreamer. Long accustomed to expressing her creativity in tangible ways—Ginna also enjoys painting and needlework—she finally decided to try putting her fantasies and wild imaginations down on paper. The result? The mother of two now spends eight hours a day as a full-time writer.

Don't miss Ginna's exciting new novel, *The Prodigal Daughter,* due out next month from MIRA Books!

Chapter One

More than a dozen policemen stood vigil in the corridor outside the hospital operating room. Every few minutes, more officers arrived to join the silent watch. When one of their own took a hit, the men and women in blue rallied around.

Less than an hour earlier, the frantic call had gone out over the police radio frequency.

"Shots fired! Shots fired! Officer down! We need assistance!"

Within seconds, every available man and woman on the Houston police force had raced to aid the besieged detectives at the scene of a drug bust gone bad.

Now, grim-faced and tense, those same men and women waited for news of their fellow officer's condition.

John Werner and Hank Pierson, the two men who were closest to the wounded officer, paced like caged lions, their faces dark and stony.

Guilt and worry ate at Hank like sharp-toothed animals. Dammit, it was his duty to protect his partner's back, and he had let Matt down. Now he might die. Matt had taken two bullets, and for that he blamed himself. Under a hail of automatic weapons' fire, hunkered down behind their squad car, he had radioed in the frantic call for assistance and fired random shots at the attackers over the hood of the vehicle, but beyond that he had been helpless.

Hank suddenly stopped pacing, and with an oath, he slammed the side of his fist against the wall. Several of the other policemen eyed him askance, but no one said a word.

Lieutenant Werner understood his detective's frustration and ignored the outburst.

As chief of detectives, John Werner felt a personal responsibility for every man and woman on his squad, but he shared a special friendship with the wounded officer. John had gone through the police academy with Matt's father. Patrick Dolan had been John's best friend and one of the finest officers the city had ever had.

That it was Matt Dolan who had been shot had spread like wildfire through the Houston Police Department. The news had stunned everyone and left them shaken. Matt was a smart, straight-arrow, tough cop, a twelve-year veteran on the force. He had seemed invincible.

The double doors of the operating room swung open and every officer in the hallway sprang to attention. A middle-aged man dressed in green scrubs emerged and flashed a look around at the crowd, meeting the anxious expressions with a grim look.

"I'm Dr. Barnes. Who's in charge here?" He raked the paper scrub cap off his head and absently massaged the tense muscles in his neck.

"I am." John Werner stepped forward. Hank edged up beside him. "How is he, Doc?"

"Alive. Just barely. The first bullet nicked his right lung. The second caused severe damage to his right leg. Plus, he lost a lot of blood before he arrived here. He's a tough nut, though, I'll give him that. If he weren't, he'd never have made it this far. But he is in bad shape."

"I see." John's jaw clenched and unclenched for several seconds. At last he asked the question that was foremost on his and every other officer's mind, the question to which they all dreaded the answer. "Is Matt going to make it, Doc?"

"Barring complications, yes."

"Thank God for that."

"Yes, well…I feel it's only fair to warn you, given the condition of that leg…well…"

"What? What're you trying to say, Doc?" Hank demanded.

"Just that…well…I think you should know that it's unlikely he will ever be able to return to police work. At least, not on the streets."

Matt turned his head on the pillow and gazed out the window at nothing in particular. The lady in the mist had come to him again last night.

The fanciful thought brought a hint of a smile to his stern mouth. Nevertheless, that was how he thought of the recurring dream that had plagued him all his life: a visitation by a phantom figure.

It was strange. For the past fifteen or twenty years he'd had the dream very infrequently—once or twice a year at the most—but since awaking in the hospital two weeks ago, it had been nightly. Not even the sleeping tablets the staff administered so faithfully had helped.

Absently, Matt fingered the jagged fragment of silver that hung from a chain around his neck, his thumb rubbing back and forth over the lines etched on either side. The pie-shaped wedge had been roughly cut from a silver medallion approximately two inches in diameter.

The instant Matt had regained consciousness he'd reached for the piece, and he'd panicked when he discovered it was no longer around his neck.

The medallion piece had been returned to him only because he had threatened to tear the place apart if it wasn't. The hospital prohibited patients from wearing jewelry of any kind. Matt, however, had worn the medallion fragment since he was a small boy, never taking it off.

Matt's fingers continued to rub the etched surface and jagged edges. Somehow, merely touching it seemed to soothe him. Particularly after a night of chasing after the lady in the mist.

He smiled again. The lady in the mist. He'd named the dream that years ago. It wasn't scary or in any way threatening—just him and others he couldn't identify, chasing through swirling mist after the shadowy figure of a woman, calling out to her, reaching for her as she backed away and disappeared—yet the experience always disturbed him. Invariably, he awoke with a start, his heart pounding. Last night had been no different. He wondered, as he had countless times, if he'd ever decipher the meaning behind the subconscious message.

Pushing the futile thought aside, Matt sighed and focused his attention elsewhere.

The impersonal atmosphere of the hospital made him feel adrift, removed from the world outside, a spectator with no part to play. Which, he supposed, was appropriate, since the life he had built for himself was most likely finished.

"Dammit, Matt, are you listening to me?"

John Werner stepped between the bed and the window, blocking Matt's view of the street and giving him no option but to acknowledge him. The older man glared, his jaw thrust forward. "I've put up with your silent treatment long enough. If you think you can just clam up and pretend I'm not here, like you've been doing to me and everyone else for the past two weeks, think again. I won't stand for it, you hear?"

John was a big bull of a man, standing six foot seven and weighing more than three hundred pounds. He had a broad, menacing face that looked as though it had been hewn from oak with a blunt ax and a voice that rumbled out like the wrath of God when he was angry. Most of the detectives on his squad cringed when he got on their cases.

Matt didn't turn a hair.

"I don't know what you're talking about."

"The hell you don't. You've had a steady stream of visitors—family and friends, the guys on the force, the department psychologist, even your doctors—but you barely talk to any of them. You just turn away and tune them out. The few times you have bothered to speak was just to bite someone's head off. Well, it won't work with me. Like it or not, we're going to talk about this."

"There's nothing to talk about."

"Oh, no? How about the fact that you've refused all the offers of help you've received? Huh? How about that? Hank here has practically begged you to come stay with him and his wife while you recuperate. So have several others, but you've turned them all down flat." He nodded toward Hank Pierson, who stood on the other side of the room watching his partner with a worried expression. "Isn't that right, Hank?"

"Sure is. Look, old buddy, it's no problem. Patty and I really want you to stay with us."

"Patty's got enough on her hands with three kids to look after."

"Hey, one more won't bother Patty. Really. In fact, she insists. You know she thinks of you as family. We all do."

"Thanks all the same, but no." Matt shook his head and looked away.

"If you don't want to stay with Hank and Patty, then how about someone else?" John persisted. "Several of the other guys and their wives have offered to look after you."

"The answer is still no. I don't need anyone to look after me. Besides, I don't want to impose on my friends."

"All right. I think you're wrong and full of stiff-necked pride, but I understand. Trust me, though, like it or not, you will need someone to look after you when you leave here. At least for a while. So why don't you let the department pay for a nurse to stay with you?"

"Forget it. I don't want some stranger in my house. Anyway, I prefer to be alone. As soon as I get those discharge papers tomorrow, I'm going home."

"You're in no condition to stay in that town house alone," John roared. "Dammit, man, you've got a long recuperation ahead of you, and once your body is healed you're going to be in for some grueling rehab work before you'll be ready to return to duty."

Matt snorted. "What makes you think I'll ever be?"

"Because I know you, you bullheaded Irishman. You're not a quitter, any more than your old man was. And you love police work too much to throw in the towel without a fight."

Matt shrugged. "The doctor doesn't share your confidence."

"So what does he know? You're going to have to work your tail off for weeks, maybe even months, to pass the reentry physical, but if anyone can do it, you can."

Matt gave another scornful snort. "You have more faith in me than I do.'"

"Probably, but that will change. Now, the way I see it, you've got two choices. You can either hire a live-in nurse or you can spend the summer up at my fishing lodge on Lake Livingston."

"Your *fishing lodge?*"

"Why not? It's the perfect place to recuperate. The fresh air and peace and quiet of the country will be good for you. You can go for walks in the woods and fish off the pier at first. Later, when you're stronger, you can go sailing or take the fishing boat out onto the lake."

"Don't you have tenants at the lodge?"

"Just one right now, but that's no problem. It's a big place. You'll probably never run into each other. Anyway, you can use my quarters. There's a private entrance off the side veranda."

"I still don't—"

"This isn't a suggestion, Dolan, it's an order."

Matt bristled. "You can't order me to do anything when I'm not on duty."

Smiling benignly, the lieutenant crossed his arms over his chest and rocked back on his heels. "Oh, yeah? Don't forget, you need my permission to even take the reentry physical. You spend the summer getting well at the lodge or you can forget about working the streets again. Got that, Dolan?"

"You'd do it, too, wouldn't you?" Matt snarled. "You'd

refuse to let me take the physical for street duty and stick me behind a desk.''

John shrugged and spread his hands wide. "Hey. It's up to you, Dolan. All you have to do is recuperate and get back in shape up at Lake Livingston.''

"That's blackmail.''

"Maybe,'' John agreed with a shrug. "But I don't see it that way. I'm just trying to help one of my men get back on his feet.''

"Listen to him, Matt,'' Hank urged. "You gotta recuperate somewhere, and shoot, any way you look at it, that's not bad duty. A carefree summer at a lake in a comfortable fishing lodge. If I thought Patty would allow it, I'd almost be tempted to go out and get myself shot if it meant a summer at the lake.'' He paused and gave his partner a lopsided grin. "So whaddaya say?''

A muscle worked in Matt's jaw as his gaze slid back and forth between his two friends. Hank's expression was coaxing. John's, though pleasant, was adamant, and unyielding as granite.

"Excuse me. Am I interrupting something?''

The heads of the other two men snapped around, but Matt merely gritted his teeth. He know that drawling voice with its underlay of laughter only too well. Turning his head slowly on the pillow, he stabbed the new arrival with a hard stare.

The man stood in the doorway, one shoulder propped against the frame, an amused smile on his roguishly handsome face. Everything about him—his loose stance, the careless panache of his attire, the smooth nonchalance—made him appear friendly and harmless, but Matt knew that beneath that laid-back charm was a sharp mind and a pit-bull determination when he smelled a story.

Their gazes locked, one pair of vivid blue eyes narrowed and hard, with no trace of welcome, the other pair twinkling with curiosity and mischief and humor. Neither wavered.

"Who let you in here?" John snarled, putting an end to the silent battle. "I specifically told the staff that Matt's room was off-limits to reporters."

"C'mon, Lieutenant. Can't a guy drop by to see an old friend?"

"Just because we've known each other for a few years doesn't make us friends, Conway," Matt growled.

"All right, then, a close acquaintance. And it's been more than a few years. More like ten or eleven."

"Whatever. I still don't want you here. I have nothing to say to the press."

"You heard the man."

J. T. Conway straightened away from the doorjamb and stepped into the room, ignoring Hank's warning. "Look, I just want to do a small piece on your recovery. The public want to know how their local hero is doing."

"Yeah, right. We both know that if that was all you wanted, your paper would've sent a cub reporter, not their ace."

A rueful grin hiked up one corner of J.T.'s mouth. "Okay, maybe I was hoping to get a quote or two about the raid. Word is, the dealer was tipped off. That someone in the department is on the take. How does it feel to know that you nearly bought the farm because one of your own is dirty?"

Matt's eyes narrowed. "Get out."

"Look, Matt, I know—"

"All right, that's it. You're outta here," Hank growled. Both he and John took a menacing step toward the reporter.

"Whoa now. Look, guys, I'm just doing my job. The readers have a right to know—"

"How about I show you how it feels to eat teeth? How about that for a story? Your readers ought to love that."

J.T. looked from one determined face to the other, weighing his chances. He was a big man, matching Matt's six foot one and broad-shouldered build, but he knew when to back off. Raising both hands, palms out, he retreated. "Okay, okay. I'm going." His blue eyes darted to Matt and he winked. "You get well, buddy."

"Boy, the nerve of that guy," Hank muttered after J.T. left.

The lieutenant, with his usual tenacity, turned his attention back to Matt. "If you go home to that town house of yours, you can expect more of that sort of thing. And there won't be anyone there to run interference. If you go to the lake, you'll have privacy. No one but Hank and me and a few others will even know you're there."

"Jeez! Don't you ever give up?" Matt groaned. "Oh, all right! I'll go to your damned fishing lodge."

John beamed. "Good, good." He rubbed his palms together. "I'll make the arrangements. Hank will go by your place and pack your clothes, then be here tomorrow at checkout time to drive you up to the lake."

"I'm thrilled," Matt drawled.

"We'll get out of here now and let you rest," John returned, ignoring the sarcastic comment. "C'mon, Hank."

Out in the hallway Hank fell into step with the lieutenant. When they were out of earshot of the room, he cleared his throat and asked, "Uh, does Matt know who your tenant at the lodge is?"

"Nope. We made our deal after he was shot."

"That's what I thought. Are you sure you know what you're doing boss?"

They reached the bank of elevators and John punched the down button. The doors of the waiting elevator opened and the two men stepped inside.

"Absolutely. I've given this a lot of thought," John replied, punching the button for the lobby. "Matt's like an injured animal right now, snapping and snarling at everyone and trying his best to curl up in the dark alone and lick his wounds. Well, I'll be damned if I let him."

The lieutenant leaned back against the elevator wall and shot his detective a self-satisfied look. "Tender loving care and nurturing—that's the best medicine for what ails him. In other words, what Matt needs most right now is a good dose of Maude Ann."

Chapter Two

Matt felt every pothole and bump as the car bounced along the dirt road through the woods. Clutching the armrest, he gritted his teeth against the pain and tried to maintain a stoic expression, but a hard jar made him groan. "Ahhh...damn, doesn't the lieutenant ever grade this excuse for a road?"

"Sorry." Hank slanted him a sheepish look. "I'm going as slow as I can. Hang on. The lodge is just around the next bend."

"Yeah, I know." Matt had been to the lodge with John several times to fish.

He looked around at the thick woods on either side of the road. Through the trees on the right he caught an occasional glimpse of the lake, but there were no houses or people in sight. That was the main reason he had agreed to come here. The lodge was about two miles down the gravel road from the highway and the only structure on this finger of land, so he would have plenty of privacy.

John had inherited the lodge and all the land between it and the highway from an uncle. At present he was merely renting out a few boats, and occasionally a tenant occupied the building. When John retired, his plan was to reopen the place as a fishing lodge and run it himself.

"You know, I really do envy you, getting to spend the summer here," Hank said as he brought the car to a stop in the circular drive in front of the lodge. "This is a real nice place, in a rustic sort of way."

The large, two-story building sat in a clearing about a hundred yards from the lakeshore. Made of rough cedar, it had a covered veranda that ran all the way around, with porch swings and groupings of wicker furniture at intervals so that the fishermen who came here could sit and enjoy the view. John's uncle had built the lodge to cater to people who preferred a quiet place where they could go fishing and boating, and just relax and enjoy good family-style meals and the peace and quiet of the country.

In addition to John's quarters, the place had a huge living room, kitchen and dining room on the first floor and eight bedrooms and six bathrooms on the second floor.

"It's easy to see why the lieutenant is so proud of it," Hank continued. "You're gonna be real comfortable here."

Matt doubted that. These days he wasn't comfortable anywhere. His wounds still throbbed and ached, and every step he made was pure agony, causing the mutilated muscles and tendons in his thigh to scream in protest.

With assistance from Hank and leaning heavily on a cane, Matt climbed the veranda steps. However, when he reached the top he was so wobbly he had to sit down in the first swing he reached, while Hank unloaded his bags from the car and carried them to his room. In no time his partner reappeared. "There's something that smells delicious cooking in two big pots in the kitchen, but other than that there's no sign of John's tenant."

"Good. I hope it stays that way."

Hank looked away and shifted uneasily from one foot to the other. "Yeah, well, I guess I'd better be heading back so you can unpack and get settled. Is there anything else you need before I go?"

"Don't think so." Matt knew his partner was worried about leaving him alone, but the truth was, that was exactly what he wanted. He was in no mood for socializing, not even with his best friend. "Look, don't worry about me, okay. I'll be fine."

"Well…if you're sure. And remember, if you need anything—anything at all—you just give me a call."

As his partner drove away, Matt looked around. In addition to being a fisherman and guide, John's uncle had been an avid gardener. Though isolated on wooded lakeshore, the lodge was surrounded by a neat lawn and a bed of roses, and other flowers Matt couldn't name bordered the porch all around. From previous visits, Matt knew that there was also a vegetable garden out back, plus a large garage and storage shed.

Along one side and across the back, the forest came right up to the yard but a small, open meadow separated the lawn from the woods on the west side. At the front of the lodge the lawn went all the way down to the lake. The boat dock and fishing pier was a quarter mile or so farther along the shore, out of sight of the lodge and reached by a path through the woods.

It was a great place, and under other circumstances, Matt would have enjoyed being here to soak up the sunshine and nature, but now he resented being forced to stay when all he wanted was to go home and shut out the world.

The lieutenant had been right about one thing, Matt thought, looking around at the peaceful scene. He certainly shouldn't have any trouble with nosy reporters out here in the boonies.

The sound of voices drew Matt's attention to the woods along the east side of the yard just as a woman and a gang of children emerged. Annoyance firmed his mouth as they headed across the lawn toward the lodge. Great. Just what he needed.

They were either lost or trespassing, since all the land between there and the highway belonged to John Werner. Either way, Matt intended to send them packing.

The children were of different ages and, from what he could tell from that distance, different ethnic backgrounds. Dressed in shorts, T-shirts and dirty tennis shoes, they were sweaty, grubby and bedraggled. Oddly, each child carried a pan or bucket.

It was the woman, however, who drew his attention. She also wore shorts and a T-shirt, but on her, the common garments were unbelievably sexy, showing off full breasts, long legs and a curvy figure that made a man's mouth go dry. Her auburn hair, a wild mane of curls that billowed around her face and shoulders, glinted red in the sunlight. It was that slow, hip-rolling walk, though, that distracted him most. Just watching her approach, he felt a surge of heat in his loins. It was the first time he'd experienced that particular reaction since he'd been shot, and it both pleased and annoyed him.

Putting as much weight as he could on his cane, Matt struggled to his feet. As the group drew nearer and he was about to launch into a blistering lecture about intruding on private property, the woman waved to him and called out, "Hi, there! I'm sorry we weren't here when you arrived."

Matt stiffened, his eyes narrowing as an uneasy feeling crept up his spine. There was something vaguely familiar about the woman, but she wasn't the kind of female any red-blooded male was likely to forget.

"Hey, mister! Lookit what we gots," a little blond cherub with a dirty face exclaimed.

Before he could stop them, the pack of children clambered noisily up the porch steps and the woman followed. The little blond cherub held up her bucket for him to admire, but the rest of the kids just eyed him with suspicion, as though he was the one who shouldn't be there.

"All right, kids, take your blackberries inside and rinse them in the colander with cold water. Debbie, sweetheart, don't bother the man." She shot him a grin. "Sorry about that. She's just proud of picking so many berries."

Before he could reply, the woman turned back to the kids and clapped her hands. "Okay, introductions will come later. Everybody inside. Marshall, you and Yolanda see to the younger ones. And Tyrone, you and Dennis knock off that shoving."

Matt stared at her, his uneasiness growing.

She turned back to Matt and cocked one auburn eyebrow. "Detective Dolan? You haven't said a word. Is something wrong?"

"I know you from somewhere, don't I?"

The woman tossed back her head and laughed, and instantly he knew who she was. No man could ever forget that low, husky sound.

"Goodness. I know it's been a couple of years, but surely I haven't changed that much."

Matt's eyes narrowed. "You're Maude Ann Henley,

Tom Henley's widow. You're that shrink who used to work for the department.''

And she had changed all right. The woman he remembered had been reserved and perfectly groomed at all times, her makeup flawless. She'd dressed in tailored suits, wore her hair pulled severely back in a chignon and exuded an air of cool professionalism. Now she stood before him in ragged cutoffs, a form-fitting T-shirt, her hair a cloud of unruly curls, and apparently not wearing a speck of makeup. There was even a splattering of freckles across her nose, for Pete's sake.

''Yes. Although, my name is actually Edwards. Dr. Maude Ann Edwards to be exact. I kept my maiden name for professional reasons. And just so you know, Detective, I prefer the term *psychiatrist* to *shrink*.''

''Just what the hell are you doing here, *Dr.* Edwards?''

She looked taken aback, whether by the question or his curt tone he neither knew nor cared. He just wanted an answer. Then he wanted her gone. He had avoided her when she worked at the precinct. He sure as hell didn't want her around now.

''Why, I live here. Didn't Lieutenant Werner tell you?''

''You live here? No, he didn't tell me,'' Matt ground out through clenched teeth. ''Somehow he neglected to mention that particular piece of information. He just told me he had one tenant. I assumed it was a summer fisherman. That son of a—''

''Detective Dolan, please. I must ask that you refrain from cursing in front of the children.'' Noticing that the kids hadn't moved, she shooed them toward the door. ''Go on in and wash those berries like I told you. Jane will be back from the store soon. If the berries aren't ready, she won't be able to make that cobbler you want for dessert. So get. All of you."

The departure of the younger children sounded like a herd of wild mustangs clattering across the wooden porch. Amid shouts and squeals and a round of pushing and shoving to see who could be first, and the repeated squeak and bang of the front door, they disappeared into the lodge. A few of the older children, however, were reluctant to leave, They dragged their feet, looking balefully at Matt as they shuffled inside.

When the last straggler disappeared through the door, Maude Ann turned her attention back to Matt.

"Actually, to be fair, Lieutenant Werner didn't lie to you, Detective. I am the only tenant at the lodge."

"Why are you here?" She opened her mouth to reply, but he held up his hand and stopped her. "No, don't bother. It's obvious. Well, you can tell the lieutenant that I don't need anyone to play nursemaid, and I sure as hell don't need a shrink. So this little scheme of his was a waste of time."

Laughter twinkled in Maude Ann's whiskey-colored eyes. "My, my, what an ego you have, Dolan. Funny, I worked with you for two years and I never realized that. It so happens that my being here has nothing whatever to do with you. I leased the lodge from the lieutenant to house the foster home I established for abused and neglected children who have been taken away from their parents or guardians. I call it Henley Haven, in honor of my late husband."

"A foster home? You mean, that mob of kids *lives* here?"

"Yes. And they're hardly a mob. There are only seven children here at the moment. Henley Haven can accommodate ten easily. A dozen in an emergency. But whatever the number, the children keep me much too busy to have time to spend on you. Actually, it should relieve your mind to know that I no longer see patients. I prefer to use my training and experience helping these children adjust and heal, so you needn't worry that I'll be analyzing you."

"You're not going to get the chance, lady."

"Good. I'm glad that's settled. When the lieutenant called he merely asked if I would mind if you stayed in his quarters while you recuperated and drive you into Houston for your checkups. I go into Houston regularly anyway, and since he's giving me a good deal on this place, I couldn't very well refuse. Besides, his room isn't part of my lease agreement. That's always kept ready for him when he visits, so you're not putting anyone out.

"I did agree that you could eat with us. Jane and I must cook for the children, anyway, so even that isn't an imposition. I assure you, meals, housekeeping and an occasional ride into town are all the help you'll receive from me."

"I won't be needing those, either," he snapped. "Dammit, I only agreed to come out here to soak up some sunshine and peace and quiet. Instead, what do I find? A lady shrink and a bunch of rug rats."

"Hey, pig, who you calling a rat?"

"Tyrone!" Maude Ann admonished as a small black boy charged out onto the porch.

The door banged shut as he stepped between Matt and Maude Ann. Assuming a challenging stance that was comical in a youngster, he glared at Matt and thrust out his chin.

Surprise shot through Matt. He recognized the kid instantly. Tyrone Washington was the child of a female junkie from the section of Houston known as Denver Harbor.

Only seven, the kid was already headed for trouble. Most of the time his mother was stoned out of her mind, and Tyrone ran virtually wild through the slum neighborhood. The kid had a mouth on him like a longshoreman's and an eye for larceny. Tyrone might be only seven, but in the ways of the world he was about forty-five.

Matt looked the kid up and down and returned his glare with a cynical half smile. "Well, well, well, if it isn't Tyrone Washington. The Denver Harbor tough guy."

"That's right, pig, an' there ain't nothin' you kin do 'bout it, so kiss my a—"

"Tyrone!" Maude Ann admonished again. "You're to watch your language, young man. Furthermore, you are not to call Detective Dolan by that derogatory name. Do you understand?"

The boy looked back at her over his shoulder. "Daroga what? Whazzat mean?"

"Derogatory. It means insulting and degrading. You're new, but you've been here long enough to know that we don't treat people that way."

A perplexed frown wrinkled Tyrone's forehead. "Not even stinkin' cops?"

"No. Especially not cops. Remember I told you my husband was a policeman and a wonderful man. Now apologize."

Tyrone's face turned mulish. "I ain't gonna 'pologize to no—"

"Tyrone, either apologize or you stay here with Jane tomorrow while the rest of us go to the movies. The choice is yours."

"Ah, Miz Maudie—"

''You heard me, Tyrone.''

''Look, can we drop this?'' Matt snapped. ''I don't care if the little punk apologizes or not.''

''Mr. Dolan! I said no name calling. The rules I've given the children apply to everyone who stays here.''

''Then we don't have a problem, because I'm not staying.''

''That is entirely up to you, Detective,'' she replied with a pleasant smile. ''I have no feelings on the matter one way or another, I assure you.''

''Fine, then you won't mind if I call the lieutenant and tell him to send someone to pick me up, will you,'' he snapped back.

''Not at all. There's a telephone in your room.''

Matt gave her a curt nod. Leaning on his cane, he gritted his teeth and turned to leave.

''Humph. Good riddance,'' Tyrone muttered, but this time Maude Ann was too distracted to correct him.

She bit her lower lip and watched Matt Dolan limp away. She recalled how he used to look, striding around the station house, often without his suit jacket and his shirtsleeves rolled up. A big man with broad shoulders, a lean muscular build and a self-confident demeanor, he had emitted an aura of masculine invincibility and strength.

His back was still ramrod straight and his head high, but he had lost weight during his stay in the hospital, and his progress was so slow and so obviously painful it wrung her heart. It was all she could do not to rush forward and help him.

The only thing that stopped her was the certain knowledge that he would rebuff the offer, probably none too politely. That, and the promise she had made to herself.

When John Werner had contacted her and asked if Matt

Dolan could stay at the lodge for a few months, she had vowed she would give the man his space and not let herself become involved in his recovery in any way. She had enough on her hands with the children. Nor did she need or want to be drawn back into the world of law enforcement and the dark psychological and physical trauma that came with it.

She had left all that behind two years ago when her husband Tom had been killed during a bank holdup. Her life now was devoted to the children.

Self-deception had never been one of Maude Ann's shortcomings, and she had to admit there was another reason for steering clear of Matt. She didn't ever want to take a chance of falling for another law-enforcement officer.

Not that the risk of that happening was great. During the three years that she had worked for the HPD, Matt had been polite but distant. Maude Ann couldn't recall ever having had a personal conversation with the man, nor had he ever consulted her about any of his cases unless a superior had ordered him to.

He wasn't anything like Tom, not at all her type, and given their history, there was little danger of an attraction developing between them.

Still, Maude Ann wasn't stupid. Matt Dolan was a handsome devil, in a tough-as-nails kind of way. With his black-as-coal hair and vivid blue eyes, those chiseled features and his general ''go to hell'' attitude, he stirred something deep in the female psyche that even the most intelligent of women would have a difficult time resisting.

Yes, it was definitely best, all around, if she gave Detective Dolan a wide berth.

Chapter Three

Matt sat on the edge of the bed with the receiver to his ear, impatiently counting the rings on the other end of the line.

"Lieutenant Werner."

"You sorry, sneaky, scheming, back-stabbing bastard. You set me up."

"Ah, good afternoon to you, too, Matt. I take it you've met Maudie and her charges."

Matt ground his teeth and tightened his grip on the receiver. John didn't even try to hide the amusement in his voice. Matt could almost see him leaning back in his chair, grinning like a jackass eating briars. "At least you have the good sense not to pretend you don't know what I'm talking about," he snarled.

"Not much point in that, is there. So how is Maudie?"

"Maudie is fine. I'm mad as hell. I swear, Werner, if I was there right now, I'd knock your teeth out."

"C'mon, Dolan, in your condition you couldn't whip a flea, and you know it. Of course, you're welcome to try, but if I were you I'd wait until I recovered."

"Funny. Real funny. Did you really think I'd go along with this? I refused to see a shrink at the hospital, so you figured you'd maroon me in the boonies with one. Maude Ann Edwards, for Pete's sake! I steered clear of the woman when she worked for the department. Why the devil would I want to spend time with her now? Radio Hank right away and tell him to turn around and come get me. I'm outta here."

"No way, Dolan. We have a deal and you're sticking to it. Look, don't go jumping to conclusions. Maudie doesn't take patients anymore. But she is a doctor. I figured if you needed medical attention, she would be handy to have around. That's all. She's too busy with her kids to bother with the likes of you, boyo, so just relax, will ya?"

"Forget it. I'm not staying here with that woman and all those kids. You got that? Send Hank back for me. Now."

"No can do, buddy. Tell Maudie hi for me and call me at the end of the summer. We'll talk then about you coming back for that physical."

"Wait a minute! Don't you—"

A click sounded and the dial tone droned. Matt jerked the receiver away from his ear and glared at it, then slammed the instrument down so hard it jumped off the base and he had to hang it up again.

With a frustrated growl he flung himself back on the bed and turned the air blue with curses. He didn't give a rat's nose if Dr. Maude Ann Edwards heard him. In fact, he hoped she did. Maybe she'd give him the boot.

"The children will be down in a minute," Maude Ann announced as she returned to the kitchen. "I left Yolanda supervising their hand-washing."

"Humph, somebody has to," Jane said. That scamp Dennis acts like soap and water are poison. So does Tyrone."

Maude Ann's throaty laugh rolled out. "I know. Dennis just tried to convince me his hands weren't dirty because he'd kept them in his pockets all day."

Jane rolled her eyes. "What those two don't think of the devil hasn't invented yet." Standing in front of the big, six-burner commercial stove, she stirred a pot of gravy. "If that policeman fella is going to join us for dinner he'd better shake a leg, 'cause it's almost ready."

Maude Ann removed an enormous pan of biscuits from the oven. Steam rose from them filling the kitchen with a delicious aroma. She glanced at the door that connected Matt's room to the kitchen. "He hasn't so much as stuck his head out of there, has he?"

"Nope. I got back three hours ago and I haven't seen hide nor hair of the man. Haven't heard a sound outta him, either. You sure he's in there? Maybe he decided to walk up to the highway and hitch a ride back to Houston."

"Not likely. In his condition he wouldn't make it a hundred yards." Maude Ann chewed on her lower lip. "I suppose I should knock on his door and let him know it's dinnertime."

"Humph," Jane poured the gravy into a gravy boat and set it on the table with a decisive thud. "I'd let him stew in his own juice, if it was me. Never could abide a foul-tempered man."

"Detective Dolan isn't foul-tempered, exactly. He's just...well, intense is the word, I guess." Maude Ann pulled two crocks of butter from the refrigerator and placed one at each end of the table. Unable to resist, she picked off a chunk of hot biscuit and popped it into her mouth, and immediately closed her eyes in ecstasy. "Mmm, heaven. Jane, you really are going to have to teach me how to make biscuits like these."

"I'm willing. The problem is you never have a spare minute."

Maude Ann sighed. "True." She glanced at the closed bedroom door again and resigned herself. "Well, I guess I'll have to call him. I can't let him skip dinner. In his condition he needs all the nourishment he can get."

"Suit yourself. While you roust him out, I'm going to go see what's keeping those young'uns. It's too quiet up there by far."

Jane marched out of the kitchen with a militant step and headed for the stairs.

Wiping her hands on the towel slung over her shoulder, Maude Ann went to the door and tapped on it lightly. "Detective? Dinner is ready."

She waited a few seconds, but there was only silence on the other side of the door. "Detective Dolan?" she called again.

She hesitated, then turned the knob, eased the door open and stuck her head inside. "Detective Dolan, are you in here?"

The sun had almost set and the light coming through the windows was rosy and dim. At first Maude Ann thought the room was empty, but as she crept inside she saw him through the gloaming, lying back motionless across the bed, his arms flung over his head.

Her heart leapt with fear and guilt. Dear Lord, was he dead? If so, it was her fault. How could she have let him stay in here by himself for so long without bothering to check on him? The man had just gotten out of the hospital a few hours ago.

Holding her breath, she moved closer to the bed. When she finally stood over him and spotted the steady rise and fall of his chest, she closed her eyes. Thank God. He had only fallen asleep.

She opened her eyes and stepped even closer, intending to nudge him, but she hesitated. Tipping her head to one side, she took shameless advantage of his unguarded state to study him.

As her gaze ran over his face, her own softened and her tender heart contracted. He looked so exhausted, so pale. So defenseless. How sad it was, she thought, for this proud, strong man to be reduced to a state of near helplessness.

He had incredibly long eyelashes for a man, she noticed for the first time. They lay like feathery black fans against his skin. Beneath their sweep, bruiselike shadows formed dark circles under his eyes.

Her eyes trailed down his body and her concern deepened. Though a big man, Matt had always kept himself trim, but now he looked much too thin.

Never in a million years would she have thought to see Matt Dolan brought down to such a state. How very close he'd come to losing his life, Maude Ann thought. As her darling Tom had two years ago.

Through Matt's light blue shirt she could see the faint outline of a bandage on his right side and the bulge of another one beneath the denim covering his right thigh.

They were sure to need changing regularly, yet she knew that any offer to help him would meet with a curt refusal.

Suddenly Maude Ann realized that Matt must have fallen into a deep sleep, no doubt involuntarily, soon after making his telephone call. His sneakered feet were still flat on the floor and around his body the cream-colored chenille bedspread was undisturbed.

Compassion softened her face. Poor man. The trip from Houston must have exhausted him. Apparently he hadn't moved so much as a muscle in more than three hours.

She hated to disturb him. Still, to regain his strength he needed nourishment. Bending over, she reached out to touch his shoulder, but she drew her hand back when he jerked and mumbled something in his sleep. From the way he was thrashing around on the bed, he appeared to be having a nightmare.

"Detective? Detective Dolan, wake up."

His hand shot up like a striking snake and clamped around her wrist, and Maude Ann let out a shriek as she was jerked down on top of him.

The sound cut off almost before it started as his other hand clamped over her mouth.

Matt's head came up off the mattress, and Maude Ann's eyes widened above his fingers as she found herself looking into his dark, furious face, just inches from the end of her nose.

His wounds may have weakened him, but there was still a surprising amount of strength left in those powerful arms and shoulders.

"Just what the hell do you think you're doing, sneaking around in my room?"

She tried to answer, but her words came out in an indecipherable mumble against his palm. She gave up and glared at him, and he finally got the message and removed his hand.

Maude Ann shook back her hair and tried for a haughty look, which was difficult to achieve when one was sprawled, half-dressed, on top of a man. "I was *not* sneaking around in your room,'' she informed him. ''I came in to tell you that dinner is ready.''

''Yeah, right. Have you ever heard of knocking?''

''I did knock. Several times. But you didn't answer. I was worried that something had happened to you, so I came inside to check. You seemed to have been having a bad dream.''

Those deep-set blue eyes narrowed as he searched her face for the truth. In the rosy glow of sunset they glittered like sapphires in his dark face. After a time he seemed to come to a decision and gave an almost imperceptible nod.

''I'm fine, as you can see.'' He paused, his eyes locked with hers. Suddenly the air seemed thick, and an odd tautness surrounded them. ''And feel,'' he added.

Maude Ann's eyes widened. Horrified, she realized several things at once. First, that he still gripped her right forearm in an unbreakable hold, and his other hand was splayed across her bottom. Second, not only was she sprawled on top of him, her bare right thigh was nestled intimately between his legs, and his body had responded to the contact. He might have been weakened by the gunshot wounds, but there was certainly nothing wrong with his sex drive.

Heat raced through Maude Ann like a warm flood, and to her dismay, she felt her own body tighten. Even in the dim light, she could see that Matt was aware of her reaction.

Color flooded her face. She told herself to get up, but she seemed to have lost the power of movement. She could feel his heat all along her body, his breath feathering her face, warm and moist, that masculine hand kneading her buttocks ever so slightly.

Her own breathing was shallow and drew painfully

through her constricted throat. With every labored breath
her breasts swelled against the solid wall of his chest.

Had her life depended on it, Maude Ann could not have
looked away from his hot stare. Just when she thought she
would surely burst into flames, Matt broke eye contact. She
experienced a momentary relief, but when his gaze slid
downward over her face and zeroed in on her mouth, her
heart took off at a gallop.

He stared at her lips for what seemed like forever. His
eyes darkened. Maude Ann swallowed hard. Slowly, Matt
tipped his head to one side and raised it closer to hers, and
her heart began to boom.

Her eyes drifted shut. She felt his breath caressing her
mouth and her entire body tingled with anticipation. Before
contact could be made the sound of clattering feet and high-
pitched chatter announced the arrival of the children in the
kitchen.

Aghast, Maude Ann jerked back and tried to scramble
off Matt, but at the first move he groaned. She froze.

"Oh, I'm sorry! I'm so sorry! Your wound! Did I hurt
you?"

A grimace contorted his face. "I'm…okay," he ground
out through gritted teeth. "Just…take it…slow and easy."

"Yes. Of course. I should have realized—"

"Ah, jeez! Watch that knee, will you?"

A fresh wave of color climbed Maude Ann's face, but
she bit her lower lip and eased up off him. She was acutely
conscious of the open door and the children taking their
places at the table in the next room, of Jane issuing orders.
She prayed that no one looked this way, or if they did, that
they couldn't see anything in the fading light.

With excruciating slowness, she got to her knees beside
him on the mattress, then backed off the bed and regained

her feet. She smoothed her hair away from her face and brushed at her shorts, more out of nervousness than need.

Then she noticed that Matt still lay flat on his back with his eyes closed and his face contorted.

"Are you all right? Do you need help getting up?" She stepped closer and held out her hand, but he opened his eyes and gave her a baleful look.

"No, I don't need your help," he growled. "I'm not so pathetic that I can't get up off the damned bed by myself." He grabbed hold of the brass railing at the foot of the bed and tried to haul himself up, but his face clenched with pain and he couldn't hold back a groan.

"Oh, for heaven's sake!" Her patience at an end, Maude Ann bent over and slipped her arms around his chest and tugged him upward. "You men and your stubborn pride! It doesn't make you any less of a man to need a little help now and then, you know," she admonished as she gently assisted him to his feet.

"I don't like to be a burden," he gasped when he could catch his breath.

"No one does, but sometimes it can't be helped. Although, I must say, that was foolish of you to jerk me down like that. You could have reopened your wounds."

His gaze met hers. "If those kids hadn't arrived when they did, I probably would have."

Maude Ann felt a blush heat her cheeks again. She hoped it wasn't visible in the dimness, but even if it was, she wasn't one to back away from a challenge. Tossing her head, she gave a throaty chuckle. "In your dreams, Detective. At this point you haven't got the strength for an amorous encounter. But since you brought it up, let me make this much clear. You are welcome to stay here and recuperate for as long as it takes, but I am not part of your physical therapy. Now, if you don't mind, dinner is ready, and Jane and the children are waiting.''

She turned to leave the room, but he grasped her forearm and stopped her. ''Just a minute, Dr. Edwards. I woke up and found someone hovering over me. Grabbing you was a perfectly natural reflex reaction.'' He paused a beat, then added, ''Just as what happened after that was a natural reaction when a man finds a woman lying on top of him. I don't apologize for that.''

Pursing her lips, Maude Ann considered that. After a moment she nodded. ''All right. I can accept that.''

''Good. And just to set the record straight, I wasn't the only one on that bed who was aroused.''

Never one to play games or prevaricate, Maude Ann gave him a rueful half smile and a nod. ''Fair enough. So why don't we just chalk up what happened as a freak occurrence? Propinquity, if you will. Despite your wounds, you're still a red-blooded male, and there hasn't been a man in my life since Tom died.''

A startled look flashed in his eyes, but she ignored it. ''Add to that combination a dimly lit room, a bed and close contact, and naturally one thing leads to another. We know it didn't mean anything, so let's just forget it happened, shall we?''

Pulling her arm free of his grasp, she smiled cordially and tipped her head toward the kitchen. ''Now we really had better get out there before Jane comes looking for us.''

Without waiting for a reply, Maude Ann turned and strolled out, aware of Matt's gaze drilling into her back.

She had already taken her seat at the head of the table when Matt emerged from his room.

Instantly the childish chatter around the table ceased and a tense silence descended. Seven pairs of wary young eyes watched Matt's slow progress as he leaned heavily on his cane and limped to the table.

When he was seated, Maude Ann, acting as though Matt's presence was nothing out of the ordinary, smiled at her charges and said, "Children, this is Detective Matthew Dolan. He works for the Houston Police Department and he's going to be staying with us while he recovers from an injury."

"You mean he gots an ouchie like me?" the tiny blond girl asked. She raised her arm and proudly displayed a wide Band-Aid on her elbow.

"Yes, Debbie. Only Detective Dolan's ouchies are really bad ones, so he's going to be staying with us until they get all better."

The child turned big, pansy-blue eyes on Matt. "You needs to put a Band-Aid on 'em. I can show you where they are. Miz Maudie has all kinds of pretty ones. Some even gots flowers and fairies on 'em."

Despite his foul mood, a smile tugged at Matt's mouth. He resented being stuck here. He especially resented being here with a shrink and a pack of kids. However, he would have had to have a heart of iron to resist those innocent blue eyes and that face like an angel.

"Dumb girl," Tyrone muttered. "He ain't got that kinda ouchie. He's prob'ly been shot."

Gasps and frightened exclamations erupted around the table.

"That's quite enough, Tyrone. You're scaring the other children."

"Yes'um, Miz Maudie," he replied in a meek voice, ducking his head. Under his breath he added just loud enough for Matt to hear, "Fool shoulda got his head blown clean off, messing with them guys. I sure wouldn't'a cried none if he had. Be one less pig on the streets.''

The boy cut his gaze toward Matt and stuck out his chin. Matt met the boy's surly gaze steadily.

"What was that, Tyrone?"

He turned his head and looked at Maude Ann with an expression of wide-eyed innocence. "Nothin', Ms. Edwards. I was just sayin' how lucky he was."

"Hmm." The glint in Maude Ann's eyes said that she did not believe him, but she let the matter slide.

"My mommy got shot," the girl of about six or seven sitting next to Maude Ann said quietly. She sat staring at her clasped hands resting against the edge of the table. Then she turned her solemn gaze on Matt. "My daddy did it. I saw him. My mommy died."

Matt didn't know what to say. The blank expression in the child's eyes was chilling. Dammit, it wasn't right that a kid should witness such grotesque violence. "I'm... sorry."

Maude Ann reached over and laid her hand over the child's smaller one. "It was a horrible thing, but Jennifer is going to be okay, aren't you, sweetheart?"

The blank look left the little girl's eyes, replaced by trust and abject adoration as she met Maude Ann's reassuring smile. She nodded. "Yes, ma'am."

She wasn't a pretty child. Not like the little blond cherub, Debbie, Matt thought, but she appeared so fragile and vulnerable just looking at her made your heart contract.

Deftly, Maude Ann diverted everyone's attention by making introductions, starting with Jane Beasley, the chunky, middle-aged woman who was her assistant, and working her way around the table.

In addition to Tyrone, Debbie and Jennifer, there was

ten-year-old Marshall, his eight-year-old brother, Dennis, an eleven-year-old Mexican girl named Yolanda and five-year-old Timothy.

Matt sat through the introductions in tight-lipped silence, acknowledging the children and Jane Beasley with no more than a curt nod. He had no desire to know any of them. He may be stuck there, but he intended to keep his distance.

When dinner was over, the children cleared the table, then Maude Ann sent them off to brush their teeth, though not without protests.

"Ah, do I gotta, Miz Maudie?" Tyrone groaned.

"Yes. Now shoo. All of you. And don't think you can pull a fast one on me, either, because I'm going to inspect those teeth when you're done."

Muttering under his breath, Tyrone shuffled out, deliberately dragging his feet on the brick kitchen floor and trailing the other children.

Matt sipped his coffee and watched them go. When their footsteps faded away, he switched his gaze to Maude Ann. "If you're hoping to reform that kid, you're wasting your time. Take it from me—he's bad news."

"Nonsense." Dismissing his comment, Maude Ann left the table and joined Jane at the sink, where she picked up a towel and began drying dishes.

"Do you know anything about his background?" Matt probed.

"If you mean do I know that his mother is a drug addict who never took care of him, yes."

"Do you also know that at seven he's already got a rap sheet? The kid's been picked up for everything from shoplifting to acting as a lookout for a couple of thugs who robbed a liquor store. Being a minor, there's nothing we can do to him, and he and his friends know it. Judges won't even send him to Juvie at his tender age. That's why the older guys like to use him.''

"So? All that proves is he's a little boy who's had a horrible life so far.''

"Lady, Tyrone Washington is a juvenile delinquent in the making. Six months ago I caught him acting as a numbers runner for a gang running a bookmaking operation. I grabbed the kid by the scruff of the neck and hauled him down to the station house myself.''

Maude Ann stopped drying a plate and shot him an accusing glare. "You arrested a seven-year-old boy?''

"I didn't cuff him and throw him in a cell, if that's what you mean. I just to tried to scare the kid. Anyway, it didn't work. A few days later he was running errands for the same gang.''

"All the more reason for removing him from that environment. Tyrone needs love and guidance and structure in his life. He needs to be shown that someone cares and will be there for him, that life doesn't have to be the squalid existence he's known.''

Matt shot her a sardonic look. "Watch those rose-colored glasses, Dr. Edwards. They distort your vision.''

"Sounds pretty cynical to me,'' Jane said, speaking up for the first time. "What's the matter, Mr. Dolan—don't you like kids?''

Matt shrugged. "I like them okay. Actually I haven't been around children a lot, so I haven't thought much about it one way or another.''

"Ah, I see,'' Jane said as though that explained everything, and turned back to the sinkful of dishes.

"Look, this has nothing to do with me. Those kids are your problem, not mine. I just thought you ought to know Tyrone's background.''

"Thank you, Detective. However, I assure you, I am apprised of every child's case history before he or she ever comes here."

"Fine. Suit yourself. It makes no difference to me." Matt downed the last of his coffee and struggled to his feet. "It appears I'm stuck here whether I like it or not. You're probably not any more thrilled than I am, so I just want you to know that, other than mealtimes, I'll stay out of your way. I'd appreciate the same courtesy in return."

Gritting his teeth against the vicious stabs of pain, he limped to the doorway that connected his room to the kitchen. There he paused and turned back to look at Maude Ann.

"As for the kid, just don't say I didn't warn you."

Chapter Four

Matt didn't come out of his room the rest of the evening, nor did Maude Ann catch so much as a glimpse of him during the next four days, except during meals.

At those times he was distant, speaking only when necessary. He made no effort to join in the mealtime conversations. Inexplicably, little Debbie seemed to find him fascinating, but he barely acknowledged her chatter, and he ignored Tyrone's muttered digs. Matt simply ate his food as quickly as good manners allowed and left.

Maude Ann told herself that was fine with her. If he did not want to be sociable, then she, Jane and the children would keep their distance.

His physical condition troubled her. He was in a great deal of pain, she could tell, and it did not seem to be lessening, nor was he regaining strength as he should. However, she reminded herself repeatedly that Matthew Dolan was not her responsibility. Besides, Matt made it crystal clear with every word, look and action that he did not want her help.

It wasn't easy for Maude Ann to remain aloof. Nurturing came as naturally to her as breathing, and no matter how antisocial his behavior or how hard she tried not to, she still worried about him. Whether or not he wanted to accept it, he did need help.

Still, Matt was a proud man, and she knew any offer of help would not be appreciated. Maude Ann promised herself that she would respect his wishes and leave him alone.

Her resolve held only until his fourth night at the lodge.

That evening, after cleaning the kitchen and supervising baths and teeth brushing, Maude Ann, Jane and the pajama-clad children settled down in the huge living room as they did every night. While the younger ones watched an animated movie on television, Maude Ann and the older boys and girls played a board game. Jane sat in a rocking chair by the massive stone fireplace, contentedly crocheting an afghan.

Maude Ann was feeling smug and proud of herself for the self-restraint she had shown. Not only had she resisted the urge to aid Matt in any way, she had behaved as though she wasn't even aware of his struggles.

However, as had happened every night since he'd been there, while she laughed and talked with the children, she found that she was also keeping one ear cocked for sounds of distress from Matt's room.

Between chores and play and picking berries in the woods, the children had worn themselves out that day. When all her exhausted charges were settled in for the night, Maude Ann went from room to room for one last peek, pausing in each to gaze at the sleeping children snuggled in their beds, their young faces slack and vulnerable and so heartbreakingly innocent. As she studied them, her chest swelled with emotion.

Henley Haven was an enormous responsibility that required long hours of hard work, patience and sacrifice. Many people thought she was crazy for taking on such a burden, and there were times when she questioned her own sanity. Yet, as always at night during this quiet time, she knew a sense of peace and fulfillment that erased all doubt and made it all worthwhile.

Maude Ann closed the door on the last pair of sleeping children and made her way down the hall to her own quarters.

There she filled the tub and treated herself to a long hot soak. Afterward, she showered and shampooed her hair, then crawled into bed, sighing with pleasure. Though only a little after ten, it had been a busy day and she was exhausted.

The clean smell of soap and bath talc clung to her skin and mingled with the fresh, outdoorsy scent of cool cotton sheets that had been dried in the sunshine. Smiling, she closed her eyes and snuggled her face into the down-filled pillow and waited for sleep to claim her.

An hour later she was still waiting. Finally, thoroughly irritated, she threw back the covers donned her robe and stomped, barefoot, out of the room. She loped down the stairs, her clean hair dancing around her shoulders with each impatient step, and her long batiste gown and robe fluttering out behind her.

In the kitchen she started to flip on the overhead light, but thought better of it after a glance at the closed door of Matt's room. She had forgotten about him.

A line of light shone from under the door, and she heard

the faint sound of the shower running. She wasn't going to wake him, at least. However, neither was she anxious to have any contact with him. Forcing herself to move with more caution, she crossed the room and turned on the dim light above the kitchen stove.

A few minutes later she had just removed a mug of warm milk from the microwave when she heard a thud from Matt's room, followed immediately by a groan.

Acting on instinct, without stopping to think of what Matt's reaction might be, she put the mug down, dashed to the door of his room and burst inside.

"Detective Dolan? Are you all right?" she called, darting a quick look around.

The bedspread was turned down, but the bed was empty. The lamp on the nightstand gave off a pale glow that barely illuminated the room, but the door to the en suite bathroom stood ajar, and a narrow rectangle of bright light spilled out. Maude Ann headed in that direction. Halfway there another groan sounded.

"Detective, are you—" She gasped and jerked to a halt in the bathroom doorway.

Matt lay sprawled facedown on the shower floor, struggling to climb to his hands and knees. Overhead the steaming spray beat down on him full force. Every time he tried to gain purchase on the slick tile, he slipped and fell flat again, with painful results.

The shower stall had been built to accommodate John Werner's massive proportions, making it bigger than many small bathrooms. Prone in the middle of the floor, Matt could not reach the sides or anything else on which to brace himself.

Recovering her senses, Maude Ann rushed forward and

snatched open the shower door. "For heaven's sake, wait! Don't try to get up by yourself!"

"Hey! What're you…doing in here?" Matt groaned. "Get the hell out. I'm naked."

"Most people are when they shower."

"Funny. Now, will you leave? I can…manage on my own."

"Oh, yes, I can see that," she replied, giving him a dry look. "Really, Detective, you're being foolish. I am a doctor, after all. I have seen naked men before."

"You're a head doctor. And you haven't seen me."

"Oh, please." She made an exasperated sound and rolled her eyes. She reached in and turned off the shower, wetting the front of her gown and robe in the process, and stepped inside. Immediately she skidded and almost fell. "Whoops! Good grief, this thing is slick as goose grease on glass. Why didn't you tell me? I'm surprised you haven't already broken your neck."

"It wasn't important. Now will you…get out of here?" he gasped.

"No. I'm not going anywhere until we get you on your feet and out of this skating rink, so you're just going to have to deal with it."

Holding on to the built-in towel rack, she leaned down and hooked her other hand under his arm. "C'mon, now, just hang on and let me do the lifting. Will you stop pulling away! You're just making it more difficult."

"Dammit, at least get me a towel before you haul me up."

"Oh, honestly!" Releasing his arm, Maude Ann eased out of the shower and snatched a wine-colored towel off the rack, then quickly climbed back inside and dropped the cloth over his bare backside. "There, that should protect your modesty. Now can I have a little cooperation here?"

Groaning, Matt rolled first to one side, then the other and after several tries finally managed to knot the towel around his lean middle.

"Ready now?" She hooked her hand under his arm again and tugged with all her might, hauling him to his knees, but not without causing him to wince and suck in his breath.

"Are you all right?"

"I'm…okay. Just give me a minute." He closed his eyes and breathed hard for several seconds, then he grasped her arm. "Okay, I'm ready. Let's go."

As Maude Ann pulled, Matt braced his other hand on her hip and strained to lever himself up. The agony in his face was awful to see, and her heart squeezed in sympathy.

"Easy, easy. Don't put any weight on that wounded leg."

Matt shot her a blistering look. "You just hold on to that rack and let me worry about my leg. Jeez, are you always this bossy?"

"Sorry." She gave him an abashed grin. "Comes from dealing with children all day, I guess."

"Well, in case you haven't noticed, I'm not ten years old."

Oh, she'd noticed, all right. It was difficult not to, under the circumstances. Still fresh in her mind's eye was the sight of those tight buns of his.

Despite his recent weight loss, Matt's broad shoulders and arms were corded with muscle. So was his impressive chest and flat abdomen and long, powerful legs. Water-beaded tanned, glistening skin and more droplets clung to the jagged piece of silver he wore on a chain around his neck and the mat of dark curls that covered his chest. She could not help but notice how the silky hair arrowed downward to swirl around his navel, then narrow into a thin line that disappeared beneath the maroon terry cloth slung low around his hips.

She was seeing much more of Matt Dolan than she had ever expected to see, and he was most definitely not a boy but an adult male. A very attractive, well-built, virile adult male.

It wasn't easy, but after a lot of struggle and slipping and sliding, she finally managed to pull him to his feet. "Here, just hang on to me," she instructed. Looping his arm over her shoulder and wrapping her free arm around his waist, she carefully stepped out of the shower with him.

The instant his feet touched the bathmat, he released her and grabbed the edge of the basin for support. Stiff-armed, he braced himself against the sink and hung his head, clenching his jaw. Beneath the tanned skin, his face was pale, and his muscles quivered with fatigue.

Without a word, Maude Ann grabbed another towel and began to pat his torso dry, working so briskly she was almost finished before he could protest.

"Hey! Stop that! Look, I can manage from here okay."

"Nonsense. You're so exhausted you can barely stand. You need to lie down before you fall down. Again." Squatting beside him, she ran the towel down one of his legs and up the other before he could dodge her hands, then she tossed the towel onto the rack and grasped him around the waist again.

"Come along, let's get you to bed."

Out of the corner of her eye, she saw his jaw set, but this time he didn't argue. Beneath her encircling arm, she felt his muscles tremble, and she knew by the way he leaned against her that his strength had reached low ebb. She also knew that a man like Matt Dolan would hate for anyone, especially a woman, to see him in such a weakened state.

His cane was propped against the wall, and she grabbed it and hooked it over her arm as they passed by.

Their progress across the large bedroom was slow and painful, but finally they made it.

"There, you go," she said brightly, lowering him onto the side of the bed.

While Maude Ann lifted his feet onto the mattress, Matt gave a sigh, closed his eyes and collapsed on his back with one arm crooked over his head and the other flung wide.

Straightening, Maude Ann stood beside the bed, debating what to do next. Lines of pain and fatigue etched Matt's face, and his skin had a grayish cast. His black hair was tousled and wet, and a lock hung down over his forehead. Her fingers itched to smooth it back off his face, but she resisted the urge.

Her gaze slid downward over the arm flung over his head, tracing the tender underside to its juncture with his body. For no reason, her attention was caught by the tuft of damp, dark hair under his arm. As she stared at it, she felt her stomach tighten.

Helpless to stop herself, she ran her gaze over his shoulders and throat, the sculpted beauty of his collarbone. A glint caught her eye, and she zeroed in on the jagged piece of silver nestled in the thatch of dark hair on his chest. She wondered what it was. It must be important, because he wore it all the time, even while bathing.

The mystery diverted her only seconds before her gaze was again drawn downward, trailing over his ribs, which moved rhythmically up and down with each heavy breath he drew.

Maude Ann's mouth went dry. Lord, he was a magnificent male specimen. She knew she should look away, but she could not. Mesmerized, she continued her study, following that intriguing line of dark hair down over his belly and lower.

Then her gaze encountered the angry, puckered wound on his right leg. Instantly the sensual spell was broken.

Before she could stop herself she sucked in a sharp breath. Quickly she glanced at Matt's face to make sure he hadn't heard and found he was watching her, his eyes steady and glittering beneath half-closed lids.

Hot color rose in her neck and face, but for an interminable moment neither moved nor spoke. They simply stared at each other, their gazes locked.

The air in the room seemed thick, almost suffocating, magnifying every sound. Maude Ann could hear the wind-up clock on the bedside table ticking, the whir of the cicadas outside the window, the thrumming of her heartbeat in her ears. She wondered if Matt could hear it, too.

"See something you like, Dr. Edwards?"

Maude Ann swallowed around the tightness in her throat. "I was just looking at your wounds. They need tending. I'll, uh…I'll rebandage them for you, if you like."

"What are you going to do? Kiss them and make them all better, like you do Debbie's ouchies?"

"Hardly." She forced a chuckle, fighting to regain control of the situation and her wayward senses. "You're not four years old."

She turned to go in search of his medical supplies, but his hand shot out and clamped around her wrist like a vice, jerking her to a halt. His blue eyes glittered dangerously, and when he spoke his voice dropped, becoming rough and steely.

"That's right. I'm not one of your wounded chicks that you can cluck over and mother. I'm a man, with a man's appetites."

His gaze dropped to her chest, and his eyes darkened. Maude Ann was about to protest, but instead, a downward glance made her gasp and clamp her free arm over her breasts. The front of her gown and robe were still sopping wet, and the thin batiste clung to her body like a second skin. The air-conditioned air had cooled the wet cloth, causing her nipples to pucker and harden. They thrust against the wet gown, clearly visible through the semitransparent material.

"Right now I'm not in any shape to do anything about those appetites, but I will be soon. Remember that the next time you come waltzing in here uninvited. You may get more than you bargained for."

Blushing from her hairline to her toes, Maude Ann stammered, "I got wet helping you. I didn't realize...I certainly didn't mean to flaunt myself. Anyway, I was only trying to help."

"Oh? Is that what you were doing just now? *Helping* me?"

"Well, I—"

"Just keep in mind that the next time you're tempted to look at me with that hungry gleam in your eye, you better be prepared for the consequences."

Denial never even occurred to Maude Ann. Though it hadn't been intentional, she had been admiring his body, and she'd been caught red-handed. She nodded. "Fair enough."

She started to move away, but Matt's grip on her arm tightened. She looked at him and arched one eyebrow.

Matt rubbed his thumb over the delicate skin on the inside of her wrist, and his eyes grew slumbrous. "Unless, of course, you'd like me to satisfy that hunger of yours."

Her sense of humor and down-to-earth common sense, neither of which was ever far from the surface, came bubbling up. That she would find herself in such a situation with Matt Dolan, of all people, struck her as absurdly funny. He was the most intimidating, overwhelmingly masculine man she'd ever encountered. When she had worked for the HPD, even before she had met and married Tom Henley, Matt had paid her no more mind than a piece of office equipment.

That had suited her just fine. From their first meeting she'd had the good sense to know that someone like her, a simple homebody at heart, had no business getting involved with an intense, complicated man like Matt.

Shaking her head, Maude Ann gave a throaty chuckle and pulled her arm from his grasp. Matt's eyes narrowed, his expression going from sensual to surprised, then annoyed. Clearly, he had not expected that reaction.

"Tempting as it is, I think I'll pass on that offer, Detective. I may be a frustrated widow, but I know when I'm in over my head. Now if you'll excuse me, I'll go get some bandages for those wounds."

"Don't bother. I can manage."

"Fine. Then I'll say good-night." Only moments ago she would have argued, but now a hasty withdrawal seemed the wisest course.

The instant Maude Ann pulled the door shut behind her, she leaned back against the kitchen wall and fanned her face with her hand. "Whew! That is one potent man," she whispered.

The encounter with Maude Ann served as a wake-up call for Matt.

What his doctor's repeated lectures and weeks of his friends' pleas and cajoling had failed to do, the humiliating episode in the shower accomplished in mere minutes, firing in him an iron-willed determination to regain his strength—and with it, the life he'd had before he'd been shot.

He had allowed the doctor's pessimism to infect him, to rob him of a sense of purpose. He had wanted a guarantee that he would recover. When he didn't get one, he refused to try. It was easier to accept defeat from the start than to fight and struggle for weeks, maybe months, and fail, anyway.

He had been so mired in bitterness and self-pity he couldn't see what a pathetic loser he'd allowed himself to become—not until he'd found himself sprawled helpless as a newborn baby on the shower floor, completely dependent on a woman to help him out.

It had stung to have Maude Ann see him so weak and helpless. So had that husky laugh of hers and her blunt honesty. The easy way she had twice dismissed the flare of desire between them had been downright insulting. Labeling her feelings nothing more than frustration had made it painfully clear that it wasn't him she wanted; her reaction would have been the same with any man. Abstinence, not attraction, had prompted that smoldering inspection she had given him.

Intellectually Matt knew he shouldn't let the incident bother him. Men, after all, had been guilty of the same impersonal lust for eons. The problem was, coming from a warm and sensual woman like Maude Ann, it had seemed doubly insulting to be relegated to nothing more than a sex object.

What the devil. She wasn't his type, anyway, and he sure as hell wasn't interested in getting involved with the woman.

Still…her attitude had rankled.

The way Matt figured it, the sooner he got back in shape and got out of there, away from the maddening woman and her ragtag bunch of kids, the better.

The morning after the shower incident, Matt rose early and did his exercises, this time with vigor, pushing himself almost beyond endurance.

Before going into the kitchen for breakfast, he braced himself for awkwardness, but it was a wasted effort; Maude Ann wasn't there.

Loath to ask where she was, Matt pretended not to notice her empty chair, but the kids had no such inhibitions.

"Where's Miz Maudie?" Tyrone demanded the instant he took his seat.

"Yeth, where ith she?" Debbie echoed.

"She's gone into Cleveland to do some shopping," Jane replied. "She'll be back in an hour or so. Now you kids eat your breakfasts. Soon as we clean up the kitchen we're going to do some chores."

That brought groans all around the table, especially from Tyrone. Fighting the urge to laugh, Matt ducked his head and ate his waffles in silence.

After breakfast he went for a walk, taking the path through the woods that he'd seen Maude Ann and the kids use. Every step was agony. He limped along, sweating and breathless from the exertion and pain, putting most of his weight on his cane and forcing one foot in front of the other.

Jane was in the kitchen when he staggered in at last to get a drink. She looked up from icing a cake and raised an eyebrow when she saw his flushed, sweaty face.

"Gracious me, you look like forty miles of bad road. What on earth have you been doing, Detective?"

His mouth tightened. He crossed to the sink, the soft thud of his cane almost silent on the brick floor. He had made no attempt to cultivate a friendship with the woman or anyone else in the house, but Jane Beasley didn't let that stop her.

She was a gregarious woman with a sometimes caustic forthrightness about her. She didn't believe in formality and had no time for it. Everyone who came within her sphere she treated exactly the same. You could like it or lump it, it made no difference to her.

"I went for a walk in the woods." He drew a glass of water, chugged it down in three long gulps and filled the glass again.

"Are you sure you're up to taking walks just yet? You look ready to keel over to me."

"I'll be fine. I just need some water is all. I got kind of dehydrated."

"Mmm, I'm not surprised, in this heat. Next time take a bottle of water with you. Oh, by the way, your shower is fixed. Maude Ann put some adhesive non-skid strips on the shower floor as soon as she got back from town."

"She told you what happened?"

"Just that you took a fall last night. 'Course, Maudie being Maudie, she fretted about it all night. Took off at first light to buy those strips to remedy the situation. I swear, that woman's a born mother hen."

"*That's* what she went shopping for so early?"

"Sure. What'd you expect?"

He hadn't expected anything, really. Certainly not that she would make a special trip into town just for him.

Jane swirled the last dollop of icing on top of the cake with a flourish. Wiping her hands on a towel, she gave Matt another long look. "Why don't you go out on the veranda and sit in the shade and rest a bit? You look plum peaked. I'm real glad you're making an effort to recover, but it's not good to push yourself too hard, you know. Particularly at first."

"Funny, I don't recall asking for your opinion," Matt said in the cold voice he used to keep people at arm's length.

"Well, you got it, anyway. No charge." She waved both hands in a shooing motion. "Now go on out there and sit down before you fall down."

He was tempted to refuse, just because she'd ordered him, but the veranda did look inviting. Besides, he was tired of being cooped up in his room.

"All right, all right. I'm going."

The first thing Matt saw when he stepped out onto the back veranda was Maude Ann and the children working in the vegetable garden, about thirty feet behind and to one side of the lodge.

He gingerly lowered himself into a swing and settled back against a pillow to observe Maude Ann and her crew of pint-size gardeners.

As he followed her movements, his first thought was the same one he had over and over for the last four days. What the devil was she doing with this motley bunch of kids and only Jane Beasley to help her?

It didn't make sense. She was an educated woman, a

doctor. She could have a successful and lucrative career in Houston. She wasn't his type, but she was an attractive woman. She was also incredibly sensual and responsive. He had firsthand knowledge of that. So why had she buried herself out here in the middle of nowhere?

Despite the nagging questions, a smile teased Matt's mouth when he noticed that every one of the kids wore a straw hat. More of Maude Ann's mothering, no doubt. Probably slathered them all with sun block, as well.

Most of the kids were working diligently. All except Tyrone. He merely leaned on his hoe, looking bored.

All Matt could see of Maude Ann was the top of her straw hat bobbing among the tall stalks of corn. Suddenly two corn stalks parted, and she stuck her head through the opening

"Tyrone, those weeds aren't going to jump out of the ground, you know. Get busy."

"I don't want to hoe no weeds." He shot her a look, his mouth set in a mulish pout. "I ain't no farm boy."

"No, you're not. But you are a boy who likes to eat. Around here everyone does their part, so either get busy with that hoe or come over here and help me with the corn."

For a moment Matt thought the boy would refuse, and he sat up straighter in the swing, preparing to lend a hand if the little hoodlum gave her any trouble. Then Tyrone threw down his hoe and stomped over to the corn patch, high-stepping over the rows of plants and muttering under his breath. He was a city boy, he groused. He didn't belong here.

For the next fifteen minutes or so the seven-year-old miscreant trudged along behind Maude Ann, looking sullen and ready to revolt, while she broke ears of corn off the stalks and dropped them into the basket he carried. By the time she finished, Tyrone's load had grown so heavy he was gripping the handle of the basket with both hands.

Maude Ann wiped her brow with her forearm and arched her back. "Tyrone, sweetie, take the corn into the house and give it to Jane."

"Yes, ma'am!" Before she got all the words out he headed off as fast as the heavy basket would allow. "And come straight back!" she called after him.

Watching the boy move away, Maude Ann shook her head, but a smile curved her mouth.

Turning her attention to the other children, Maude Ann moved around the garden checking their progress, assisting some and correcting technique where necessary.

"She's something, isn't she?"

Startled, Matt looked up and found Jane standing beside the swing holding a tray containing a pitcher of lemonade and glasses, her gaze fixed on Maude Ann.

Matt turned his attention back to the garden and said nothing, but that didn't deter Jane.

"That gal's a natural with children. She's never met one she didn't adore. And they love her back, too. Even the problem ones like Tyrone come around after a while. You ask me, it's a darned shame she and her husband didn't have any of their own. A woman like that should have a houseful."

Matt had to agree, but he merely shrugged and said, "There's time. She's still a young woman."

"Huh. Fat lot of good that does. She hasn't been out on a date with a man since Tom was killed, and she ain't likely to go anytime soon. Where is she going to meet a man, stuck out here in the country with a passel of young'uns seven days a week, I'd like to know? She never takes a day off, though the good Lord knows, I nag her about it enough." Jane glanced his way. "I was hoping when you showed up that something might happen between you two, but I can see now that you're not suited."

Matt frowned. He agreed, but somehow, hearing it from Jane annoyed him. "Really? What makes you say that?"

"Well, it's obvious, isn't it? She's a warm, loving woman who adores children. Pardon me for saying so, Detective, but you're about the coldest, most unfeeling man I've yet to meet. You act as though the children don't exist. Why, that poor little angel, Debbie, chatters away at you all the time, and you ignore her. If there's an ounce of tenderness or love in you, I've yet to see it. No insult intended, but Maudie deserves better.

"Now then, I'd best be getting back to work. Those young'uns are going to be starving when they're done in that garden. Here's your lemonade." She plunked down the tray on the wicker table beside the swing and went back inside.

That was certainly plain talk, Matt thought, frowning after her. Oh, well, he did ask.

Matt turned his attention back to Maude Ann. It was funny—when she'd worked for the department, he would never have pegged her as a nurturer. He had assumed that all psychiatrists were cool, analytical people who stood a little apart from the rest of the world, observing, rather than participating. That was part of the reason he'd steered clear of her. That and the fact that he had always preferred chic blondes with a bit of an edge.

Maude Ann, however, was neither cool and distant nor chic and sophisticated. She was totally natural and unaffected. She was a woman who went around barefoot in cutoff jeans and T-shirts without a speck of makeup. A woman who opened her arms to children with problems. A woman who was compassionate and loving and maternal, a natural born earth mother.

Her husky laugh rang out, and Matt saw her grab Debbie up and swing her around.

He'd seen her do that sort of thing constantly since his arrival. Daily, she gave each child an equal amount of attention and time, listening to their earnest chatter as though it was the most important thing she'd ever heard, laughing with them and giving them smiles and praise. He'd noticed, too, that she constantly touched the children, ruffling their hair, patting their cheeks or their shoulders, giving them hugs and kisses or squeezing their hands.

No doubt, that sort of thing was important to a child's emotional well-being. The kids certainly seemed to eat it up.

What baffled Matt was, why the devil did those simple actions suddenly seem so damned sexy?

Chapter Five

He was getting stronger. He could feel it.

Matt hobbled along the path through the woods, determination and a feeling of satisfaction driving him on.

Every day he pushed himself a little harder than the day before, walking farther, forcing himself to depend less and less on the cane, and the effort was beginning to pay off. Mostly he used the walking stick for balance, leaning on it only now and then when he stepped wrong and received a jab of pain in his leg.

He went around a bend and through the trees saw the lodge up ahead. Matt chugged down the last of his water, and when he emerged from the woods, he headed for the back steps. On the veranda he paused to do a few cool-down twists and stretches.

He took these walks in the mornings, and in the afternoons he did the exercises and stretching that the hospital's physical therapist had recommended, only Matt did more than prescribed, and he was gradually stepping up the pace and intensity. The pain was still there. So was the limp, but both were gradually lessening.

It had been two weeks since he'd started applying himself to getting back in shape, and already he could walk half a mile or more without undue suffering. Jane's excellent cooking had put back some of the weight he'd lost, and the color had come back to his skin. If he continued to improve at the same rate, he figured he could switch from walking to running within a couple of months.

When he reached that goal, he would get Hank or one of the other guys on the force to bring his set of weights to the lodge so he could begin some strength training.

It was mid-June. By Matt's calculations, he should be ready to return to Houston and take the reentry physical by the end of September. October at the latest.

The back door opened, then banged shut, and footsteps thudded on the wooden boards of the porch, but Matt didn't look around. Grimacing, he grasped his right ankle and pulled his leg up behind his body. More perspiration popped out on his forehead and the tendons in his neck stood out as he stretched the injured thigh muscle as far as he could bear. He couldn't quite bring his heel into contact with his buttocks yet, but he was determined to get there.

"I brought you some water," Jane announced. "If you don't stop torturing yourself and drink it, I'm gonna pour it into my geranium pot."

Matt released his ankle and grinned at her over his shoulder as she plunked the tray down on a wicker table.

"Nag. Nag."

Chuckling, Matt looped the towel around his neck and took the tumbler of water she offered. He chugalugged the water, and when Jane refilled it he drank half without stopping.

Over the past couple of weeks more had changed than just his physical condition. He had made peace with Jane. You could even say they had become friends, if their sparring could be classified as a show of friendship.

He spent a lot of time in her kitchen talking to her while Maude Ann and the kids were outdoors doing chores or playing games or whatever it was she did with them on their daily outings. Jane was plainspoken and saw to the heart of things with crystal clarity, and she wasn't in the least shy about expressing her opinions. She'd given Matt hell often enough about the way he kept his distance from the kids.

Matt knew Tyrone's background, and he'd learned about Jennifer's the first evening he was there. From Jane, he'd learned that Marshall and his brother, Dennis, had been orphaned when their mother had committed suicide, that Timothy had been repeatedly beaten and nearly starved, that Debbie had been abused by her stepfather and that Yolanda had simply been abandoned on the side of a freeway. As yet, the police had no clue who her parents were.

Though Matt pretended indifference, Jane's comments about his treatment of Debbie and the other children bothered him. He didn't want to hurt the little girl—or any of these kids. They'd had enough hard knocks in their young lives already.

Matt knew it was important for a kid to have a role model, an adult they could idolize and learn from. Hell, he'd thought that Patrick Dolan had hung the moon in the sky.

But he saw no point in allowing the children to form an attachment to him. He would be leaving in a few months, after all. Besides, he had his own problems to deal with.

"Where's your boss and her flock of chicks?" he asked

Jane casually, but he didn't fool her. The look in her eyes said she knew exactly why he'd asked.

"Inside, cleaning house. She's assigned them all a job. The little ones are dusting and Maudie and the others are doing the rest."

"Really? What's Tyrone's job?"

Wry humor twinkled in Jane's eyes. "Cleaning toilets."

Matt laughed so hard he had to lean against one of the veranda posts. "Oh, that's rich," he gasped when he caught his breath. "I can just imagine how much he likes that."

"Well, let's just say he's not too happy right now."

"I can imagine."

"You could stick around and see for yourself, if you wanted to, but we both know you won't."

The look in her eyes challenged him to deny the charge, but he merely smiled. "Actually, I'd planned to go fishing."

Jane sniffed. "Figures." Giving him a disgusted look, she picked up the tray and stomped back inside.

Matt shrugged off her disapproval and went to the storage shed behind the garage, where he gathered what he needed from Werner's large stock of fishing gear. Ten minutes later he settled himself in his favorite spot on the end of the long, T-shaped boat dock.

Lake Livingston covered many square miles, and the boat dock sat in a secluded cove. At this hour the tall pines that lined the shore still shaded the pier. Water lapped against the pilings. Farther out, sunshine danced on the water, flashing like diamonds. A bird flew low and skimmed the water.

The dock was a peaceful spot to relax and think or just enjoy the quiet and solitude. When John Werner had inherited the place and announced his plan to retire here, Matt had thought he was crazy. After the fast pace of Houston and the challenge and stimulation, the occasional adrenaline rush of police work, how could he even consider burying himself in the boonies? However, during the past few weeks, Matt had come to appreciate the lieutenant's desire to live here.

He had been fishing for almost an hour when the hammer of footsteps on the wooden dock interrupted his solitude.

Scowling, Matt looked over his shoulder and saw Tyrone carrying a pole and a bucket. Worms, no doubt.

The boy raced out onto the pier, then spotted Matt and pulled up short.

Matt made no effort to hide his annoyance, and Tyrone glared right back at him. Matt had a hunch that Tyrone had known all along that he was there and was taking spiteful pleasure in interrupting his solitude.

Bold as brass, the boy marched out to the end of the pier and plopped himself down on the opposite side of the T from Matt.

"Where'd you get that rod and reel?" Matt demanded

"Same place as you. Outta the shed."

"Oh, yeah? Well the difference is, I have the owner's permission to use his gear."

Tyrone shrugged.

"I thought you were cleaning toilets."

"I'm done with that," the boy muttered in a surly tone that matched his scowl.

An awkward silence fell. For a long time the only sounds were the lap of the wavelets against the pilings beneath the pier, the caw of a crow in the woods, the soft whir, plop, whir when Matt cast his line out and reeled it back in.

Keeping his gaze straight ahead, Matt ignored the boy. After a while, realizing he had not heard Tyrone casting, he glanced over to see what the little hooligan was up to.

He was surprised to discover the kid was still struggling to thread a worm onto his hook.

The tip of Tyrone's tongue stuck out of the corner of his mouth and he scowled with intense concentration.

Matt frowned. He started tell him that he was doing it all wrong, but he changed his mind and cast.

A splash to his left close to the pier drew his gaze back to the boy. Tyrone had finally impaled the worm on the hook, but his first cast had gone no more than a few feet.

Muttering a string of colorful curses no seven-year-old should know, the boy reeled in his line. When the hook and sinker cleared the water he spat out a vivid obscenity. His overzealous cast had slung the worm off.

It took him another ten minutes to rebait his hook, and when he cast he got the same result as before.

Between casting and catching two good-size trout, Matt watched the boy out of the corner of his eye and shook his head. It was obvious the kid had never fished before in his life. Which, he supposed, wasn't so surprising. Until Tyrone came here, he had probably never been more than a mile from that dump where he and his mother had lived. There weren't many fishing holes in the city slums.

Matt tried to ignore the kid, but Tyrone's vivid cursing and mutters made that impossible. Every now and then he glanced over at the boy, and his frustration grew. Finally, when Tyrone got the granddaddy of all backlashes, Matt could stand it no longer.

"Oh, for Pete's sake! Don't yank at it like that—you're just going to make it worse," he snapped, struggling to his feet. "Here, let me show you."

"I don't need no help from you, pig."

"Well, too bad, punk. You're getting it, anyway. I'm tired of listening to you cuss."

"I'll cuss if I wanna. An' I know how to fish."

"Oh, yeah. Then why is it all you've done for the past twenty minutes is fling worms into the lake?"

Ignoring the boy's glare, Matt eased down next to him on the pier and took the rod from his hands. "Jeez, this looks like a bird's nest."

Tyrone muttered a choice expletive about the quality of the rod and spat into the lake.

Matt picked patiently at the tangled mess. "You'd better watch that mouth of yours. It'll get you into big trouble with Dr. Edwards."

"Huh. I ain't scared of Miz Maudie."

Matt kept his gaze on the tangled line and pulled apart another knot. After a while the boy looked out across the lake and swung his legs back and forth over the edge of the pier.

"You do know that you have it pretty good here, don't you, kid?"

Tyrone swung his legs harder. "Yeah. I know," he admitted grudgingly. He let several seconds tick by, then added, "But I still hate cleaning toilets."

Chuckling, Matt pulled another knot loose. "I got news for you, kid, everybody does, but it's just one of those nasty jobs that's gotta be done. Life's full of 'em. In a big family like this one everybody has to take their turn."

"We ain't no family."

"Really? Sure looks like one to me."

"Naw. We're just a bunch of kids nobody wants."

"Is that right? It appears to me that your Miss Maudie wants you. Otherwise, why would she bother to run this place? She doesn't have to, you know."

"Huh. She's just doin' it for the money the state pays her. That's what all fosters do."

"Are you kidding me? Shoot, kid, that's chump change compared to what Dr. Edwards could make seeing patients in Houston. The lady is a psychiatrist. Most of them charge over a hundred dollars an hour.''

The boy frowned. ''Then why ain't she doin' it, instead of taking care of us?''

Matt gave him a long, level look. ''You're a smart kid. You figure it out.''

He returned his attention to the backlash, but he could feel Tyrone's gaze on him as he untied the last knot and rewound the line. Reaching across the boy, he took a worm from the can. ''Okay now, pay attention. Here's how you bait a hook.''

Tyrone rolled his eyes and tried to look bored, but his sharp, sidelong gaze followed every move Matt made.

''All right, now stand up and I'll show you how to cast.''

Kneeling behind the boy on his good leg, his other knee bent and his foot flat on the pier, Matt put his hand over Tyrone's on the grip and guided his arm. ''When you cast, don't throw the rod like you're cracking a whip. All that does is sling your bait off and create a backlash. Draw back and swing forward in a smooth, continuous motion, like so and thro-o-ow it out there. Nice and easy. And control the reel's spin with your thumb, like this. You got a backlash because the reel was spinning off line faster than the weight on the bait end could carry it out.''

He guided Tyrone through the motion three more times, explaining the finer points as they practiced. ''Okay, you got that?''

''Yeah, yeah, I got it,'' the boy muttered.

''Fine. Let's see how you do.''

Scowling with concentration, Tyrone bit his bottom lip, drew his arm back, swung it forward and sent the baited hook sailing out over the water. When the hook and sinker hit with a gentle plop, he shot Matt a wide-eyed look over his shoulder, his grin growing wide. ''I did it!''

"Yeah. Now reel it in. Hey, not so fast! Jeez! How are you going to land a fish if he can't catch the bait? You want him to think that worm is just swimming along without a care."

"I gotcha. You mean like an easy mark. Like some dude struttin' down Lyons Avenue with his wallet stickin' up outta his back pocket, just askin' for somebody to lift it."

Matt rolled his eyes at the analogy. "Yeah, well, something like that. Okay, now you got the hang of it. Bring it in nice and easy now."

When Tyrone reeled the line all the way in and the hook cleared the water with only the worm attached, he looked crestfallen. "There ain't nothin' on it," he said, shooting Matt an accusing look.

"Of course not. If you'd gotten a bite you would've known it. And you don't catch a fish every time you cast, kid. Fishing is an art and it takes patience. Sometimes you can cast all day, but if the fish aren't biting you're not going to catch anything. You just have to keep trying."

On the third try Tyrone had reeled the line in barely halfway when it tightened and the bobber disappeared under the water, nearly jerking the pole out of his hands.

"Hey!"

"You got one!" Matt shouted. "Release the pressure on the line and let him run."

"But he'll get away!"

"No he won't. Not if you do it right. Keep the end of that rod up or you'll lose him!"

"It…ain't…easy, man," the boy gasped, hauling back on the pole with all his might.

"That's right," Matt agreed, reaching over Tyrone's shoulder to lend a hand. "But then, few things in life worth doing are."

Matt doubted that Tyrone heard the subtle moral in the

comment. The boy was so caught up in the excitement of catching his first fish he wasn't aware of anything else.

The fish jumped out of the water, a silver flash, twisting and arcing, and the reel spun with a rapid whir. "Oh, man! Look at that sucker go!" Tyrone shouted gleefully, pulling back on the rod with both hands as his catch took off and the pole bent in an even sharper arc.

"It's a big one, ain't it, Dolan?"

"Sure seems like it," Matt agreed, his excitement only slightly less than the boy's. "And, man, can that devil fight. Give him his head, son," he coached. "But keep that line taut. Now reel him in a little. Just a little. That's it. That's the way. Now play him out again. Let him know he's in a battle. Atta boy. You're doing fine. Just fine."

Over the next two hours, Matt caught five more fish, but threw four of them back because they were too small. Tyrone landed three more keepers and threw one back, though Matt had quite a job convincing the kid to give it up.

The boy was having the time of his life. When Matt announced it was time to quit, he protested loudly.

"Aw, man, I'm just getting started. You can quit if you want to, but I'm staying."

"I don't think so. You know the rules. You kids aren't supposed to go near the water unless an adult is with you. Besides, it's lunchtime. Anyway, fishing is best in the morning and the late afternoon. Fish don't bite much in the middle of the day. So come on, let's go."

"Aw, ma-a-an," Tyrone groused, but he reeled in his line, and when Matt took the pole from him and handed him the stringer full of fish in exchange, the boy slung it over his shoulder and fell into step beside him.

Maude Ann ran down the path to the boat dock, her heart hammering against her ribs. Fear nearly consumed her.

Matt fished off the pier nearly every morning, so she didn't have much hope that Tyrone would be there. Those two avoided contact whenever they could. But she'd looked everywhere else.

"Oh, God, please let him be there. And please let him be all right," she implored. "Please. Please."

What if, despite her rules to the contrary, Tyrone had gone down to the lake by himself and fallen in and drowned? It would be just like him to disobey. What if he'd climbed a tree and fallen and hurt himself, and she had walked right by him when she'd searched the woods? What if he'd broken a leg or gotten a concussion? Or cut himself and bled to death?

Sweet heaven, what if he'd run away and tried to hitch-hike out on the highway, and some pervert had picked him up?

Panic threatened to choke her. Whimpering, Maude Ann hastened her steps. The instant she tore around the next bend she could have wept with relief. Up ahead, Matt and Tyrone came walking toward her.

One look at her disheveled appearance and panic-stricken face and Matt obviously could tell that something was wrong.

He hurried to meet her as fast as his injured leg would allow. "What is it? What's happened?" he demanded, but she barely heard him. Her entire being was focused on the small, dark-skinned boy tripping along beside Matt as though he hadn't a care in the world.

"Tyrone!" Profound relief washed through Maude Ann, nearly turning her legs to rubber. The instant she reached the child, she dropped to her knees and snatched him into her arms. "Tyrone. Oh, thank God you're all right. Thank God, thank God," she gushed, squeezing the startled boy to her bosom in a bear hug.

The kid was dirty and smelled of sweat and fish, but she didn't care. Between raining kisses over his temple and cheek she babbled an almost incoherent stream of gratitude and endearments. Finally, laying her cheek against his sweaty head, she closed her eyes and began to rock the squirming child back and forth, hugging him fiercely.

"Miz…Maudie. Miz Maudie…leggo 'a me! I can't breathe!"

"Oh, I'm sorry!" She released him from the hug, but could not bear to break physical contact with him just yet. She ran her hands and her gaze over his shoulders, his arms, his chest. Framing his face with her palms, she inspected him, reassuring herself that he was, indeed, all right.

"Oh, sweetie, you nearly scared me to death."

"Me? How come?"

"How *come?* Tyrone, I didn't know where you were. Neither did Jane or any of the children. I was so worried. I thought something terrible had happened to you. I spent the past two hours searching the woods."

Tyrone looked dumbfounded. "I was fishing down at the pier with Dolan. See." A grin brightened his face, and he held up the stringer of fish and thumbed his chest. "*I* caught the biggest one." he announced proudly.

Maude Ann's mouth dropped open. Her stunned gaze went from the boy to the fish, then to Matt. "He was with *you* all this time? I've looked everywhere but the pier. I knew you were there fishing. It never occurred to me that Tyrone would be with you." She closed her eyes. "I've been worried sick."

"Tyrone, why the devil didn't you tell anyone where you were going?" Matt snapped.

Immediately the boy bristled. "Why should I? Back home, I went where I wanted, an' I didn't have to tell nobody, neither. My momma, she didn't care."

The statement, issued with such childish bravado, innocently revealed the grim, loveless existence of Tyrone's life before coming to Henley Haven. Maude Ann felt as though her heart were slowly tearing in two.

"Yeah, well, look at the kind of mom—"

Maude Ann flashed Matt a warning look over Tyrone's head, cutting off whatever disparaging remark he had been about to make. This was dangerous ground and they had to tread very carefully. She knew that no matter how awful or neglectful a parent was or how indifferent a child strove to appear, children still loved their mothers and fathers. They needed to love them, needed to believe their parents loved them back, if only a little. She would not strip any child of that illusion.

Cupping the boy's cheek, she looked at him tenderly. "Tyrone, your mother had problems that prevented her from giving you all the attention you needed. But she loved you, and I'm sure if she could have, she would have looked after you better."

"Shoot, she didn't love nothing but crack." Fixing his sullen stare on the ground, Tyrone drew circles in the dirt with the toe of his sneaker. "Told me if I didn't stay outta her sight, she was gonna give me away."

Anger flared inside Maude Ann that any mother, no matter how stoned she was, could say such a horrible thing to a child. A quick glance at Matt told her that he was as appalled and furious as she was.

She battled down the raw emotions and continued in a soft voice, "Maybe she just didn't want you to see what the crack did to her."

Tyrone looked up, and Maude Ann's chest squeezed painfully at the flash of hope in his chocolate-brown eyes.

"I care about you, too, sweetie. I care very much. That's why it's important to me that you are safe and happy. And when I don't know where you are or what's happened to you, I can't help but worry.'' She gave him a coaxing smile and stroked his hair. ''You don't want to worry me, do you?''

Tyrone looked at his sneakers again and shook his head. ''No, ma'am.''

''Good. So from now on you'll ask permission before you go off somewhere, okay?''

''Yes, ma'am.''

''Thank you, Tyrone,'' she said, and hugged him again. This time, he hugged her back.

Holding him close, Maude Ann closed her eyes and smiled, her heart swelling with love for this neglected, difficult child. For a few seconds, she allowed herself to relish the feel of his small, warm body, the scrawny arm clamped around her neck, his sweaty, little-boy smell, but when tears threatened, she released him and stood up.

''Now why don't you run along and take those fish to Jane before they spoil,'' she said briskly, giving him a little push toward the lodge.

Tyrone needed no more urging. He took off at a run, the stringer of fish flopping and bouncing against his backside.

Brimming with emotion, Maude Ann watched him until he rounded the bend and disappeared from sight.

''You are really something, lady.''

She gave a start and turned to see Matt studying her. Until he spoke she had almost forgotten he was there. ''Pardon?''

Matt walked toward her, slowly, purposefully, his slight limp almost undetectable.

Maude Ann watched him, and her heart began to boom. Something in his eyes, something glittering and intense that turned them several shades darker, sent a frisson of apprehension feathering down her spine. Some sixth sense told her to move, to flee while she had the chance, but her feet wouldn't budge.

Then it was too late.

Coming to an abrupt halt just inches away, Matt dropped the two fishing rods, reached out and clamped his hands on her shoulders and jerked her against his chest.

His smoldering gaze zeroed in on her mouth and stayed there.

Despite her best effort to control them, her lips quivered under that intense stare. Nerves danced along her skin, and suddenly she felt parched as a desert. She swallowed hard and licked her lips with the tip of her tongue.

Something flared in the depths of his blue eyes. For the space of several heartbeats, Matt stared at her. His grip on her shoulders tightened, and she felt herself being drawn closer, saw his head tilt ever so slightly and his eyelids grow heavy. Her heart lurched to a stop, then took off at a gallop. All the while his fiery gaze remained fixed on her mouth.

Then he looked into her eyes and stiffened. His black brows came down in a frown.

"Why the hell don't you get married again?" he snapped, and released her so quickly she stumbled backward.

Dazed and confused, Maude Ann touched her mouth with trembling fingers and watched him stomp away. "Now, what in the world was that all about?" she whispered.

Chapter Six

The memory of the encounter with Matt niggled at Maude Ann all during lunch. He had been about to kiss her, she was certain of that. She was no fluttery, naive girl; she knew when a man had amorous intentions. So why had he stopped and stalked off? Not that she *wanted* him to kiss her, but it was a puzzle.

It bothered her that she had no idea whether his actions had been driven by anger or passion. She was a psychiatrist; she was supposed to know these things. However, with someone as intense and moody as Matt, it was difficult to tell.

He had certainly seemed angry when he left, but the fire in his eyes had definitely been sensual. So which had it been? And what had he meant by those cryptic parting words? Her marital state had never before been of any interest to Matt Dolan.

He, of course, wasn't any help at all. Throughout lunch

Matt didn't so much as glance her way, nor did he take part in the conversation, but there was nothing new about that. To Maude Ann's chagrin, from the way he acted, you would never know that sizzling encounter just half an hour earlier had even occurred. Without coming right out and asking him, which she wasn't about to do, it appeared she was never going to find out what that little scene had been all about.

Mealtime with seven active children was not conducive to introspection. With a sigh, she decided that trying to analyze this remote, complicated man was more trouble than it was worth, and she put the matter aside and turned her attention to her charges.

She had promised them that if they were good and did their chores with no arguing, she would take them into town that afternoon to see a movie. By the end of the meal, they were so excited at the prospect they could barely sit still.

"Can we go now, Miz Maudie? Can we?" Jennifer asked, looking at Maude Ann hopefully.

"First clear the table, like always."

A chorus of cheers and the scrape of seven chairs on the brick floor erupted as the children hurried to comply.

"Hey! Take it easy!" Matt barked when Marshall nearly knocked him off his chair darting around the end of the table.

"Sorry, sir," the ten-year-old responded automatically, but he didn't slow down.

Watching them scramble to the sink with their plates and glasses, Maude Ann smiled, but inside dread squeezed her chest at what she was about to do. Still, she had no choice.

"All right now, all of you go wash your hands and meet me on the front veranda. Everyone except Tyrone, that is," she added quickly when they took off for the hallway door.

Tyrone skidded to a stop, his glee vanishing. "Why can't I go too?" he asked, eyeing her with wary suspicion.

The other children slowed their exit just long enough to dart sympathetic glances his way, then clambered out, pushing and shoving to be first through the door.

"I'm afraid you can't go with us, Tyrone. You sneaked out and went fishing this morning without doing your chores. Now you're going to have to stay here and finish the job while the rest of us go to the movies."

"That ain't fair! I promised that little snitch, Dennis, five bucks to clean 'em for me. 'Stead, he ratted on me. He's the one who didn't do the job, so he's the one you oughtta punish."

"To start with, Dennis did not tell on you. I caught him doing your job and made him stop. You cannot buy or bribe your way out of doing your share of the work around here, Tyrone. And by the way, just where did you plan to get this five dollars you were going to give Dennis?"

Tyrone focused his sulky gaze on the floor and shrugged. "I dunno. I'd get it someplace."

"Translation—he was going to lift it from your or Jane's purse," Matt drawled, entering the discussion for the first time. Leaning back in his chair, he sipped his iced tea and eyed the boy over the rim of the glass. "Isn't that right, Tyrone?"

If looks could kill, the one Tyrone aimed at Matt would have toppled him on the spot, but he didn't deny the charge, which in itself was an answer.

"I see." The disappointment in Maude Ann's voice made the boy wince and lower his head again until his chin touched his scrawny chest. "You didn't pull your weight today, Tyrone. On top of that, you bribed another boy and apparently you plotted to steal. You're lucky your punishment isn't more severe."

"But I hate cleaning toilets!" he wailed.

"I know. I feel the same. Nevertheless, we all have to take turns doing it, and this week is your turn, so you'd better get busy. You'll find the cleaning supplies in the bathroom at the top of the stairs where you left them."

His brown eyes snapped fury. For a moment she thought he was going to stage an all-out rebellion. Then what would she do?

"You said you cared 'bout me. I knew you was lying. I knew it! You're just like everybody else!" he accused. "I hate you! I *hate* you!"

"No, that's not true. I do ca— Tyrone, wait!" Maude Ann called, but he ignored her and ran from the room.

She started to go after him, but Matt got to his feet first. "Stay here. I'll go talk to him."

"You? Oh, but—"

"Just sit tight and let me handle this."

Panic surged inside Maude Ann as she watched Matt limp out of the room. No sooner had he disappeared through the doorway than she jumped to her feet to go after him, but Jane put a hand on her forearm and stopped her.

"Now, Maudie, give the man a chance. Could be what that boy needs most is a man to guide him."

"I know, but Matt's so harsh with the boy."

"He may be a little crusty on the outside, but he's a good man. And a fair one. He'll do the right thing. Trust me."

Maude Ann chewed her bottom lip and stared at the empty doorway, worry and misgivings chasing across her face. At last she sighed and sank back down on her chair. "Maybe you're right."

She tapped her foot and drummed her fingers on the table and glanced at the clock four times in fifteen seconds. It was no use.

"I can't stand this," she announced, and shot to her feet again. "I have to know what's going on."

Hurrying out of the room before Jane could stop her, she raced to the large foyer, swung around the newel post and took the stairs two at a time. At the top she spotted Matt standing a few feet away in the open doorway of the first bathroom.

He looked totally at ease, leaning on the cane with one shoulder propped against the jamb, the fingertips of his free hand stuck in the back pocket of his jeans. The casual stance allayed some of Maude Ann's fears. At least he hadn't stormed up here and lit into the boy. Not yet, anyway.

Eavesdropping was not an admirable activity, nor was it one in which Maude Ann would have engaged under normal circumstances. However, her concern for Tyrone drove her to it as she crept closer.

"I done told you—go away, pig."

Standing a few feet behind Matt, Maude Ann couldn't see Tyrone's face, but she heard the surliness in his voice. The child kept his back to the door and scrubbed the bowl of the commode furiously with a long-handled brush.

"Look, punk, you did wrong and you were busted. It's as simple as that."

"Yeah, well, I'm gonna blow this place first chance I get."

Maude Ann's heart lurched. She clasped her hands in front of her and pressed her lips together.

"Now that'd be kinda dumb, wouldn't it? This place and Dr. Edwards are the best thing that ever happened to you. Are you gonna blow it just because you're mad you got caught breaking the rules?"

The boy shot a searing glance over his shoulder. "Whazzit to you, pig?"

"Nothing, really. I just hate stupidity, that's all. This place is your chance at a decent life, kid. All you have to do is keep your nose clean and follow a few simple rules, and you'll be fine. It's not that difficult."

The boy's scrubbing slacked off to a less-intense rhythm, and this time his backward glance held the first sign of relenting. Maude Ann pressed her clasped hands tight against her breasts and said a silent prayer.

"Look, I'll make a deal with you. You don't give Dr. Edwards any more trouble, and I'll take you fishing whenever you want for as long as I'm here."

Tyrone stopped scrubbing altogether and turned. "You mean it?"

"Yeah."

"What if I wanna go every day?"

Matt shrugged. "Then we'll go every day. I fish most mornings, anyway. Afternoons, too, sometimes."

A calculating gleam entered the boy's eyes. "Will you take me out on one of them boats down in the boathouse?"

"Don't push your luck, punk," Matt drawled, but Maude Ann heard the laughter in his voice. "So how about it? Deal?"

Tyrone pursed his lips and appeared to consider. Then he shrugged and rolled his eyes. "Aw right, deal."

"Good. Let's shake on it."

Matt stepped into the bathroom with his hand outstretched. Tyrone stared at it, apparently surprised by the adult gesture, but he quickly wiped his sweaty palm on the leg of his jeans and stuck his small hand in Matt's large one. As they shook, the boy's chest puffed out and a grin nearly split his face.

Touched, Maude Ann retreated to the top of the stairs to wait for Matt.

He spotted her the instant he stepped from the bathroom,

and his mouth thinned as he limped toward her. "What are you doing here?" he demanded in a furious whisper, but he didn't wait for an answer. Grabbing her arm, he began hustling her down the stairs. "I thought I told you to wait in the kitchen."

"I don't take orders well. It's one of my many failings," Maude Ann replied with a saucy grin. She had hoped the cheerful admission would erase the scowl from his face, but it hadn't the least effect. "Anyway, I'm glad I didn't. I wouldn't have missed what just happened for the world. Oh, Matt, you were so wonderful with Tyrone!"

At the bottom of the stairs he turned her to face him. "You came upstairs because you didn't trust me to deal with the kid fairly, isn't that right? What did you think I was going to do—give him a beating? I'm not an ogre, Maude Ann."

He was angry, but she was too happy to care. She gave him a tender smile, her whiskey-brown eyes brimming with warmth as they ran over his face. "No you're not," she agreed in husky voice.

"I may not be a shrink like you, but for your information, in my own way, I've been trying to save that kid ever since he was about three years old."

"Have you? Oh, Matt, that's so sweet. I think you're making headway."

She gazed into those blue eyes and that stern face and tried to think of a way to explain how she felt, how grateful she was, how moved, but words seemed inadequate. She was brimming over with so much emotion she simply could not contain it any longer. Stepping closer, she placed her palms on his chest and gazed up at him with a melting look.

"Thank you," she whispered, and rising on tiptoe, she put her mouth on his.

Matt stiffened and went utterly still.

It was the softest of kisses, a gossamer caress of infinite tenderness and gratitude that lasted only seconds. There was nothing sexual about it—at least, Maude Ann had not intended there to be—but the instant their lips met in that feathery touch, a zing of electricity shot through her from the point of contact all the way to her bare feet.

If Matt felt anything, he gave no sign. Even as her hands curled into the front of his shirt, he stood rigid as a statue.

Shaken, she drew back and looked up into his face with a self-conscious smile, but it froze on her lips when her gaze met his. He was watching her, his eyes blazing. His face was dark and rigid with the emotions that seethed just below the surface.

Maude Ann felt her heartbeat speed up. This close she could see the tiny lines around his eyes, the pores in his skin, each individual eyelash. She could smell the musky maleness of him, the hint of outdoors and sweat, and feel his breath feathering across her forehead.

"If you're going to thank a man with a kiss, at least do it right," he growled, and before she realized his intent, he bent his head and clamped his mouth to hers. At the same time, his arms came around her, jerking her against his chest.

The kiss was powerful, stunning, and so hot and erotic Maude Ann thought surely she would melt into a puddle on the floor. His tongue stabbed into her mouth, dueled with hers, demanding surrender. His hands roamed over her back, and she felt his cane bumping against her backside. Maude Ann's head swam. All she could do was clutch his shirt and hang on.

She experienced a sudden sensation of spinning. Then her back came up against something hard and flat, and she realized he had swung her around so that her back was to the wall. With his hands braced on either side of her shoulders and his mouth still fused to hers, he leaned his weight into her and pressed against the wall.

The feel of that hard body against hers sent a shiver rippling through her. Her knees were so weak she would have slid down and collapsed on the floor had he not kept her pinned in place. Bracing on one arm, he moved his other hand to her waist and slid it slowly upward to cup her breast. When his thumb swept back and forth across her nipple, her toes curled against the hardwood floor of the hall.

At last he raised his head and released her, but he did not step away. Dazed and shaken, Maude Ann leaned weakly against the wall, her mind fogged with passion. Her breath rushed in and out of her lungs like a marathon runner's at the end of a race.

With his forearm still braced against the wall beside her head, Matt leaned in close and trailed his gaze over her flushed face. It lingered for an uncomfortably long time on her wet, slightly swollen lips, then lifted to meet her eyes. "That's the way it's done."

Straightening abruptly, he turned and limped away, leaving her stunned and disoriented.

Maude Ann had been kissed before. Many times and quite thoroughly, but never like that. Tremors still shook her body, and her heart hammered against her ribs like a wild thing.

She watched Matt move through the doorway at the back of the central hall behind the stairs. When he disappeared into the kitchen, she closed her eyes and let out a long, gusty sigh and slid down the wall until her bottom bumped the floor. Leaning her head back, she closed her eyes. She had always thought Matt was handsome in a tough-as-nails sort of way. Sexy, too. But she hadn't realized he was so...so potent. Sweet, merciful heaven. The man was lethal. If she wasn't careful, she could be in big trouble here.

Matt was having similar thoughts about Maude Ann, though his mood was far less genial.

With a barely civil nod for Jane, he stomped through the kitchen and into his room as fast as his injured leg would allow, slammed the door behind him and didn't slow down until he reached the bed. Hooking the cane on the brass rail at the foot of the bed, he flopped on his back on top of the bedspread, clasped his fingers together on top of his chest and stared, tight-jawed, at the ceiling.

He'd been without a woman too long. Kissing Maude Ann had felt too damned good.

Not that she wasn't attractive. Hell, she was beautiful— beautiful, brainy, empathetic, educated, with an earthy sexuality that made a man itch. And not just for sex, although there was that, but for other things, as well—home and hearth, family, commitment—all the things he avoided like the plague.

One thing he'd learned after twelve years with the department was that those things and police work just didn't go together.

Maude Ann was not the kind of woman suited for a casual, no-strings relationship, and he wasn't in the market for anything else.

He had seen too many of his fellow officers' marriages go sour and end in divorce. The stresses of the job, the long hours, put a strain on a marriage, or even a serious relationship, that few could withstand. Even those marriages that managed to weather the strain were less than perfect.

All his life, Matt had watched his mother worry about his father, seen the fear and dread in her eyes whenever Pat Dolan left for work. Eventually, almost inevitably it had seemed, what she had feared became reality. Matt had witnessed his mother's overwhelming grief when her husband had been killed during a routine traffic stop.

Less than a year later, she was gone, too. Congestive heart failure, the doctors had said, but Matt knew better. Maggie Dolan had died of a broken heart. Matt had no intention of ever putting a woman through that misery.

From outside came the sounds of high-pitched, excited voices. Matt rose from the bed and went to the window in time to see Maude Ann and the children heading for the minivan. She had exchanged her shorts and tank top for a swirling floral skirt that came almost to her ankles, a simple yellow T-shirt and a pair of strappy yellow sandals. Strolling along with a huge straw bag slung over her shoulder and her long auburn hair tied up in a ponytail with a yellow scarf, she looked about eighteen, instead of the thirty-four he knew her to be.

Matt watched her straighten collars and tie sashes and pat little rumps as she helped the kids into the vehicle, and his jaw clenched. There they were again, those simple, loving gestures that she handed out so naturally. He ran his hand through his hair and down the back of his neck to massage the tight muscles there. Dammit, why did he find Maude Ann's nurturing ways so appealing? It didn't make any sense.

Oh, he knew what she and her colleagues in the mental-health profession would probably make of it. No doubt they'd say he was starved for a mother's love, but Matt knew that wasn't true. Maggie Dolan had been a wonderful mother to him.

True, she hadn't given birth to him. He had been a little older than two when Patrick and Maggie Dolan had adopted him, but they couldn't have given him more love and attention had he been their own flesh and blood.

And he had loved them the same way, he thought, watching Maude Ann and her brood of misfits drive away. Which, he knew, was why that persistent dream made him feel so damned guilty.

Unconsciously, Matt touched the piece of medallion nestled against his chest. Though he didn't remember her, had no pictures of her and even in his dreams he'd never seen a face, he knew in his gut that the woman in the mist was his natural mother.

Ever since his parents had explained that he was adopted, he'd had the normal curiosity about the woman who had given birth to him. What was she like? Why had she given him up? Who was his father? Now and then Matt wondered what his biological family was like, and what course his life would have taken had his birth mother kept him.

Even so, he'd never felt any powerful yearning for her or any particular desire to search for her. The way he figured it, she had given him away. End of story.

Still, he had to admit that deep inside him was a hollow feeling, a longing that wouldn't go away. For what, he didn't know, except that it wasn't for his mother. Maggie Dolan had been all the mother he had needed. No, it was something else. It was as though something was missing, something vital.

Lost in thought, Matt continued to absently trace the outline of the medallion piece. It had been left to him by his birth mother. The jagged piece of silver was the only link he had with her.

He knew nothing about the woman. According to his parents, she had insisted on only two things when she had given him up for adoption. Being Irish American, she had wanted him to go to an Irish-American couple. Plus, she had stipulated that he be allowed to keep the medallion fragment.

Hungry for a child to call their own, the Dolans had readily agreed to her conditions. However, Matt knew that legally he couldn't be bound by their promise.

Hell, he didn't even know why he kept the thing. It was nothing but a piece of metal—useless, really. With only part of the medallion, he couldn't even make out the message etched on the back or the symbol on the front. He probably should have thrown the thing away years ago. But something inside wouldn't let him discard this last link to the woman who had given him life.

Accepting that, Matt returned to the bed and lay on his back with his fingers laced behind his head. His thoughts swung back to Maude Ann and the puzzling effect she had on him.

No, mothering was definitely not what he wanted from her. Besides, she didn't fit his image of a mother—a plump matron in an apron and a print dress who fussed and fretted over you and knitted sweaters and smelled of lavender and fresh-baked bread. It was a description, he realized, that fit his adoptive mother to a T, but not Maude Ann.

True, she was caring and affectionate with the kids and had a generous nature, but there was nothing in the least bit matronly about that luscious body and those long legs, or that sultry, hip-swinging walk of hers. Or that husky laugh that conjured up thoughts of warm summer nights, cool sheets and hot, sweaty sex. Even barefoot and wearing cutoffs and a tank top and not a speck of makeup, the woman oozed an earthy sex appeal that damn near drove a man crazy. Somehow, her giving nature only intensified that allure, sort of like the icing on a cake.

She was not, however, a woman you could love and leave, which was the only kind of relationship he wanted. Anything else, with a woman like Maude Ann, would only lead to disaster.

So what was he going to do about this attraction? he wondered as his eyes began to droop sleepily. To neutralize this chemistry between them, maybe he ought to work on building a casual friendship with her. Nobody wanted to ruin a good friendship with sex.

It was worth a shot. Keeping his distance sure as hell hadn't made the attraction go away.

"Here they come," Jane announced.

Maude Ann didn't need to ask who she was talking about. She sat the stack of plates on the table and joined the older woman at the sink. Through the window she saw Matt, with Tyrone at his side, emerge from the woods and head for the back veranda.

Thanks to the scorching weather, for the past week he had been taking his two-mile walk before breakfast, instead of after.

As soon as Tyrone had heard about it, he had begged permission to go with him.

"Why, Tyrone, I didn't think you liked Matt," she had gently teased, knowing full well that the boy's feelings about his former nemesis had shifted dramatically.

"Yeah, well...he's okay, I guess. Anyway, somebody oughtta go with him. You know, just in case he needs help."

Maude Ann had not been fooled by the transparent excuse. Since Matt had started taking Tyrone fishing, he had been a different child, and Matt had become his hero. Every chance he got, the boy followed him around like a shadow, mimicking his every move and everything he did, even to the point of getting up before dawn to walk through the woods.

Matt had changed somewhat, too. Nothing miraculous or drastic, but at least he had loosened up a bit and occasionally joined in their mealtime conversations. Only yesterday morning, he had come out to the garden when she and the children were working and shown Marshall and Yolanda the correct way to stake the tomato plants. Little Debbie had become jealous and demanded that he show her how to pick beans, which she had already been doing for weeks. Matt had ended up spending the entire morning in the garden helping the kids.

The other evening, at Tyrone's urging, he'd even joined her, Jane and the children in the living room after dinner to watch a movie on television.

Small things, really, but at least he was making an effort to be cordial, which made for a more pleasant atmosphere at mealtime. If it wasn't for those unexpected little sparks of sexual tension that flared between them, he would be the perfect house guest.

Maude Ann watched Matt brace one foot on the veranda rail and stretch his hamstring, then reverse feet and stretch the other. Muscles in his back and legs flexed and rippled beneath tanned skin that glistened with sweat, and she felt her pulse race.

Merciful heavens, but he was one delicious hunk of man.

Maude Ann sighed and silently reminded herself how inappropriate it was for her to be attracted to him. And dangerous. There had been no repeat kiss. Matt acted as though it had not happened at all. Which, she supposed, was just as well. After all, he was a cop.

"Watch it, girl." Jane gave Maude Ann a poke in the ribs with her elbow. "If you don't stop ogling the man, your tongue is going to be hanging out soon. I hate to think what kind of lascivious thoughts are going on in that head of yours."

Maude Ann grinned at her, not in the least abashed. "It doesn't hurt to look."

"True enough. Actually, I'm pleased to know a man exists who can get your motor running again."

Maude Ann shot her a look of mild exasperation, but she really couldn't argue with that, and Jane knew it. Matt was the first man to make her aware of her own sexuality since Tom. She stole another look at him through the window and sighed. "Good thing he's a cop. If he weren't, I might attack the poor man."

"You ask me, that'd be the smartest move you could make. And you could relax those rules of yours. It's possible to have a relationship with a man without marrying him, you know."

"Oh, no. Not on your life. Not me. With my luck I could date a dozen men, and if one of them was a cop, that would be the one I'd fall in love with."

"A dozen, huh? Shoot, I'd be happy if you dated just one. And so what if you did fall for another cop? Just because a man is a police officer doesn't mean he's going to go out and get himself killed. Most of them work thirty years or more and never have to fire their guns once."

"Maybe so, but I'm not taking any chances."

Jane clucked her tongue and gave her a disgusted look. "Stubborn. That's what you are. Just plain ol' mule stubborn. Oh, well. Maybe that fella you're meeting for lunch today will be single and gorgeous. He sure sounded sexy over the phone."

Maude Ann groaned. "Oh, no. That's today? I'd forgotten all about it."

"Don't even think about canceling. This is too important."

"I know, I know. It's just that there's so much to do if I'm going to make a good impression. I'd better start getting ready right now."

Two hours later, the woman who looked back at Maude

Ann from the mirror was a far cry from the casual, shorts-and-tank-top-clad foster mother the kids saw every day.

The mint-green, square-necked, princess-style dress skimmed her body perfectly and fell in a slim, straight tube from her hips almost to her ankles. On one side of the skirt a long slit from the hem to about three inches above her knee provided walking ease and a tantalizing flash of leg with each step.

It had been so long since she had dressed up for a social event—court appearance didn't count because then she always wore one of her business suits—that Maude Ann was a bit surprised herself. And pleased.

She picked up her keys and small white purse and headed for the door like a general going into battle.

She was halfway down the stairs when Matt walked in through the front door. Two steps inside the wide foyer, he spied her and stopped in his tracks.

"Maude Ann?" he said with so much shock that she chuckled, but her steps faltered under his hot stare.

Slowly, thoroughly, he took in every inch of her, from the coral-tipped toes peeking out of the sandals to the shining russet hair that swung around her face, controlled for once in a full pageboy. The inspection was blatantly sensual, the look in those vivid blue eyes sizzling. At last that bold gaze met hers, and when he spoke, the husky pitch of his voice made her skin prickle.

"You look beautiful."

The compliment caught her off guard. She had expected sarcasm. Forcing her feet to move, she continued down the stairs. "Thank you. Tom always said that I cleaned up good," she quipped.

"More than good. Spectacular."

"Are you trying to tell me something? Do I really look so awful normally?"

His gaze continued to roam over her as she descended, and when she reached the bottom of the stairs and stepped into the foyer he moved closer. "Maude Ann, you couldn't look awful if you tried. It's just that today you look really incredible."

"Good heavens. Be careful. You'll turn my head."

"I doubt that's possible. You're just about the most down-to-earth person I know." He gave her another quick head-to-toe inspection. "I take it you're going somewhere?"

"Yes. I have an appointment in Houston."

Without her noticing, Matt had somehow inched nearer while they talked. Now he stood so close she could feel his heat radiate along her bare arms. He smelled of soap and shaving cream, and sunshine and maleness. His nearness made her insides quiver and her nerves jump. She had just spent the past three hours indulging in a confidence-building grooming routine for the meeting in Houston. If she wanted to preserve her poise, she knew she had to get out of there. Now.

Maude Ann glanced at her watch. "Oh, look at the time. If I don't hurry, I'm going to be late, so if you'll excuse me…"

The twitch of Matt's mouth told her he knew he was making her nervous, but after a brief hesitation he stepped aside and let her pass. "Sure."

She hurried to the door, aware every step of the way of his gaze burning into her back.

If his expression was anything to go by, she had much the same effect on the man she was meeting for lunch as she'd had on Matt.

Maude Ann spotted him before he saw her. She had never met the man before. Their dealings so far had consisted of two telephone conversations, but since he was the only man sitting alone in the restaurant, it was easy to pick him out.

He sat at a table in a window alcove, absently fiddling with his silverware and looking bored. As she and the maître d' approached, he glanced up, and a look of surprise flashed over his face, followed by a swift but discreet appraisal and a slow smile of masculine appreciation.

He stood up as Maude Ann reached the table. ''Mr. Conway?'' she asked. ''You are J.T. Conway, the reporter with the *Houston Herald,* I hope.''

He flashed a charming smile. ''Guilty as charged.''

Chapter Seven

Maude Ann extended her hand. "How do you do."

He was a tall man, about the same height as Matt Dolan, and he had the same blue eyes and wide-shouldered, muscular build. He also looked about the same age. There, though, all similarity ended. Where Matt's hair was black as midnight, J.T. Conway's was a rich, dark brown. His eyes twinkled with teasing good humor, and she suspected that his smile could charm the hardest heart.

"I do hope I haven't kept you waiting long, Mr. Conway."

"Not at all. I'm delighted to meet you, Doctor. I've heard good things about you from several sources. It's nice to finally put a face with the name. Particularly such a lovely face."

It had been a long time since a man had flirted with Maude Ann, and J.T. Conway did it with such panache that she felt a little rush of pleasure. "Thank you," she replied with a polite smile, taking the chair he held out for her.

"Before we start, I must ask how you heard about Henley Haven. We're not listed in any telephone book and few people know of our existence. I'd like to keep it that way."

"I sorry, Doctor, I'm afraid I can't reveal my sources. But I will promise that I won't pass the information on to anyone."

She looked at him for a long moment. "Well, I suppose I'll have to settle for that."

They made small talk as they perused their menus and the waiter took their drink order.

When the man left, J.T. Conway's blue eyes twinkled at her. "You don't look at all like my image of a doctor. Or a foster mother, for that matter."

"Really? And what do you think a doctor and foster mother looks like?"

"I don't know, but you're much too young and too lovely to be either."

"Thank you, but I assure you, I am both." Maude Ann took a sip of water to hide her smile. "Which, may I remind you, is why I'm here."

"I appreciate your meeting with me." His rueful smile was charming. "I'll be honest with you. When my editor assigned this story to me, I wasn't too enthused about it. But now that I've met you, I'm glad I was given the job. So, tell me, Dr. Edwards, where exactly is this foster home of yours?"

"If you don't mind, I'd rather not say just yet."

That was why she had insisted on meeting him at a restaurant to discuss the possibility of him doing a story on Henley Haven instead of him coming to the lodge, as he had originally requested. Only John Werner and a small number of his officers, along with a few judges and social workers, knew where Henley Haven was located.

This meeting was a chance for both her and J.T. Conway to size each other up. He would decide if a story on Henley Haven would be of sufficient human interest for his newspaper, and Maude Ann would decide if she trusted him enough to allow him to write it.

"You're being kinda cloak-and-dagger about this, aren't you, Doctor?"

"Perhaps I am, Mr. Conway, but—"

"Please, call me J.T."

"Oh. Very well, then. And I'm Maude Ann. Now, as I was saying, until we reach an understanding, I would prefer not to disclose the whereabouts of Henley Haven. I appreciate your enthusiasm for this project, Mr. Con—uh, J.T., but I must warn you, before I grant an interview, there are some things we need to discuss."

His dark eyebrows rose, and Maude Ann could see that he was surprised. Apparently, not many people hedged when he wanted to do a story about them. After a brief hesitation, he shrugged and leaned back in his chair. "Maude Ann, you do realize that a big spread in the Sunday supplement, like the one I'm planning to do, will give your foster home invaluable publicity, and it's free. That can only be of benefit to the children."

"Not necessarily. It depends."

"On what?"

"On the type of story you do. And on whether or not you agree to my conditions."

"Conditions?" He laughed and shook his head. "I'm sorry, Maude Ann, but I don't allow conditions to be imposed on what I write. It's called freedom of the press."

"I see. If that's your final word, then I feel I must exercise my freedom of choice and right to privacy." Her tone was polite. So was her smile, but there was steel in her eyes. "I'm sorry, Mr. Conway, but I'm afraid there will be no story about Henley Haven. And no point in continuing this meeting. Perhaps if you would call the waiter over, you can cancel my lunch order. Good day." She picked up her purse and started to rise, but he reached across the table and grasped her wrist.

"Whoa. Whoa. Don't be so hasty. C'mon, sit down and let's talk about this, Maude Ann. Surely we can work something out."

"I doubt it. Those are my terms and they're not negotiable." Maude Ann's nature was mellow and easygoing, but when it came to the children, she could be as fiercely protective as a lioness. The look she aimed at him left no doubt of that.

J.T. eyed her shrewdly. "You operate mainly on a combination of grants and donations and the pittance the state allows foster parents, right?"

She nodded, and a look of satisfaction flickered in his eyes. He obviously thought he'd hit on the right tactic.

"Well, then, just think what a financial boon a piece like this would be."

Sitting back down, Maude Ann pulled her wrist from his grasp and met his confident gaze. "I am well aware of that, J.T. However, while I'll admit that it would be nice to have more operating capital, there are more important considerations."

He blinked, taken aback. "Like what?"

"Like the safety of the children."

They stared at each other in silence across the linen-covered table, Maude Ann's gaze level and uncompromising, J.T.'s full of disbelief and frustration. Finally he sighed. "You are one tough negotiator, lady. Okay, why don't you tell me what it is you want?"

"First of all, I want your agreement, in writing, that you will not divulge the names of any of the residents of Henley Haven in your story, or show any of their faces in the photos that will accompany the story."

"Why not? There's nothing like sad little faces to stir up public sympathy."

"For the same reason I don't give out the location of the home to people I don't know—for the children's safety. You have to understand that with the exception of a few who were orphaned under harrowing and traumatizing circumstances, these children were forcibly and permanently removed from their mother's and/or father's care. I don't want any disenfranchised parents with a grudge against our judicial system showing up on my doorstep trying to reclaim their child by force. None of them need any more trauma in their lives."

"Mmm. I guess you do have a point there. Anything else?"

"Only that you cannot divulge the whereabouts of the home to *anyone*—either in print or verbally." She waited a beat, then added, "And you must grant me the right to final approval before the story is printed."

"Whoa! Just hold it right there. That isn't going to happen. I might—just might—be able to get my editor to go along with the other conditions, but no way in hell will he allow an outsider to censor a story."

Maude Ann pursed her lips and gave him a considering look, but it was just for appearance' sake. She had expected him to balk at the last condition, which was why she had included it.

In any negotiation each party had to compromise and give in on something. So she threw in a condition that she could forgo if necessary, to which she knew J.T. and his superior would object. Chances were, if she gave in on that point, they would feel victorious and probably wouldn't object to the conditions she *really* wanted to impose.

"Well...I suppose for the sake of compromise, I have to give in on something," she said finally. "If you promise on your honor that you will write a favorable article about Henley Haven without revealing its whereabouts or the identities of the residents, I won't insist on seeing it prior to publication."

"You have my word on it. I'll run your conditions by my editor and get back to you in a few days. If that's okay?"

"That will be fine." She opened her purse and pulled out a long, white envelope and handed it to him. "This is a document outlining in detail my conditions. You can just cross out the prepublishing approval clause, and we'll all initial. If your boss agrees to the other terms, then you both need to sign the document and return both copies to me. When I've signed them, I'll return your copy."

J.T. looked flummoxed, but the waiter returned with their order before he could reply. When the man left, he raised his eyebrows and leaned forward. "You had a *contract* drawn up?"

"Yes. I told you, my number-one concern is keeping the children safe."

J.T. tipped his head to one side and looked at her with renewed interest. "You'd do it, too, wouldn't you? If I reneged on our deal, you'd use this document to sue me, wouldn't you?"

Still smiling sweetly, Maude Ann leaned closer across the table. "In a New York second, Mr. Conway. When it comes to protecting those children, I'd fight the devil himself."

The next morning, Jane awoke with a toothache, and Maude Ann shooed her off to the dentist. Preparing break-

fast for nine people on her own had her thoroughly frazzled
and dashing around the kitchen like a crazy woman, but at
last she put the meal on the table and sat down with Matt
and the kids.

"Can I haff two muffinth thith morning, Mith Maudie?"

Maude Ann looked at Timothy, and her heart wrenched
at the trace of fear in the five-year-old's eyes.

Though he had been with her for ten months, he still
expected a slap for simply asking for food. Because he had
been starved the first four years of his life, the child never
seemed to get enough to eat. Nor could he quite believe
that he was allowed to eat his fill.

Unable to resist, Maude Ann reached over and tousled
the child's blond curls and gave him a warm smile. "You
can have as many muffins as you want, sweetheart. Just
like always."

She glanced up and discovered Matt watching her, his
eyes dark with some unknown emotion. Inexplicably, her
face heated and she felt a little tingle race over her skin.

"What time are we leaving, Miss Maudie?"

Grateful for the diversion, Maude Ann turned her attention to Yolanda, only belatedly registering the barely controlled excitement in the girl's voice.

"Leaving?"

"To go out on the houseboat."

"Oh, dear!" She had been so busy since Jane left she'd
forgotten all about the excursion she'd promised the kids.
"Children, I'm afraid we're going to have to postpone our
outing until another day when Jane can go with us."

"But you promised to take us out on the houseboat today
if the weather was good!" Jennifer whined as groans went
up from the other children. "You promised!"

"I know. And if I could keep that promise I would, but

it's just not possible. Jane will be gone for hours, and I don't imagine she'll feel like doing much when she returns. I can't operate the houseboat and keep an eye on all of you by myself."

"But you promithed!" Debbie wailed while the other children muttered their own complaints.

Feeling terrible, Maude Ann sent an imploring look around the table. "Kids, I really am sorry. Honest. I know you're disappointed, but—"

"I'll go with you," Matt inserted quietly.

Maude Ann's head snapped around. "Wh-what?"

"I said, I'll go with you. I can operate the boat and you can keep an eye on the kids."

"Oh, but—"

"'Ray! We're going!" Debbie squealed.

All around the table the other children cheered and hooted and pumped their arms in victory.

"Matt, I don't think you realize what you're letting yourself in for."

Instantly the babble of elation around the table faded to a taut silence as seven pairs of eyes switched back and forth between the two adults.

"I told the children we would stay out on the lake all day. We were going to picnic in a cove several miles south of here and go swimming and maybe fish off the boat and just laze the day away. We won't get back until late."

"No problem. I've got nothing else to do. Anyway, I've been promising Tyrone for weeks that I'd take him out in one of the boats. Isn't that right, Tyrone?"

"Yeah, but I thought we was goin' out in one of them hot powerboats. Just you'n me," the boy mumbled with a pout. "Not on some dumb ol' houseboat with everybody else."

In spite of the situation, the boy's reluctance to share his hero with the other kids brought a smile to Maude Ann's lips.

"Yeah, well, you don't start with the most powerful, you know. You have to crawl before you can walk. Besides, I'm not sure I'm up to handling one of those souped-up jobs just yet." Matt reached over and cuffed the boy on the shoulder. "C'mon, punk, don't look so glum. It'll be fun."

The prospect of spending a whole day with Matt filled Maude Ann with a mixture of excitement and apprehension. No matter how appealing, she knew it wasn't a smart thing to do. The attraction between them was too strong. Whenever they were in the same room, even sitting at the table with Jane and the children around them, sexual tension sparked and crackled in the air between them. She couldn't believe Matt didn't feel it, too.

"Matt, I don't think—"

"What's the problem? You said you needed help with the boat and I'm volunteering. Unless, of course, you have some personal objection to my coming along?"

"No, of course not!" she lied. "I, uh...I'm just concerned that you'll get bored."

As one, seven little heads swiveled, and the children looked at Matt, their young faces taut and hopeful.

Leaning back in his chair, he sipped his coffee. Over the rim of the cup his eyes mocked her. "I don't bore easily, Maude Ann." He cocked one brow. "Any other reasons I shouldn't come along?"

Seven pairs of eyes swung back in Maude Ann's direction.

She tried desperately to think of something, but other than the truth, she couldn't come up with a single plausible reason. With what she hoped was a gracious smile, she bowed to the inevitable. "No, of course not. None at all."

"Good. We wouldn't want to disappoint the kids, would we?"

His gaze swept over the expectant faces. "Well? What're you all just sitting there for? Go get your swimsuits and let's get this show on the road."

The kids scattered like a covey of quail, shouting and squealing as they raced to the sink to dump their dishes and silverware. An instant later seven pairs of little feet pounded up the stairs. The decibel level was ear-shattering.

Maude Ann gave Matt a rueful look. "Just remember, you volunteered."

A half hour later they were on board the *Lazy Day,* chugging out into the cove, picking up speed a bit as they left the placid cove and the boat slipped into the lake's main current.

The kids were so excited they ran from one side of the craft to the other, peering over the sides and chattering. Maude Ann had made them all put on life jackets before they left the dock. Even so, she assigned Marshall and Yolanda the job of keeping an eye on the younger children while she went inside to stow their gear.

She put their towels, sunscreen and bug repellent in the bathroom and went into the small galley. As she searched the cabinets for lemonade mix, she wondered how she could have forgotten, even for a minute, that she had promised the children this outing on Lieutenant Warner's house boat.

The screen door slid open with a bang and Tyrone dashed inside. "Miz Maudie! Matt, he says he could sure use somethin' to drink. An' he needs you to come up to the bridge to show him where you want us to go."

"Tell him I'll be up in a bit but in the meantime to just keep heading south."

"Yes, ma'am."

He turned and raced back outside as quickly as he'd come in.

Smiling, Maude Ann shook her head. The change in the boy since Matt had taken him under his wing was nothing short of miraculous.

She wondered why Matt had volunteered to come out with them today. He had never done anything like that before. True, he had mellowed a bit lately. As his physical condition had improved so had his attitude toward her and the kids. So maybe this act of kindness was just more of the same.

That line of reasoning eased her tension, and she smiled and picked up the tray and headed for the forward deck. Apparently, the prospect of returning to Houston and the department had worked wonders on Detective Dolan's disposition.

She left the children eating their snack and climbed the ladder to the bridge.

"Where the devil have you been?" Matt demanded the instant her head poked over the top of the upper deck.

"Looking after the kids." She joined him at the console and pointed ahead. "The cove we want is right around the next bend. We've picnicked there a few times this summer. It has a sandy beach and the water is shallow for fifty feet or so out. It's a good place for the children to swim."

She glanced down at them and smiled. "I really appreciate you doing this, Matt. They're having a wonderful time."

"Like I told you, it's no problem."

Her gaze cut to him, and a little dart of awareness shot through her.

He stared straight ahead, his attention fixed on the water, both hands on the wheel. A baseball cap, dark sunglasses and a pair of boxer-style swimming trunks were his only attire. His skin was bronze from his daily walks and fishing, and it glistened with a fine sheen of sweat. He had regained almost all the weight he had lost, and his face no longer had that drawn look. Well-defined muscles sculpted his broad shoulders, chest and arms. He was an impressive-looking man.

The children's laughter and excited squeals floated up to them. Matt glanced down at the lower deck and snorted. "The way they're acting, you'd think they'd never been on a boat before."

"They haven't. Well…except for Marshall and Dennis. They claim that before he died, their grandfather used to take them out fishing in his skiff. But none of the others have been boating before."

"Why not? I thought you said you'd been here since February."

"We have, but I can't take them out by myself, and Jane is terrified of the water. She can't swim and she's leery of venturing out onto the lake even wearing a life jacket. It's taken me all summer to persuade her to give it a try so that the children could enjoy the treat."

"Why didn't you say something before now? I would have helped you."

"You? Oh, please." She shot him a wry look. "What? Do I look like a masochist?"

Matt had the grace to look embarrassed.

"Okay, okay. I'll admit I've been a bear to you and the kids since I arrived. I apologize for that. It's just that I've been so…down since the shooting. For a long time I was kind of lost, I guess. I wasn't certain of anything—whether I'd ever be able to return to active duty, whether I could live with it if I couldn't go back. Would I still be a good cop if I did? What I would do the first time I heard gunfire again? I guess I took out all my frustrations and uncertainties on you and your bunch.''

"It's okay." Touched that this strong man trusted her enough to make the admission, Maude Ann put her hand on his arm. The contact startled him, and she felt the involuntary contraction of his muscles.

She also felt the jolt she always experienced when their bodies touched. With an effort, she smiled warmly at him. "Really. You don't have to explain or apologize to me, Matt. I understand post-trauma depression."

He stared into her eyes as though searching for something. Finally he nodded. "Yeah, I guess you do."

Maude Ann told herself to break eye contact, to look away from that vivid blue stare, but she could not.

As their gazes held, a subtle tension built. She felt her chest tighten, her pulse race. She saw Matt's pupils dilate, saw the slight flare of his nostrils. A breeze caught a tendril of her hair and whipped it across her mouth. Several strands stuck to her lips, and as she lifted her hand to pull them away, his gaze dropped to her mouth.

The hungry look in his eyes made her heart skip a beat, then take off at a gallop.

Matt's mouth suddenly tightened, and he jerked his gaze away, focusing on the water ahead. His hands gripped the wheel in a white-knuckled hold. "Look, I'd like to forget these past few weeks and start over. I'd like us to be friends, Maude Ann."

Friends? She blinked several times and tried to adjust to the abrupt change in his demeanor. She had been certain he was about to kiss her again. Instead, he was offering friendship?

Was that even possible, given the chemistry between them? True, it was probably the wisest course to take. Anything else was impossible.

Finally she nodded and smiled at him. "I'd like that."

"Good." Letting go of the wheel with one hand, he stuck it out for her to shake. "Pals?"

His slow smile did devastating things to his stern face and her insides, and Maude Ann had the fleeting thought that it was a shame he didn't smile more often. Although, for her own emotional stability, perhaps it was just as well that he didn't.

Ignoring the tingly sensation that raced up her arm when she clasped his hand, she gave him a wry smile. "Pals."

Pulling her hand from his, she glanced ahead. "That's the cove."

Matt throttled down the engine, and immediately, realizing they were nearing their destination, the children's excitement level rose.

"I'd better get down there before somebody falls overboard. Give me a yell when you want me to drop anchor."

"Will do."

Being friends was for the best, Maude Ann told herself as she scrambled down the ladder. She knew that.

Even so, she couldn't seem to banish the tight knot of disappointment that caused her chest to ache.

Chapter Eight

Matt steered the flat-bottomed boat as far into the shallow cove as he dared before cutting the engine and calling down to Maude Ann to drop anchor. The kids were so excited they scampered from one end of the boat to the other, jumping up and down and squealing with delight and anticipation.

The instant the anchor splashed into the water, a babble of pleas to go swimming erupted from the children. The din was so overwhelming Maude Ann couldn't get a word in.

"Hey! Knock it off, you guys," Matt barked, hopping down the ladder on his good leg. "We're going to do this in an orderly manner. Now, I want all of you to line up over here," he ordered, pointing to a spot on the deck in front of him.

To Maude Ann's amazement, not only did the kids scramble to obey, except for a few giggles and elbow pokes, they were quiet about it. None of them appeared to be frightened by Matt's gruffness, nor did they seem to mind his dictatorial manner.

"All right now, if you can swim, raise your hand. Good. Good. Marshall, you, Yolanda and Dennis can help Maude Ann and me keep an eye on the other kids. You nonswimmers keep your life jackets on."

"Uh, Matt," Maude Ann said, "those are a bit bulky. I brought some floaties and inner tubes for the little ones to wear while swimming."

He frowned. "What the hell is a 'floatie'?"

"You'll see. I'll go get them."

When Maude Ann returned, she and Matt spent the next fifteen minutes blowing up the inflatable cuffs and putting them on the upper arms of the three youngest children.

To save Tyrone the indignity of being lumped in with the little ones, Matt slid a red plastic inner tube over his head and ordered him to stick beside him once they were in the water.

When at last they were ready, Matt jumped over the side first to test the depth of the water. Finding it came just to his waist, he signaled to the older kids to join him. Whooping with joy, Marshall picked up his little brother and tossed him over the side. As Dennis hit the water, his brother reached for Yolanda, but the shrieking girl dodged him and jumped in on her own. Marshall followed right behind.

Matt watched them for a few minutes to assess their competence. None of them were Olympic material but they were good enough swimmers to put his mind at ease.

Tyrone's gaze followed his friends with envy, but he eyed the water with a good amount of trepidation. Seeing his dilemma, Matt stepped closer to the side of the boat and murmured, "Just hold on tight to the inner tube with both hands, close your eyes and jump."

The boy flashed him a wild-eyed look. If anything, he appeared more frightened than before.

"C'mon, punk. It's not that deep here. See?" Matt held up both arms to show the boy where the water reached on him. "If you jump, your feet will probably touch the bottom for a second, then you'll bob right back up. Nothing to it."

Tyrone leaned forward and peered over the edge of the boat at the water. He caught his lower lip between his teeth.

"You can do it," Matt quietly urged. "And you know you can trust me. I won't let anything happen to you. Now c'mon, jump. Show 'em you're not afraid."

Tyrone's round-eyed stare went from Matt to the water, then back to Matt. For a second Maude Ann thought he would refuse. Then, setting his jaw, he clutched the inner tube under both arms, closed his eyes, sucked in a deep breath and took the plunge.

He hit the water with a yell and a tremendous splash, but when he surfaced, he was grinning. "I did it!"

"Sure you did," Matt acknowledged matter-of-factly. "Just don't go getting cocky on me. And stay close. As soon as we get the little ones into more-shallow water, you're going to get some swimming lessons, punk."

Tyrone looked ecstatic, and Maude Ann's heart filled with gratitude. She could have kissed Matt for his gruff kindness toward the boy.

Demanding her attention, the three remaining children hopped around on the deck as though it was on fire, squealing, "Me next! Me next, Miz Maudie! I wanna go swimmin' too!" Surreptitiously, Maude Ann wiped the moisture from her eyes and handed Jennifer and Timothy down into Matt's waiting arms. With Debbie straddling her hip, the child's arms locked around her neck in a death grip, she stepped off the side of the boat.

For the next couple of hours the older children swam and played a water game understandable only to them, while Matt and Maude Ann worked with the younger ones in the shallow water near the shore.

Matt showed remarkable patience and gentleness with the children. Within an hour they could all tread water. After two hours, Jennifer and Tyrone were happily paddling around and diving to the bottom to retrieve the coins and other objects that Matt tossed there. Even little Debbie and Timothy learned to float and do the dog paddle. What they lacked in form they more than made up for in joy and enthusiasm.

After a few hours of play, the children were ravenous and clamoring for lunch. Once they had eaten, Maude Ann issued orders that no one could return to the water for at least an hour. The children complained, but she stood her ground. When Matt backed her up, they accepted defeat and wandered off to seek other diversions.

Sitting on the picnic blanket, Maude Ann watched them play, her face soft with fondness. "They're having such a good time." She turned her head and looked at Matt. "Thank you so much for coming with us today. I wanted the children to have this day of fun, particularly Marshall and Dennis. There's a good chance they'll be leaving, so this may be their last outing with us."

Matt shot her a frown. "What do you mean? Where are they going? Jean told me that their mother committed suicide when their father ran out on them and there was no close family to take them. Ah, jeez! Don't tell me Children's Services has found their deadbeat dad and they're going to turn them over to him!"

"No, no. Judge Simpson would never do that. He's a

real children's advocate who puts the welfare of the children first. A distant cousin has petitioned the court for custody of the boys. He and his wife have two sons the boys' ages. Under the judge's orders, Children's Services has done a thorough check on them, including an extensive psychological study. They appear to be just the sort of family the boys need. The final custody hearing will be soon.''

"I see. Do Marshall and Dennis know?''

"Yes. I explained everything to them privately. Naturally, they're nervous about leaving. They feel secure here. But at the same time, they're anxious to be part of a real family again, and after our talk, I think they're okay with leaving. Last night I told the other children. There was some anxiety. Mostly fear that they, too, would have to leave someday, but that's only to be expected.''

"Do they have reason to fear? I mean, is this how it's going to be for all of them? They're here for a while, and just when they begin to feel safe, they're shipped off to strangers?''

The anger in Matt's voice caused surprise to ripple through Maude Ann. She had thought he was a cold and unfeeling man, uninterested in the children or their problems. Lord knew, with the exception of Tyrone and the occasional small kindness to Debbie, he had gone out of his way to avoid them.

A hint of a smile tugged at her mouth. Poor man. He had worked so hard to remain aloof and uninvolved, but the effort had apparently been for nothing. As she knew only too well, children in their innocence had a way of winding their little fingers around your heartstrings whether you wanted them to or not.

Touched by his righteous anger on their behalf, Maude Ann reached out and laid her hand on Matt's arm. "I won't lie to you, Matt. It's possible. For some of them, at any rate. Others, ones like Tyrone and Jennifer, may never be adopted, in which case, they may remain here. Or they could eventually be transferred to another foster facility.''

''Oh, great! So they're just going to be shuffled around from one foster home to another until they're eighteen, when they'll be booted out into the world to fend for themselves.''

''The system isn't perfect, Matt, but it's all we have.''

''It stinks! Why can't they all just stay here with you?''

''Matt, you have to understand, Henley Haven is just a temporary shelter for these kids, a place to heal and adjust until a better home can be found for them.''

''Better than this?'' he demanded with an expansive wave of his arm. ''Impossible. Hell, Maudie, your place is every kid's dream—a rambling home in the country, with a lake and woods, a bunch of other kids for company, good food, clean clothes and beds, all run by a beautiful mother figure. Trust me, for a kid, it doesn't get any better than this.''

Maude Ann gaped at him, momentarily stunned, not only by his praise of Henley Haven, but to learn that he thought she was beautiful. When he continued to glare, she blinked and gathered her scattered wits.

''Matt, that's sweet of you. I...I don't know what to say. I always thought you didn't like me. And that you disapproved of me running a foster home.''

Some of the harshness faded from his face, and she thought she saw a flash of chagrin in his eyes before his gaze switched to the ground in front of his bare feet. ''That wasn't personal. I just wanted the place to myself.'' He picked up a handful of sand and let it trickle back to the ground, watching the flow as though it was fascinating.

''I never disliked you,'' he added quietly. ''I'll admit I've never had much faith in your profession, particularly in conjunction with police work, but until recently, I was neutral about you on a personal level.''

''I see. And now?''

He looked up and his gaze locked with hers. Something in his eyes, something intense and hungry, almost desperate, sent a thrill coursing through her. His face was dark and somber. His whole body seemed taut, as though he was on the brink of making a life-altering confession. The depths of his eyes, swirling with emotion, were like a seething cauldron.

Then he blinked and it was gone, as though a curtain had been lowered. He gave her a quirky smile. ''Now? Now we're pals. Remember?''

Disappointment washed over her, but she returned his smile with a weak one of her own. ''Yes. Of course,'' she agreed, but she had the strangest feeling that was not what he had been about to say at all.

The boys came running back at that moment, Marshall in the lead and little Timothy trailing far behind and whining. Skidding to a halt beside the blanket, they were flushed from their run and smelled of sweat and sunshine.

''Miz Maudie, can me'n Marshall an' Dennis go exploring in the woods?'' Tyrone gasped, his chest heaving.

Maude Ann glanced at the thick woods that lined the shore. The kids played in the woods around the lodge all the time, but there they had trails and most of the underbrush had been cleared out. These woods were wild and thick and probably dangerous. ''Oh, guys, I don't know…''

''C'mon. Let 'em go, Maude Ann. All boys like to explore,'' Matt said with a hint of admonition in his voice.

''What if they get lost?''

''They won't. But if they do we'll find them.'' Taking her agreement for granted, he turned a stern face on the boys. ''Now listen up. You guys can go, but you're to keep the beach in sight at all times. No wandering off deep into the woods chasing a lizard or anything else. Period. You got that?''

''Yessir,'' they replied in unison. ''We won't. We promise.''

''And you have to take Timothy with you. And keep an eye on him so he doesn't get hurt.''

''Aw, do we gotta?''

''Sorry, boys. That's the deal. Take it or leave it.''

Tyrone rolled his eyes. ''O-*kay*, he can tag along.''

''So what are you waiting for? Get going.'' They took off at a run. ''And when I call you, you'd better haul your skinny little butts out here, you hear?'' he yelled after them.

Maude Ann watched them scamper into the woods, their rubber-soled shoes slapping their heels. When they disappeared from sight, she aimed a bemused look at Matt. ''How do you do that?''

''What?''

''Get them to snap to attention that way and obey your orders.''

''They're learning to recognize the voice of authority, that's all.''

She tipped her head to one side and studied him. ''I think it's much more than that. They trust you.''

Matt shrugged. ''Maybe. I don't know.''

''I do. Each of these children has suffered at the hands of an adult. You're gruff and intimidating. Your size alone should frighten them, yet they aren't in the least afraid of you.''

''Hell, I hope not. I want to command their respect, not terrorize them. Only a monster would do that.''

Wrapping her arms around her drawn-up legs, Maude Ann rested her chin on her knees and gazed out over the water. Sunlight flashed silver on the gentle wavelets, and the houseboat bobbed peacefully in the cove. A flotilla of puffy clouds drifted along as though being pulled by a string. From the woods came the raucous caw of a crow and the angry chatter of a squirrel.

"Believe me, there are plenty of monsters in the world," she said. "I've seen them in court often. As I'm sure you have. Evil has many faces."

Matt turned his head. She could feel his eyes on her, studying her, but she kept her own eyes focused straight ahead.

"Is that why you started Henley Haven?" he asked quietly. "To protect kids from monsters?"

Maude Ann huffed out a mirthless little laugh. "If only I could. No, by the time they come to me, the damage has already been done. All I can do is try to undo it—at least, to the extent that's possible. The nightmarish memories will always be there for these children—there's no escaping that. But with help, they can learn to move on and not let what happened dominate their present and future.

"What I try to do is provide some normalcy, show them that the world doesn't have to be a scary place, that there are people in it who will love them and take care of them."

A sad little grimace twisted her mouth. "Sometimes I succeed—most of the time, actually—but once in a while I don't. Every now and then there's a child who's been so savagely traumatized that I can't penetrate the shell he's built around himself. But I have to try. I have to," she added softly, passionately.

Yes, Matt thought, watching her, she would have no choice. Not Maude Ann. Her nature was too giving, her soul too sensitive, her heart too loving to do otherwise.

Little lost souls with old eyes, the timid, the frightened, hellions and budding delinquents—she welcomed them all with open arms, giving them, some for the first time in their short lives, unqualified love and nurturing, a secure home, freedom from fear and discipline tempered with caring.

He glanced down the beach at the girls, busily building their castle, then at the woods where the boys were exploring. They were not her flesh and blood, but she loved every one of them, and her valiant spirit would always demand that she protect and defend them to her last breath.

Maude Ann Edwards was an extraordinary woman.

As Matt studied her profile, his chest swelled with emotion, a dark swirl of feelings he didn't want to acknowledge, didn't want to think about, but they wouldn't go away. The longer he gazed at her the tighter his chest grew, until it almost hurt to draw breath. The urge to touch her, to put his arms around her and pull her close, to taste her lips, almost overwhelmed him.

He told himself to look away, to change the subject, but he couldn't. "The kids are lucky to have you," he replied in a husky voice.

"No. I'm the lucky one." At that moment the sound of high pitched giggles broke the silence of the cove. She looked at the girls, and her face softened with a gentle smile. "They bring such joy to my life. I would be lost without them."

"You're great with them. You should have a houseful of your own." He waited a beat, then asked, "So why didn't you and Tom start a family right away? Neither of you were exactly children when you married."

Inserting her late husband's name into the conversation had been a deliberate attempt to defuse the situation and banish the desire gnawing at him. It didn't work.

Maude Ann laughed and leaned back on her elbows. Matt had to stifle a groan. Heaven help him. Did she have any idea how sexy and desirable she looked, stretched out like that, wearing nothing but that skimpy bathing suit? All right, as bikinis went, hers was modest, but her womanly curves were delicious enough to tempt a saint.

"My, you're just full of questions today, aren't you? Actually, Tom and I did try to start a family. When we had no luck, we had some testing done and discovered that his sperm count was extremely low. We were about to undergo in vitro, but before we could arrange it, he was killed."

"I'm sorry."

Maude Ann lay down all the way on her back. Knowing he shouldn't, but unable to resist, Matt stretched out on his side next to her and propped his head on his hand. This close he could smell her womanly scent, feel her body heat.

"That's all right. It's been two years now, and I've come to terms with losing him, and with knowing I'll never have babies of my own."

"It's not too late. You should marry again."

She chuckled. "Now you sound like Jane."

"I'm serious, Maude Ann." He reached out and ran a fingertip along her jaw. He felt a tiny jolt of electricity race up his arm from the point of contact, and he knew from her start that she had felt it, too.

Her eyes widened. She lay perfectly still, staring at him. The air between was suddenly heavy, charged with sizzling awareness, with need. Matt could barely breathe, and the rapid rise and fall of her chest revealed that she had the same problem.

"You're a beautiful, desirable and vibrant woman, Maude Ann," he whispered. "It would be criminal for you to spend your life alone."

"W-would it?" She swallowed hard.

Smiling, he slid his finger down her elegant neck and she shivered. The tiny reaction sent his blood racing through his veins to settle in a hot pool in his loins.

He gritted his teeth and cursed himself for a fool. If he

had an ounce of sense he would back off now, pretend he'd felt nothing. It was the prudent thing to do.

His gaze trailed down her face and fixed on her mouth, and his eyes narrowed into slits. Aw, hell. Prudent be damned. If he didn't taste that luscious mouth soon he was going to explode.

His fingers curved around her neck. She stared up at him. At the base of her throat a pulse beat rapidly. He felt her breath feather across his jaw in erratic little puffs.

"Maudie," he whispered, leaning closer, and her eyelids fluttered shut as he lowered his head toward hers.

A bloodcurdling yell rent the air a fraction of a second before his lips touched hers. Matt's head jerked up. "What the hell?"

"Run! Run!" Marshall burst out of the woods first, carrying Timothy over his shoulder like a sack of feed. Hot on his heels, their eyes big as saucers, came Tyrone and Dennis, racing for the water.

"Run! He's right behind us!" Tyrone yelled.

"Who is right—" Matt never got a chance to finish the question, for at that moment, a wild pig came charging out of the woods with blood in his eyes.

"Ah, jeez! They've flushed out a pineywood rooter." Matt sprang to his feet and jerked Maude Ann up. "C'mon! We gotta grab the girls!"

Maude Ann took one look at the snorting animal with the lethal-looking tusks, let out a yelp and did as she was told.

The boys pounded past them, hit the water at full speed and kept going, sending up a tremendous spray. Instantly the pig changed targets and came after Matt and Maude Ann.

Sure he could feel the creature's hot breath on the back

of his legs, Matt turned on more steam, dragging Maude Ann along with him.

Without breaking stride, they swooped the girls up and bolted into the lake, Matt with Yolanda under one arm and Jennifer under the other, Maude Ann clutching Debbie. They didn't stop until they caught up with the boys, who had barreled out to the five-foot depth before they realized that their pursuer hadn't followed.

Treading water, they all stared back at the beach, where the wild pig trotted up and down along the water's edge, snorting and pawing and eyeing them with feral hatred. Unable to reach them, the animal turned and vented his fury on their belongings.'

Maude Ann, Matt and all the children watched with their mouths agape as the animal butted the picnic basket and sent it sailing out into the lake, then savaged the blanket with his tusks.

As quickly as he had erupted from the woods, the pig ran back into them and disappeared.

A stunned silence stretched out, the only sounds the gentle lapping of water.

"Man, that was one mad pig," Tyrone finally muttered in an awestruck voice.

Matt's gaze met Maude Ann's. After a moment his mouth twitched. So did Maude Ann's. Unable to hold back any longer, they both burst out laughing.

"What's so funny?" Tyrone demanded, scowling at them. "We was nearly killed by that pig."

"Yeah, that's not funny," Dennis complained, and several of the others chimed in their agreement.

Matt and Maude Ann laughed so hard they had to lean on each other for support, and it was minutes before either could answer.

Still chuckling, Matt shook his head and gripped the

boy's shoulder, but his eyes twinkled at Maude Ann. "You're gonna have to take my word for it, kid. That was funny."

The outing in the cove marked a change in Matt's attitude toward the children and in his relationship with Maude Ann.

After that day, he continued to help with the children, accepting without question his daily participation in their activities, just as though that was his purpose in being there.

If Maude Ann took the kids berry picking or for a walk through the woods, Matt went along. He taught them to play catch with both a softball and a football, took them fishing on the pier, nailed a hoop on the side of the garage and taught them, girls and boys alike, the finer points of basketball. When they played, it was all the kids against Matt, and it usually turned into a squealing, shouting free-for-all.

He helped out in the garden and around the house. In the evening after dinner he began joining them in the living room, and he participated in board games or whatever else was going on.

The children loved having Matt around—having both of them around. Maude Ann knew that she and Matt had somehow become surrogate parents, the kind every last one of these kids had probably always wished for but never had. That was the only thing about Matt's participation in their lives that worried her. How, she wondered, would they would react to his departure?

There was no question that he would be leaving soon, probably in a couple of months, maybe less. His chances of returning to active duty were looking brighter all the time, as daily he grew stronger and his limp had all but disappeared.

In those quiet moments late at night, Maude Ann admitted to herself that she loved having Matt around as much as the children did. Foolish and self-destructive as it was, she knew that day by day she was slowly losing her heart to the man, but there didn't seem to be a thing she could do to stop it.

All she could do was make sure Matt didn't know. If now and then, when they accidentally touched or their eyes met for a few seconds too long and that spark jumped between them, well, so be it. She would keep a tight hold on her wayward emotions and savor their summer of friendship. If there was heartache in her future, she would deal with it when it came.

The call from J. T. Conway came late one afternoon, nine days after their lunch together. Matt and Tyrone were out rowing on the lake somewhere. The weather was unbearably hot, and as a result, the children were cranky and listless, and Maude Ann had spent most of the day breaking up squabbles. She had been about to take the kids to the creek for a swim to cool off when the telephone rang.

She had expected to hear from J.T. sooner, but she suspected he had deliberately made her wait. Maude Ann didn't care. As long as she got what she wanted.

"It went pretty much as I thought it would," J.T. told her. "My boss doesn't like it, but he's willing to accept your first three conditions. However, he won't budge on the prepublication approval. I'm sorry, Maude Ann."

No, you're not, she thought, chuckling to herself. There wasn't a reporter in the entire country who would allow an outsider carte blanche to censor his work. "I see," she said doubtfully, and immediately J.T. rushed on.

"But you have my word, Maude Ann, that I'll write an

upbeat story. One that will have people begging you to take their money, I swear it.''

"Thank you, J.T. Uh…you and your boss *did* sign the contract I gave you, didn't you?''

"Yes. I was hoping I could bring it out today.''

"That would be fine.''

When she'd given him the directions, J.T. went on in a casual tone, "I was thinking I could come out around five and you could show me around the place, let me get acquainted with the kids, that sort of thing. Then afterward, maybe I could take you out to dinner.''

"Oh, J.T., I'm not sure that's—''

"I thought you could fill me in on some background stuff,'' he went on quickly before she could refuse. "You could even help me decide what angle to take with the story.''

"I see.'' Maude Ann doubted that was his main reason for wanting to take her to dinner, but the chance to perhaps influence the direction his story would take was too tempting to pass up. Besides, an evening out with an attractive man might help her current predicament. If she was ever going to get over Matt, she might as well start now before her heart was completely lost. And what better person to help her than J. T. Conway? He was an intelligent, charming and witty companion. And he was handsome, to boot.

"All right. If you get here by five that should allow plenty of time for me to introduce you to the children and show you around before we leave for dinner.''

Matt's back and shoulder muscles were screaming as he rowed the last few feet to the pier. When the skiff bumped the piling, he pulled in the oars and secured them, then stood up, rolling his shoulders and flexing his back muscles while Tyrone threw a mooring line around the piling.

"You did real good today. We musta rowed ten miles!" the boy exclaimed, flashing Matt a wide grin. "Man, we was flying across that water like we was a rocket."

"What's this 'we' stuff, punk?" Matt asked. He shot the boy a teasing look and rotated his shoulders one last time. "I didn't see any oars in your hands."

"Hey, man, I was helpin'." Tyrone lifted his chin at a cocky angle and thumbed his chest. "I'm your trainer, remember. Anyway, I was ballast. Without me to balance the boat, you'd'a never made it that fast."

"Izzat so? That's big talk for a pipsqueak."

"A pip what? Whazzat mean?" Tyrone scowled. "Is you bad-mouthing me, pig?"

Matt laughed and put his hand on the boy's shoulder to guide him up the path to the lodge. "Don't get your shorts in a wad, punk. I was just jerking your chain. C'mon, let's get a move on. Jane'll have dinner ready soon and I'm starving."

They kept up a steady stream of teasing insults as they walked along the path. When they emerged from the woods and Matt saw the strange car parked in front of the lodge, he felt a stab of annoyance. Who the devil...?

"Looks like Miz Maudie's got company," Tyrone remarked.

"Yeah." Matt frowned, trying to place where he'd seen that car before.

Just as he and Tyrone approached the front steps, the door opened and Maude Ann stepped out onto the veranda. The first thing Matt noticed was that she was wearing a dress and high heels. Then his gaze fell on the man who followed her.

Matt jerked to a halt, fury turning his face hard as granite. "What the hell are you doing here, Conway?"

Chapter Nine

"Well, well, well. If it isn't our wounded warrior. How's it going, Detective? Long time, no see."

"Not long enough."

"Matt!" Maude Ann exclaimed.

He ignored her. "Who told you I was recuperating here, Conway?"

"You're kidding me. This is where you've been all this time? No wonder I couldn't find you."

"Knock it off, Conway. I don't buy that innocent act. I want the name of the person who told you where I was."

Alert to the discord between the two men, Tyrone stood by Matt's side, avidly taking it all in, his sharp gaze skittering back and forth between them.

Farther down the porch, the girls sat in a circle, playing a game of jacks. They barely glanced the men's way.

J.T. met Matt's hostility with his usual lazy grin. "No, really, no one told me a thing. Not that I didn't ask, mind you. But your buddies down at the precinct either didn't know where you'd disappeared to, or they just weren't telling, and no one else had a clue. I've been beatin' the bushes all around Houston trying to find you. I was beginning to think you'd fallen off the earth.''

"If no one told you, how did you find out I was here?''

J.T. chuckled. "I didn't. This is just pure dumb luck. I'm here to do a story on Henley Haven.''

Matt turned his furious gaze on Maude Ann. "You've agreed to meet with this jerk?''

"Hey! I resent that,'' J.T. protested, but the amused smile still lingered around his mouth.

Before Maude Ann could answer, a look of sudden understanding flashed over Matt's face. His eyes narrowed. "That's where you went a couple of weeks ago, wasn't it? That so-called business you had in Houston was a lunch date with Conway, wasn't it?''

Maude Ann blinked at him, dumbfounded. He made it sound like an accusation. "Yes, it was. Although I don't see why you're so upset about it. Mr. Conway had contacted me about possibly doing a story on Henley Haven for the Sunday supplement. I met him in Houston and we discussed the matter.''

"And I suppose you're going to let him do the article?''

"Yes. Yes, I am. It will be good publicity. The exposure could help raise money for the home.''

"Dammit, you might have had the decency to discuss it with me before you gave him the go ahead.''

"Why should she consult with you?''

Matt stabbed his finger in J.T. direction. "You stay out of this, Conway. I'm talking to Maude Ann.''

The harshness of his voice drew the attention of the girls. Their jacks game forgotten, they stared with wide-eyed apprehension at the three grown-ups.

Not Tyrone. He seemed to find the hostile exchange exciting. His gaze flashed to J.T., eager for the next volley.

Noticing the children's reactions, Maude Ann winced. Learning the reason for the confrontation no longer mattered. She had to put a stop to it before the children became more upset.

J.T.'s good-natured smile vanished. "Listen, Dolan, I've had about enough of your attitude. I don't want to tangle with an injured man, but…"

Bristling, Matt started up the steps. "Don't let that stop you. On my worse day I can handle you, Conway."

"Aw *right!*" Tyrone cheered. "Git 'im, Dolan! Punch his lights out!"

"That's it." J.T. braced as Matt gained the porch, but before either man could take a swing, Maude Ann stepped between them and put a hand flat against each chest to keep them apart.

"Stop it! Just stop it right now!"

"Get out of the way, Maude Ann."

"Listen to the man, Doc. This is between Matt and me."

Over the top of her head the two men's gazes clashed.

"No! I most certainly will not! How dare you behave like this in front of these children," she all but hissed. "Haven't they been through enough without witnessing such a disgraceful exhibition? Look at them. Just *look* at them. You're frightening them."

Instantly Matt and J.T.'s gazes shot down the veranda to the girls' stricken faces. Against her palms, Maude Ann felt a slight easing of tension in both men's bodies.

"Ah, damn," Matt spat. Taking a step back, he stood at the veranda railing with his shoulders taut, his fists clenched at his sides.

J.T. tried to mumble an apology, but Maude Ann cut him off with a sharp look and a curt, "I don't want to hear it.

Not another word out of either of you. Not until the children are inside."

"Shoot! Whadja go'n stop 'em for?" Tyrone grumbled.

"And that's quite enough out of you, too, young man. You go inside and wash up for dinner."

"Aw, Miz Maudie—"

"Now."

Maude Ann was normally the most easygoing of women, but when she used that tone, not even Tyrone dared to argue. Grumbling, the boy ducked his head and started for the door.

She turned to the girls with as pleasant an expression as she could muster. "Girls, it's time to wash up for dinner."

Unlike Tyrone, they scrambled to obey, gathering up their jacks and ball and scurrying inside.

As soon as Maude Ann was certain they were out of earshot, she turned to the two men.

"It's obvious that you two know each other and there's no love lost between you, but that's no excuse for that childish display you just put on. I want an explanation, and I want it right now, so one of you had better start talking."

"Matt has a problem with reporters," J.T. volunteered. Good humor returning, he aimed a cocky grin Matt's way.

Matt's gaze still burned with anger. "Not all reporters. Just pests like you." He turned to Maude Ann. "Whenever a crime occurs, he barges in, interfering with police investigations, harassing victims for comments at inappropriate times, digging up confidential information any way he can and publishing it with no regard to how he's jeopardizing our case."

"Hey. Ever heard of freedom of the press?"

"Ever heard of the right to privacy?" Matt shot back. His gaze sought Maude Ann again. "When I took a bullet, this guy practically beat me to the hospital. No sooner had

I woken up from surgery than he started trying to worm a story out of me about the drug bust.''

J.T. spread his hands wide. ''Hey, I'm just doing my job.''

''Yeah, well, you've got a lousy job, Conway. And I'm warning you, if you so much as mention my name in your article, I'll make you wish you'd never heard of Henley Haven.''

His angry gaze switched to Maude Ann. ''I came here for privacy and to get away from people like him. It's bad enough that you've destroyed that by bringing a reporter here, but exploiting these kids for money is low. And to think I believed you when you said you wanted to protect them. Nice going, Dr. Edwards.''

''Matt, you don't under— Matt, wait!'' She stepped forward, reaching out to him, but he ignored her and stalked into the house. Maude Ann flinched as the door slammed behind him.

''Oh, dear.''

''Ah, don't worry. I've known Matt for over ten years. Believe me, his bark is worse than his bite. He didn't mean that stuff about the kids—he's just ticked off. When he cools down he'll probably apologize.'' J.T. paused. ''Of course, he'll get angry all over again when the article comes out, but don't worry, he won't kill me.''

Her head snapped around. ''What do you mean? You're not going to mention him in the article after what he just said, are you?''

''Sure I am.''

''But why? Do you hate him that much?''

J.T. looked shocked. ''I don't hate him at all. To tell the truth, I kinda like the guy. Don't ask me why. He's hard-nosed and crusty as hell, and he sure isn't fond of me or my profession. Still, I can't help but admire him. Go figure."

"If you feel that way, then why are you going to write about him when you know he'll hate it?"

A wicked twinkle entered J.T.'s eyes. His slow grin was pure devilment. "Partly because I enjoy rattling his cage."

"J. T. Conway, that's terrible."

"Yeah, I know," he replied, not in the least repentant. "Anyway, liking the guy is one thing, business is something else. It'll make a great hook for the piece. You know, a headline like, 'Wounded officer finds healing peace at Henley Haven.'"

"I won't let you do that."

"Now look—"

"You signed a contract, and I'm going to hold you to it."

"C'mon, doc, that agreement was for the kids' protection."

"It states that you will not mention the name of any resident of Henley Haven. Matt lives here. That makes him a resident. So help me, J.T., if you print his name or even allude to his presence here, I'll slap you with a lawsuit."

He gaped at her. "This is crazy. It's not as though I'm going to malign him. Matt's a hero. A fallen member of the thin blue line. That makes him newsworthy. Besides, the readers want to know how he's recovering."

"That doesn't mean he has to satisfy their curiosity—or sell newspapers for your boss. Matt, like everyone else, has a right to privacy. And you will respect that right. Do I make myself clear?"

J.T. shook his head slowly, a look of amazement on his face. "Like crystal. Jeez, lady, you are one tough negotiator."

He glanced at the door through which Matt had stormed

moments before, then looked back at Maude Ann with a speculative gleam in his eye. "Am I missing something here? Do you and Matt have a thing going? Is that why you're protecting him?"

"No, of course not!" she snapped quickly—a bit too quickly, judging from the way J.T.'s eyebrows shot skyward. "I simply think that in this case he's right and you're wrong."

He grinned and gave her face another quick study. "Whatever you say. Now, shall we go?"

"You still want to take me to dinner?"

J.T. grasped her arm and led her down the steps and along the gravel walkway toward his Jeep Cherokee. "You bet. Now more than ever. I like a woman who sticks up for her man."

"*What?* J.T., I just told you, there is nothing going on between Matt and me. We're just friends, that's all."

"Okay. If you say so."

"No, really. It's true."

She continued to protest all the way to the restaurant, which was near the yacht club, several miles down shore from the lodge. She might as well have saved her breath.

Each time J.T. responded with "Uh-huh," but the wicked twinkle in his eyes said he didn't believe her. By the time their dinner arrived Maude Ann was so frustrated she gave up and changed the subject.

After a while, once she had dismissed the matter from her mind and relaxed, she began to enjoy herself. Though J.T. was an outrageous flirt and a tease and didn't seem to take anything seriously, he was also handsome, charming, witty and intelligent, all of which made him a thoroughly delightful companion.

After she had answered his questions about Henley Haven and told him all her plans and hopes for the foster home, their conversation turned to other things. J.T. was a master at wheedling information from people, and before she knew it she was telling him about her college and med school years and what a struggle it had been. She told him about going to work after graduation for the Houston Police Department, and how she had met Tom there and married him, and about the pain of losing him. J.T. listened attentively and sympathetically. It turned out that he had met Tom a few times but hadn't known him well.

"So, you've known Matt for years, then?" he asked.

"Yes. Though, until he came to the haven to recuperate, I never really got to know him well."

"I'll bet." J.T. chuckled and shook his head. "He's as honest as they come and a damned good cop, but he's not exactly the most outgoing guy around."

He tipped his head to one side and studied her. "I can't imagine you working in that environment. You don't seem the type. You're too…too open. Your emotions are too unprotected. My guess is the brutality and senselessness of violent crime would tear you up inside."

"You're right. It did. When my husband was killed, I couldn't take any more. That's when I decided I would put my training and energies to use helping victims of crime. The most vulnerable are innocent children. After investigating the foster system, I realized that I could help abused and abandoned children, not just physically, but emotionally and mentally, as well. So I started Henley Haven."

"Mmm. Lucky for those kids you did. You're really great with them."

"Thanks."

J.T. had a store of fascinating tales and anecdotes, most connected with his work, which kept her laughing. Maude Ann enjoyed the tales, but she noticed that none of them revealed anything personal about him. Whenever she tried to steer the conversation in that direction, he deftly side-stepped and changed the subject. Finally her only recourse was to come right out and ask.

"I've been boring you all evening with my life story. Why don't we talk about you for a change?"

"There's not much to tell." He smiled the same charming smile he'd been giving her all evening, but she noticed the discomfort in his eyes.

"Oh, I'm sure there is. Why don't we start with where you were born?"

"Right here in Houston."

"You've lived here all your life?"

"Yep. Except for four years in Austin when I was going to U.T. But look, Doc, you don't want to hear this. It's really boring stuff."

"Why don't you let me be the judge of that? So, when did you decide you wanted to be a reporter?"

"I didn't." He gave a lame chuckle at her look of surprise. Then, for the first time that evening, his face sobered. "Actually, my dream was to become a novelist. I was sure I was going to write the great American novel. The only reason I took journalism in college was to help me hone my writing skills."

"That sounds reasonable. Did you ever write your book?"

"Naw. I started it, but I didn't get very far."

"Why not?"

"Well, for one thing, when I graduated from U.T., reality set in and I realized that I had to earn a living. I couldn't expect my parents to support me while I wrote. They were middle-aged when they adopted me, and by then they were ready for retirement."

"So after college you got a job with a newspaper."

"Yeah. But I had a plan. I was going to live frugally and save all I could. When I had enough put by to last a couple of years, I was going to quit the paper and work on my book full-time."

"And did you? Save your money, that is?"

"Oh, yeah. I have a tidy nest egg put aside. If I was careful, I could probably live on it for eight or ten years."

"Then why are you still working as a reporter?"

A rueful smile twisted his mouth. "The usual reasons. You get in a rut. The familiar is comfortable and safe. It's difficult to give up a steady paycheck. I've put in twelve years on this job. Made a name for myself, so why throw it away—that sort of thing."

"Mmm."

He frowned. "What does that mean?"

"Nothing. Just mmm."

"Dammit! I'm thirty-four years old. It's too late to make a major life change."

"Is it? People have done it in their forties and fifties. Even their sixties and seventies."

"I have a good job that provides me with a comfortable life style. I would have to be an idiot to give that up for a pipe dream."

Maude Ann spread her hands wide and gave him an innocent look. "Did I suggest that you do so?"

"You were thinking it."

"Not really." She let that soak in, then added softly, "But apparently you were."

He scowled at her across the table for a long time. Then his good humor resurfaced, and he chuckled and shook his head. "Damn, you're good, lady."

It was after ten when J.T. brought her home. When he switched off the engine, he turned partway and laid his arm across the back of her seat. "I'm glad you said yes to dinner. I enjoyed tonight."

"So did I."

The interior of the car was lit only by the yellow glow of the porch light. Above the dark shapes of the trees, lightning lit the night sky in the distance.

"Storm's coming," J.T. murmured as they watched the flickering display. The faint rumble of thunder followed moments later.

"Yes." Maude Ann felt his fingers toying with the ends of her hair. Her nerves skittered. For something to do, she pushed the button and lowered the passenger window.

The wind had kicked up, and the smell of approaching rain hung in the air. Abruptly, the whir of the cicadas ceased, and the only sounds were the whispery soughing of the wind through the pines and the faint slap of waves against the shore. When she turned her head, her gaze met J.T.'s.

"You're pretty special, Maude Ann," he murmured.

Gazing back at him, she didn't move or say a word. J.T. smiled softly and his lips settled over hers.

That he was experienced with women was evident by his easy confidence and expertise, his finesse.

The kiss was exquisitely tender, as though he was taking great care not to rush or frighten her. It was actually quite pleasant, but to her disappointment, it aroused in her none of the heart-pounding, head-spinning passion for which she had hoped. The kind Matt's kiss never failed to produce.

When J.T. sought to deepen the kiss, she leaned in and pressed closer, desperate to light a spark between them, but it was no use.

Maude Ann could have wept.

She had hoped that her reaction to Matt's kisses had been

merely the result of prolonged celibacy. How much easier her life would be if she could fall for a man like J.T.

When he broke off the kiss, he drew back and looked at her with a rueful smile. "It's just not happening for us, is it?"

"Oh, J.T., I'm so sorry, I—"

"Shh. There's no need to apologize. There's nothing anybody can do about chemistry. It's either there or it's not. Although…in this case, I think Matt's the biggest obstacle."

"J.T.," she groaned, "I've told you—"

"I know what you told me, Doc. But take it from me, you can't lie worth spit. Anyway, I've seen how you look at Matt."

"Whaaat?" she said on a rising note of horror, staring at him.

"Oh, don't worry. I doubt that Matt's noticed. He's not as observant as I am when it comes to women." He grinned at her stricken expression. "C'mon, Doc. Admit it. You've got the hots for Matt, don't you?"

Maude Ann shot him a quelling look, but his grin merely widened. Finally she gave up and slumped back in the seat, sighing. "Oh, all right, so I'm attracted to Matt. So what. Nothing can ever come of it, so what's the point of this discussion?"

"Why not? I can't imagine that Matt isn't just as attracted to you. He'd have to be stupid not to be."

"For one thing, I don't want to get involved with another law officer."

"Okay. I can understand how you feel, but you must know we don't always get to choose who we fall in love with."

"I know," she replied in a small, dejected voice. "But

even if I could live with his job, Matt just isn't the marrying kind.''

''You sure about that?''

''He's thirty-four years old and never been married.''

''So am I, but I haven't ruled it out.''

''Back when we worked out of the same precinct, I heard him say many times that he wanted no part of marriage. And his actions bore that out. He dated a lot of women, but none seriously.''

''That's what men do, until the right woman comes along. Maybe all he needs is a prod in the right direction. I could—''

She put her fingers over his mouth to hush him. ''No. I don't want you to do anything. Matt will go back to Houston soon and I'll get over him. I have the children and my work with them. That'll be enough.'' She sighed and looked at J.T. wistfully. ''I wish it could have been you. I really do.''

Grasping her wrist, he pressed a kiss against her fingers, then removed her hand. ''So do I.''

When his gaze lifted to her eyes again, there was regret and a touch of sadness, but in a blink it was gone, replaced by his usual teasing twinkle.

''But hey, just because it's not in the cards for us to be lovers doesn't mean we can't be friends.'' He gave her chin a playful cuff, his eyes crinkling at her through the dim light. ''I like you, Doc. And I like what you're doing for these kids. If you have no objection to me hanging around, I wouldn't mind dropping by now and then, maybe give you a hand entertaining the little munchkins.''

Relief and gratitude filled her. Maude Ann smiled, more sorry than ever that she could not lose her heart to this man. ''I'd like that. I'd like that a lot.''

"Good." His slow grin was a slash of white in the dim interior of the car. "It'll drive Matt nuts."

"J.T.! That's terrible," she scolded, but she couldn't help but laugh at the devilment dancing in his eyes.

"I know, but it's so darn much fun to rattle his cage now and then. Now c'mon. I'll walk you to the door."

"No, don't get out," she said, stopping him when he reached for the door handle. Before he could insist, she thanked him for the evening, gave him a quick kiss on the cheek and climbed out of the car. At the door she waved as he drove away, then turned back and fitted her key into the lock.

"Did you enjoy your date?"

Maude Ann shrieked and spun around. Her heart nearly leapt right into her throat as a man emerged from the dark shadows at the end of the veranda.

Her relief as he entered the circle of yellow light was so great her knees threatened to give way beneath her.

Sagging back against the door, she put her hand over her booming heart and closed her eyes momentarily.

"Matt, for heaven's sake! You nearly scared me to death! What were you doing, sitting out here in the dark at this time of night?"

"Enjoying the cool of the evening. You see some interesting things at night. You didn't answer me. Did you have a good time?"

"As a matter of fact, I did."

"Yes, I thought so. You sure seemed to enjoy his kiss."

She sucked in her breath. "You were *spying* on me?"

Her outrage didn't touch him. He came to a stop in front of her. His blue eyes glittered like two chips of ice. "Tell me, did you get all hot and bothered and melt against him the way you melt against me when I kiss you?"

"Stop it, Matt. You're being insulting. I know you're

still angry with me for letting J.T. write that article, but I don't deserve this.''

"Don't you? The way you go from one man to another, I'd say you deserve worse.''

She gasped. ''That's it. I don't have to stand here and take this.'' She spun around, flung the door opened and hurried inside.

Matt stormed after her. Catching up with her halfway across the foyer, he grabbed her arm and spun her back to face him. ''Dammit, answer me.''

"This is ridiculous. You said you wanted us to be friends, but you're acting like a jealous lover. What is *wrong* with you?''

His face was tight and he was breathing hard. She saw his jaw clench, his nostrils flare and quiver. His gaze dropped to her mouth and he ground out, ''Dammit, why did you let him kiss you?''

Maude Ann was suddenly as furious as he was. She jerked her arm free and glared right back at him. ''Why? I'll tell you why. Because I'm in love with you and I don't want to be. I was hoping J.T.'s kiss would snap me out of it!''

Matt flinched as though she had struck him. Shock drained every vestige of anger from his face. For a full ten seconds, he stared at her with his mouth agape.

The instant the words were out, Maude Ann could have kicked herself, but she couldn't take them back. All she could do was hold her head up and brazen her way through the next few humiliating moments.

Matt's stunned stare never left her. After what seemed like forever he whispered, ''Did it?''

Maude Ann's anger evaporated as quickly as it had come. She huffed out a long sigh, her shoulders sagging. She shook her head and looked at him sadly. ''No,'' she whispered back.

Chapter Ten

Matt couldn't move. He'd never experienced so many conflicting emotions at one time. They swirled and buzzed inside his chest like a swarm of angry bees.

Maude Ann loved him.

Joy shot through him like a rush of adrenaline.

Fury followed.

Then came fear, longing, confusion, hope—and the most searing happiness he'd ever known.

This last brought fury rushing back.

No! No, dammit! This wasn't right. He hadn't asked for this.

But Maude Ann loved him.

The thought made his heart hammer, his throat tighten. His first instinct was to put his arms around her and never let go, but conflicting emotions and ingrained caution held him back, and in the end he waited too long. He saw the flash of despair and humiliation in her eyes an instant before her chin came up.

"I...that is—"

"No. It's all right, Matt. You don't have to say anything. I know this isn't what you bargained for when you came here. I also know how you feel about serious relationships. You've always been quite open about that."

"Maude Ann—"

"No, please. Don't worry about it. This isn't your problem, it's mine. I'm a grown woman, and I'm responsible for my own actions and emotions, not you. Don't worry, I'll work through this. Life goes on no matter what. Soon you'll go back to Houston, and I'll stay here and continue my work with the kids. I'll be okay. Maybe not right away, but eventually I will be. Really."

"But—"

An ear-piercing scream cut him off.

"What the hell?"

"Debbie!" Maude Ann cried.

She took off before the name left her lips, pounding up the stairs at top speed.

Matt followed as fast as he could. The child's shrill screams continued unabated. By the time he gained the upstairs hall, they had reached a hysterical pitch and ran together into the most chilling sound he had ever heard. At the very least, he thought someone was trying to murder her.

He skidded to a stop at the open door of the bedroom that Debbie and Jennifer shared just as Maude Ann scooped the shrieking child up into her arms.

At first Debbie was as rigid as a post, pushing against the arms that held her, but after a few seconds Maude Ann's gentle voice got through to the child. Debbie's little arms clamped around Maude Ann's neck in a stranglehold, but her cries continued, only fractionally quieter now.

"Shh, sweetie. Shh. It's all right. Maudie's here," she crooned, holding the child close. "I've got you now. You're safe. Nothing's going to hurt you, baby."

Sinking onto the edge of the bed, Maude Ann rocked the child back and forth, murmuring a steady stream of encouragement and endearments. "It's okay, baby. It's okay, little love. Everything is going to be all right."

Matt sat down on the bed beside them. Concern wiped every other thought from his mind. He had never seen a child so upset. Debbie's tear-streaked face was the color of a beet and hideously contorted. She kept her eyes squeezed shut, and her tiny body shook from head to toe. She seemed caught in some terrible hysteria, oblivious to everything and everyone except the safe harbor of Maude Ann's arms. Wailing every breath, the little girl burrowed against her as though trying to climb right inside her skin.

Across the room in the other bed, Jennifer slept on without so much as a twitch. Matt looked at Maude Ann and tipped his head toward the other child. "How does she sleep through this racket?" he mouthed.

"Children can sleep through any noise," Maude Ann mouthed back.

Raising his voice to be heard over the incessant wails, Matt looked at Debbie again and asked, "What's wrong with her?"

"Nightmare. There, there. C'mon, sweetheart. You're okay. Maudie won't let anything hurt you."

Leaning her cheek against the top of Debbie's head, she continued to rock the little girl, stroking her back over and over in a continuous, soothing motion. Maude Ann's gaze met Matt's. "When Debbie first came here, she had nightmares every night, but as she came to feel safe, they gradually stopped. It's been months since she's had one.''

Matt frowned. ''I wonder what brought them back.''

''I suspect the argument we had earlier. Raised voices frighten her. It probably caused some horrible, deeply buried memory to resurface.''

Stricken, Matt stared at her, then the child. ''Ah, hell.'' Feeling like the lowest form of life, he reached out and stroked the little girl's arm. ''Hey, Debbie, don't cry, sweetie. You're gonna make yourself sick, carrying on that way. C'mon, honey.''

Gradually the little girl's wails diminished to choppy sobs, then little hitching breaths, muffled against Maude Ann's shoulder, but she didn't move or acknowledge his presence in any other way.

''Look, sweetie,'' Maude Ann murmured. ''Matt's here. He's worried about you. Don't you want to talk to him?''

Debbie turned her head just slightly and slanted an accusing peek at him out of one eye. ''N-no,'' she said. ''M-Matt's mean. He y-yelled at you.''

''Oh, I don't think he meant it, did you, Matt?''

''No! No, I was just letting off a little steam. That's all. I swear it. And I'm real sorry about it, too. I shouldn't have yelled that way.''

''See there. What'd I tell you?''

Knuckling her eyes and wet cheeks, Debbie sat up and eyed Matt with sulky suspicion.

''C'mon, pumpkin, don't you know I'd never hurt Miss Maudie? Or you? Or any of the kids? Never in a million years. And I'd throttle anyone else who tried.''

''Promith?''

''Cross my heart and hope to die,'' he said, making an X sign across his chest. He held out his arms to her. ''Now, how about giving me a hug?''

It was all the invitation Debbie needed. She lunged into Matt's waiting arms and clutched his neck so tightly that he laughed and pretended to choke. "Hey, take it easy, kid. You're strangling me."

Watching them, Maude Ann looked close to tears herself.

The child leaned back and looked him in the eyes, her small blotchy face serious as a judge's. "You're not mad at Mith Maudie anymore?"

"No, I'm not mad at Miss Maudie." His hand looked dark and huge against her face as he tenderly wiped away her tears. When he was done, he placed a soft kiss on her little rosebud mouth, pulled back and smiled.

She beamed. "Good. I don't wants you to be mad at Mith Maudie. I wuv her. An' I wuv you."

Matt's gaze darted to Maude Ann. He could see in her eyes she was remembering, as he was, that she had made the same declaration to him just minutes before.

Matt smiled at Debbie and tucked a blond curl behind her ear. "I love you, too, kiddo."

He was rewarded with another choking hug. When she released him, she said innocently, "Now give Mith Maudie a kith, too."

"Uh..."

"You gots to. So she won't think you ith still mad at her."

"Uh, sweetie, Matt doesn't have to do that. Really. I know he's not mad at me anymore."

Debbie's chin wobbled and her tears threatened to return. "But he gots to," she wailed. "Thath the way you're th'poth to 'pologize."

"Okay, okay. I'll do it. Don't get upset," Matt pleaded. He couldn't take another round of crying.

Mollified, Debbie sniffed and gave him a watery grin,

well pleased with herself, then settled back in his arms to watch.

Matt's gaze met Maude Ann's. In her eyes he saw the same turmoil of doubt and longing that he was feeling. The air between them seemed suddenly thick, making breathing difficult. Outside the storm broke with a clap of thunder that made Debbie jump, and rain began pelting the metal roof like a crazed drummer. The sounds barely registered on the two adults.

As Matt leaned toward Maude Ann, his heart thudded with a slow rhythm that was almost painful. His gaze dropped to her lush mouth. It quivered ever so slightly, and her eyes fluttered shut. His heart picked up speed, chugging like a steam locomotive leaving the station, as he touched his mouth to hers.

It was the most delicate of caresses, the slow, soft press of warm lips, a gossamer exchange of breath, a subtle taste, nothing more, but it brought a rush of sensations so exquisite they were nearly unbearable. His chest ached and his heart pounded so hard it almost suffocated him.

Debbie clapped her hands, giggling, bringing Matt back to reality with a jolt. When he broke off the kiss, she beamed at both of them.

As kisses went, that one had been as pure and chaste as the driven snow, yet it had packed a punch that left Matt shaken.

The confusion in Maude Ann's eyes told him he was not the only one affected.

He watched her blink several times, then straighten her spine and shake off the miasma of feelings, but when she reached for the child, her hands trembled. "Okay, little one, it's time for you to go back to sleep."

Instantly, Debbie's pallor returned and terror filled her eyes. She clutched Maude Ann's neck in a death grip. "I don't wanth to go to thleep. The bad man will hurt me again,'' she whimpered, her chin quivering.

"No, he won't. He's all gone now."

"No. No! He'll come back!"

"I don't think so, but tell you what. If it will make you feel safer, you can sleep with me tonight," she said before the child could work herself up into another frenzy. "Hmm? How would you like that?"

"Yeth. I wanth to sleep with you." The words came out in a rush, muffled as the terrified child clung tight and burrowed her face into Maude Ann's shoulder.

She stood up with the child in her arms, and after checking to be sure Jennifer was okay, she headed for her own room, which, Matt discovered, was the right across the hall. At the door she paused and turned to him, but her gaze didn't quite meet his.

"Thanks for your help."

"Yeah, sure. No problem." He cast a worried look at Debbie, who was already falling asleep on Maude Ann's shoulder. Matt smoothed a lock of baby-fine hair off the child's cheek and tucked it behind her ear. "Is she going to be all right?"

"She'll be fine." Maude Ann seemed to grow taller as her chin came up and she met his gaze squarely. "We'll both be fine. There's nothing for you to worry about here. Good night, Matt."

He found himself looking at a closed door. He stared at it for several seconds, not certain he liked being dismissed so summarily. His inclination was to knock on her door until she opened it again, only he had no idea what he would say to her when she did. Left with no choice, he went downstairs.

In his room he merely glanced at the bed as he walked

straight through to the outer door and stepped out onto the veranda.

The rain had settled into a steady downpour. It drummed on the roof and gushed through the gutters and out the downspouts at the corners of the veranda. It peppered the lake in an erratic dance. The air was clammy and warm, redolent with the smells of rain and mud and wet pine trees, mingled with the sweet scent of wild honeysuckle.

Leaning forward from the waist and gripping the veranda railing with both hands, Matt braced himself and stared out through the falling rain, unmindful of the splatters that hit his face and upper body.

Maude Ann loved him.

He closed his eyes and tried to sort through the knotted tangle of feelings in his gut.

Not for an instant did he doubt the veracity of her feelings. Maude Ann was the most down-to-earth, most forthright, honest woman he'd ever known. She didn't play games or exaggerate, nor was she likely to mistake infatuation for the real thing. Maude Ann analyzed, weighed, thought things through and came to a logical and honest conclusion. If she said she loved him, then it was true.

He closed his eyes. Oh, God, she loved him.

Did he love Maude Ann? Never before had he allowed himself to even consider that question in regard to any woman, and it unnerved him to do so now, but he had no choice.

Groaning, he pinched the bridge of his nose between his thumb and forefinger. Ah, hell, he didn't know.

He wasn't even sure he knew what love was. He'd wanted a great many women, and he'd made love to his share. A few he'd even been fond of, but there had been no one he could imagine waking up next to every morning for the rest of his life.

He thought about that and frowned. Oddly, he could imagine that with Maude Ann.

Did that mean he loved her?

He wanted her more than he'd ever wanted any other woman. A helluva lot more. Still…there was more to his feelings than merely wanting her. He couldn't deny that.

He enjoyed just spending time with her. Enjoyed her conversation, her company. He loved the way she looked with all that glorious auburn hair rioting around her face and shoulders. For that matter, he liked it just as much up in that girlish ponytail.

Any man with blood in his veins also had to admire the way Maude Ann filled out a pair of shorts and a tank top, and those long, shapely legs and narrow feet. That husky laugh of hers could drive a man crazy with wanting. And Lord, how he loved to watch her move. Maude Ann had a loose-limbed, unselfconscious grace about her that made even the most mundane action seem sexy.

And there was another thing. Never before had he been possessive of a woman, but he hated the thought of J.T., or any man, so much as touching her.

Was that love? Or was he just being territorial?

Impatient, Matt paced to the far corner of the veranda and back. What did it matter anyway? Even if he did love her, that didn't change anything. He still didn't think police work and marriage mixed. He couldn't offer her a future.

Not unless he failed the reentry physical.

The insidious thought sent a chill rippling through him.

No! No, he wouldn't let himself even think that. He was going to pass that physical. Pass, hell, he was going to ace it. He was a law officer. That was what he did. What he was. It was the only thing he'd ever wanted to be. He couldn't imagine a life not on the force. Didn't want to imagine it.

But, you jerk, Maude Ann loves you.

Too restless and torn to remained confined to the veranda, he muttered an oath and loped down the front steps into the rain-swept night.

Before he'd gone a half-dozen paces, he was soaked to the skin, his dark hair plastered to his head and hanging down in his face in strings. He kept going, oblivious to the storm and the chill of the wet clothes clinging to his body, the soggy squish of his athletic shoes.

He stalked down to the lake and stood on the bank in the rain and stared out across the pockmarked water.

Having the love of a woman like Maude Ann was no small thing. He may have dodged the emotion all his adult life, but he knew that much. Maude Ann was special. Unique. Maude Ann was…Maude Ann.

Intelligent, honest, sexy, fiercely loyal, beautiful, down-to-earth—she was a woman of many virtues, not the least of which was her capacity for love.

In his heart, Matt felt incredibly humbled, incredibly blessed and totally undeserving.

He groaned and tipped back his head, letting the rain slap his face. Lord, he didn't want to hurt her.

Maude Ann dumped more ice over the two dozen watermelons cooling in the galvanized washtubs lined up on the side veranda, but her gaze was fixed on Matt. Early that morning, before it had gotten too hot, he'd used the riding mower to cut the weeds in the meadow that separated the lodge from the woods on the west side. Using a bag of ground chalk to mark off a softball diamond, he poured the white powder in long, straight lines on the fresh stubble.

Marshall, Yolanda and Tyrone were supposed to be helping, but mainly they just trailed behind him as if he were the Pied Piper, carrying the square, sand-filled burlap bags she'd sewn for base markers and dropping them where Matt instructed.

Squealing and laughing, the four younger children streaked around the yard and field in a frenzy of excitement at the prospect of visitors and a cookout. Even Jennifer, who was usually so quiet, was racing around with the others.

Matt's laughter rang out. He ruffled Marshall's hair and gave Tyrone's shoulder a playful cuff. Watching him, Maude Ann's eyes narrowed. Never would she have pegged him as the kind to evade a problem or sticky situation. The hardworking detective she remembered from her days with HPD had always been a "take the bull by the horns" type.

To ignore a problem in the hope it would go away seemed to Maude Ann the coward's way, and Matt Dolan had never struck her as a coward. Yet, for the past two weeks, that was exactly what he had been doing—ignoring the problem.

He acted as though that humiliating scene in the front hall had never taken place, as though nothing had changed. In a temper, she had foolishly blurted out the truth and bared her heart to him, but no one would ever know it, the way he acted.

Not once had he tried to discuss the matter, as she had expected. There had been no awkwardness between them, at least not on his part, no polite brush-off, no pitying looks. Nor did he make the slightest effort to avoid her.

He hadn't even had the decency to try to use her love for him to get her into bed!

It would have been easier for her had he reverted to the bad-tempered recluse he had been when he first arrived at the lodge. But oh, no. Matt was relaxed and friendly as could be, damn him. He continued to help out around the place and involve himself with the children just as he'd been doing.

The only time in the past two weeks that he'd made himself scarce was the day J.T. and the photographer spent at the lodge taking pictures for the newspaper article. That, she knew, had nothing to do with her. He simply did not like or trust J.T.

Maude Ann huffed out a dejected sigh, the brief flare of anger fading. It seemed that friendship *was* all Matt had to offer her.

Well, so be it. As she had told him that night, her emotions were her responsibility, not his. She was hurting right now, but she was a strong woman. She would get past this. Eventually.

If Matt didn't want her love, that was his loss. Someday, somewhere, she would find a good, decent man who would.

In the meantime, she had the children.

For today, though, she was grateful she would have the distraction of guests.

Finished with the softball preparations, Matt snagged Jennifer as she darted by, and the usually quiet child shrieked with delight when he swung her high in the air. Immediately Debbie tugged on the leg of his jeans, demanding he swing her, too, and he laughingly obliged. When he was done, he settled the child on his shoulder and headed for the lodge with the other children trotting along beside him.

His limp was barely noticeable now. In another month it would probably be gone.

And so would he.

The thought brought a fresh wave of pain that nearly doubled her over, but she refused to give in to it.

Telling herself she had things to do, Maude Ann turned away and walked around to the back veranda, plumping the cushions on the chairs and lounges as she went. She had only just returned to the front veranda when the caravan of cars came bumping down the rutted road, horns blaring. As they drew nearer, windows came down and several of the men poked their heads out, waving and shouting raucous greetings.

"Whooie, Maudie! Lookin' *good!*"

"Hey, Doc! How's it going?"

"Long time no see, Doc!"

"Yeah! Did ya miss me?"

Maude grinned and waved, the heavy weight around her heart lightening a bit as she went down the steps to greet Lieutenant John Werner and his men.

At the same moment, Matt and the children came around the corner of the lodge. After swinging Debbie to the ground, Matt hooked his thumbs in the front pockets of his jeans and sauntered over to where the cars were pulling up.

"Hey, Matt! You big ugly son of a bi—" Detective Tony Volturo, the squad's twice-divorced Italian lover, glanced at the wide-eyed kids standing in a close huddle by the porch steps, and grimaced. "Uh...son of a gun. How ya doin', buddy?"

Before Matt could answer, his friend snatched him into a bear hug and thumped him soundly on the back. Behind them, the occupants of the other cars tumbled out, calling greetings.

"Pretty fair, all things considered," Matt replied to Tony. "That is, if you don't crush my ribs."

Laughing, Tony gave him one last thump and stepped back, his dark eyes dancing as they ran over Matt in a quick inspection. "I told all these yahoos not to count you out. Man, you're looking great. Just great. This country air must agree with you."

He winked at Maude Ann, who was standing behind

them, a little to one side, and gave Matt a jab in the ribs. "'Course, if you had a lick of sense in that hard Irish head of yours, you wouldn't be in such a hurry to get back in condition. I know I wouldn't be if the doc was nursemaiding me.''

Matt frowned, but Maude Ann laughed. "Still the same incorrigible flirt, I see.''

A come-hither smile split Tony's handsome face. "Ah, Maude Ann. You wound me. Don't you know you're the love of my life? If you'd just run away with me, I'd never look at another woman.''

"Liar.'' Still laughing, she stepped forward with her hands outstretched. He took them, but only to pull her into his arms and plant a thoroughly lascivious kiss on her mouth.

The other detectives gathering around Matt whistled and hooted and let loose with catcalls.

"Here, now! Unhand that woman, you damn pervert, before I call the cops.''

"Uh-oh. Now you've done it, Volturo.''

"Hey, Lieutenant, where're you going? You haven't even said hello to Matt yet.''

Tony broke off the kiss and winked at Maude Ann's astonished face, then aimed an unrepentant grin over his shoulder at John Werner, who was shoving his way through the crowd around Matt.

All around, the others laughed and hooted, and though red with embarrassment, Maude Ann nevertheless joined in.

"To hell with that. I'm not wasting time on that ugly Mick when there's a beautiful woman standing right here. Now get out of the way, you lot, and let me give my god-daughter a hug.''

John grasped Tony's shoulder and spun him around.

"And as for you, Casanova," he snarled into the younger man's face, only half kidding, "back off. Maude Ann is off-limits to the likes of you."

Planting a beefy hand on Tony's chest, John shoved him away, then turned with a beaming smile for Maude Ann, swept her up into his arms and swung her around.

Laughing, she hung on tightly and returned the hug. When at last he set her on her feet, he held on to her shoulders to steady her, using the opportunity to give her a quick once-over. "Girl, you sure are a sight for these tired old eyes. I swear, you get prettier every time I see you."

"Which isn't nearly often enough, but thanks for the compliment."

He gave her a rueful look. "I'm real sorry I haven't been out to see you before this, Maude Ann, but lately down at the station, we've been busier than a one-armed paperhanger. Between the heat and the full moon, the bad guys are runnin' amuck. Anyway, Matt was so ticked off at me when I sent him here, I figured I'd better stay away till he cooled off some."

"How wise of you," she drawled. "I don't imagine it helped his temper any that you neglected to tell him about me and the kids being here."

John Werner had the grace to look embarrassed. "Sorry about that, Maudie, but I was desperate. That hardhead never would have come if I had. Speaking of the kids, from what I saw when we drove up, he seems to be getting along with them okay."

"Actually, Matt's wonderful with the children. It took him a while to warm up to them, mind you, but once he did, he waded right in. He's been a huge help."

"And how're the two of you getting along?"

"Oh, just fine." Anxious to change the subject, Maude

Ann slipped her arm through John's and urged him toward the others. "Now then, let me go say hello to everyone and then we'll get this party started."

"I sure hope you don't mind us barging in on you like this, but I thought it was time for Matt to touch base with the guys."

She slanted him a wry smile. What John really meant was, he thought it was time to give Matt a nudge and start him thinking about returning to duty soon, but she let it pass.

"Not at all. I was delighted when you called and suggested it. It'll be good for Matt, and it's also important for the kids to be around other people, particularly ones with children of their own, so they can see what a real family is all about. Plus, two of the children are leaving tomorrow to go live with a relative. The other kids are a bit upset about that. The cookout will give the boys a nice send-off and maybe, for a while at least, take the other kids' minds off tomorrow's parting."

John had brought with him four married officers and their wives and children, plus Gus Jankowski and Tony, the single guys in the group, and Tony's son, Vic, from his first marriage. All together, the children numbered eleven, ranging in age from one to thirteen.

The seventh officer, Gloria Davies, was a twice-divorced, stunning brunette with the face of an angel, a salty tongue that put the guys to shame and, if rumor was to be believed, an appetite for hot, no-strings sex.

At the moment Detective Davies had her arms draped around Matt's neck and her sexy body plastered against his.

Although Matt wasn't exactly encouraging her, he didn't look as though he minded. Experiencing a stab of pain so vicious she had to bite her tongue to keep from crying out, Maude Ann pasted a smile on her face and turned her attention to the women. She greeted them with an almost desperate warmth and enthusiasm, far more than she normally would have done. While she had worked at the precinct she'd met all the women at one time or another, but they were merely acquaintances. Through work, she had developed much closer friendships with their husbands.

Nevertheless, the officers' wives responded to her with open friendliness. Maude Ann chatted with them for several minutes, though she could not have told you what she'd said. She was much too aware of Matt and Gloria Davies. Though it was like probing a sore tooth with your tongue, knowing all the while that it was going to hurt, she could not stop herself from glancing over her shoulder at the pair every few seconds. To her dismay, the woman continued to hang on Matt like wet laundry.

Maude Ann desperately needed a diversion, and she found it by helping to break the ice between her charges and the other four children.

Before long, with Tyrone in the lead, all the children except the two babies took off at a run, laughing and chattering as though they'd known one another for years.

Chuckling, John patted Maude Ann on the back and grinned at the other women. "See? Didn't I tell you she has a way with kids?" Turning to his men, he motioned with a wave of his beefy arm for them to follow and bellowed, "C'mon, you bunch of sorry gold bricks, let's get this show on the road. We've got food to cook."

"My, my," Anna Huttsinger murmured, hoisting her baby higher on her shoulder as they all started around to the side yard. "Isn't it amazing what wonderful cooks men are when all the prep work has already been done?"

They had taken just a few steps when the sound of an approaching vehicle drowned out the women's laughter. Everyone stopped and turned around.

"I don't believe it!" Tony said furiously. "It's that damned reporter."

Suddenly the mood of the party changed as every last man stepped forward, braced for a fight.

The car crunched to a halt on the drive behind the others, and Maude Ann looked around in time to see J.T. climb out. "Hey, Maude Ann, I got something for you," he called, waving a paper in the air, but before he could take a step, Hank, Tony and Gus had him pinned against the side of his car.

"What the—"

"You got some nerve, Conway," Hank snarled in his face.

"Get your hands off me, you ape."

"Watch it, creep. You're just about a half a minute from getting that pretty face of yours bashed in."

"No! Stop it! Stop it right this minute!" Maude Ann rushed in and pulled at the officers' arms. "Let him go."

"Not on your life. Maude Ann, this guy's a reporter with the *Houston Herald*."

"I know that, Hank. He also happens to be a friend of mine."

"Aw, *jeez,* Maude Ann. Somebody's gonna have to do something about your taste in friends."

"You could be right." Linking her arm firmly through J.T.'s, she gave Tony and the other two men a challenging smile. "After all, I am friends with the lot of you."

Chapter Eleven

"Look, Maude Ann, don't think I don't appreciate your stepping in back there," J.T. muttered as they approached the others. Tony, Gus and Hank trailed after them, thoroughly disgusted and muttering dark insults at J.T.'s back, which he ignored. "But I really wish you hadn't. I could've handled those guys."

"Oh, please," she groaned, "not you, too. I've had just about all the macho nonsense I can take for one day." She heaved a sigh, then relented, giving his arm a squeeze and smiling at him. "But I am glad you came by. I could use a friend right about now."

He raised an eyebrow at that, but they reached the others before he could question her.

"Ladies, I'd like you to meet my friend, J. T. Conway," Maude Ann began brightly before any of the men had a chance to speak up. Ignoring the less-than-friendly male eyes boring into them, she introduced J.T. to all the wives and to the two bouncing infants. "You probably know Lieutenant Werner and the other guys," she said when done.

"Yeah, I think so. How's it going, fellas? Ms. Davies?"

"What're you doing here, Conway?" Matt demanded. Gloria still hung on his arm, but he appeared not to notice.

J.T. grinned and held up a rolled cylinder of paper. "I dropped by to give Maude Ann an advance copy of the Sunday supplement. I thought she might like to see it before it hits the streets tomorrow."

"Oh! Let me see!" Maude Ann snatched the paper out of his hand, unrolled it and gasped. "It's the cover story!"

"Yeah, my boss thought it was a real heart-grabber, so he went with it."

Flush with excitement, Maude Ann held up the magazine to show the others. "J.T. did a story on the haven for tomorrow's paper. We're hoping it will bring in a ton of donations."

A full-page picture of herself with a child cradled in her arms, rocking in one of the porch swings made up the cover of the magazine. The soft-focused photograph had a melancholy look about it that tugged on the heartstrings. So did the title: HENLEY HAVEN. A REFUGE FOR THE INNOCENT.

The women crowded around for a closer look, but the men barely gave the paper a glance.

"I'd read it carefully before I got too excited if I were you," John warned, keeping a suspicious watch on J.T. "This guy has a real flair for twisting things around."

"I tried to warn her, but she wouldn't listen," Matt said.

Too excited to pay attention to the remarks, Maude Ann opened the magazine. The article covered three pages and included four more photographs, each as emotionally evocative as the one on the cover. Quickly, she scanned the text, her gaze flying from column to column. Looking over her shoulder, Patty and Marylou read along, while the other women pressed closer, trying to do the same.

When Maude Ann finished and looked at J.T., her eyes glittered with moisture. "Oh, J.T. This is beautiful."

He shrugged. "No big deal. Actually, it was a piece of cake to write."

Relinquishing the magazine to the other women, Maude Ann surged up on tiptoe and kissed his cheek. "I love it. And trust me, it's a *huge* deal."

Not only had J.T. written a heart-wrenching story, he had honored their agreement to the letter. Not anywhere in the article did he even hint at the location of the Henley Haven or reveal any of the children's names. The pictures were all shot either from the back or from an angle that revealed so little of their faces it would be almost impossible for anyone to recognize them.

Though he tried to act blasé about the praises, Maude Ann saw the bloom of pink beneath his tanned skin. The flush deepened when the other men looked up from the article to shoot him surprised glances.

Laughing, she grasped J.T.'s arm and gave it an affectionate squeeze. She was pleased when he agreed to stay for the cookout.

She urged everyone around to the side yard where lawn chairs were set out under the trees and the brick barbecue pit smoldered in readiness. Out of the corner of her eye, Maude Ann could see Matt and Gloria, walking close together, deep on conversation. Maude Ann grasped J.T.'s arm. "I'm so glad you drove up today and that you're staying."

"Hey, no way I'm going to pass up a chance to spend the day with you and the kids." Then he grinned and, leaning closer, murmured, "Besides, it'll drive Matt nuts."

"I should have known."

* * *

It was a perfect day for a cookout, Maude Ann thought a few hours later. It was scorching hot, but the breeze off the lake made it bearable. Over head the leaves of the giant pecan tree stirred with a swishing sound. The smell of hickory smoke and grilled burgers and hot dogs still hung in the air, mingling with the sweet scent of newly mown grass. Puffball clouds drifted across the blue sky and a squirrel chattered and scolded from the high branches of the pecan tree.

She smiled as the children streaked by again. Everyone seemed to be having a good time—except her.

To Maude Ann the day seemed endless. Never in her life had she worked so hard at enjoying herself, or at least at giving that appearance.

She'd smiled until her face hurt. She'd circulated among her guests and played the gracious hostess. She'd helped Jane and the other women serve the food and clean up afterward, she'd chased after rambunctious toddlers, laughed when the men recounted funny incidents that had occurred while on duty and exchanged girl talk with their wives. She'd joined in a watermelon-seed-spitting contest and pitched horseshoes with gusto and, to the delight of the children, had gotten into a wild water-balloon fight with Tony that had left her looking like a drowned rat.

She tried not to care that Gloria hadn't left Matt's side since she arrived or that he didn't seem to mind. After all, Maude Ann knew she had no claim on the man, and he couldn't have made it plainer that he didn't return her feelings. Matt was a free agent, and if Gloria was what he wanted, it was none of her business.

It was a humiliating and depressing thought that stung her pride. What had she been thinking? It should have occurred to her that Matt might not be unattached. He was a healthy, virile male with the kind of rugged good looks most women found irresistible. Though he shied away from serious relationships, in the time she had worked at his precinct, he had seldom been without a casual lover. If she had remembered that, maybe she wouldn't have made the mistake of falling in love with him.

But then again, maybe not.

Maude Ann sighed and took another mouthful of the ice cream she was eating to console herself. What a foolish, foolish woman she was.

Still, it hurt. Every time she heard Gloria's sexy laugh or saw her touch Matt in that intimate way, she felt her heart break a little more.

"Hey, Doc, great party." Plopping down on the lawn chair next to hers, J.T. shot Maude Ann his relaxed smile. "Even if your friends are trying to make me feel like the bastard at the family reunion."

Maude Ann shook her head. "Well, I'm glad you're having a good time," she said in a dry voice.

"Mmm." Slouching, his head propped on the edge of the chair back, his long legs stretched out and crossed at the ankles, he rested his beer bottle on his flat belly and contemplated it through half closed eyes. "I can see why you thought you needed a friend." He rolled his head on the chair back and looked into her eyes. "Don't let Matt and detective Hot Pants get under your skin, Doc."

Despite her misery, she had to laugh. "You're terrible. Her name is Gloria, as you very well know. And she's a nice person. A little…free spirited, maybe, but nice. Actually, I've always liked her. And I'm okay. Really."

"Good, because he's just trying to make you jealous, you know."

"Oh, I doubt that. I think he and Gloria are lovers."

"Mmm. At one time, maybe. At least, that's what I

heard, but that's been over for a while. I think she's just at loose ends and trying to fan an old flame."

"Well, it seems to be working." She'd tried for flippancy, but even to her own ears, the comment sounded pathetic.

J.T. reached across and put his hand over hers. "Hey, Doc, there's no game that two can't play. If you want to bring out ol' Matt's green-eyed monster I'm at your service."

Turning her hand over, she gave his a squeeze and managed a wan smile. "Thanks, J.T., but I don't think so. If Matt prefers Gloria, that's his right. Anyway, it's not as though there was ever really anything between us."

She had merely laid her heart and soul bare to him and humiliated herself, but that was the price you sometimes paid for honesty.

J.T.'s eyes said he thought she was crazy, but he returned the gentle pressure. "If that's the way you want it. Just remember, if you change your mind, the offer stands."

As the day wore on, Maude Ann was sorely tempted to take him up on the offer. But she could not bring herself to play games with another person's emotions. That did not mean, however, that she had to let the world see how much she was hurting. She had her pride, after all.

When Gloria gave Matt a sizzling kiss after he'd tossed a ringer in horseshoes, Maude Ann laughed right along with everyone else.

When the woman sat on his good leg and shared her ice cream with him, Maude Ann ignored them and cheerfully set about organizing everyone into two teams for softball. As captain of one team, she picked J.T. first and ignored Matt.

During the top of the second inning, Matt's team had two outs and two players on base when it came his turn at bat. Gloria gave his butt a pat as he stood up and headed for the plate. At second base, Maude Ann punched her glove and chanted vociferous encouragement to Tony to strike him out, as though that was the only thing that mattered to her.

After the first game, which Maude Ann's team won, Gloria didn't want to play anymore and persuaded Matt to quit, as well. They watched a few minutes of the second game, then walked off the field, hand in hand, just as J.T.'s bat cracked against the ball in a line-drive single. Maude Ann jumped up and down and cheered like a maniac.

Her turn at bat came next. She took her place at the plate, held her bat up and wiggled her hips to test her stance.

Immediately, a chorus of wolf whistles and cries of "Shake it, baby, shake it!" came from the bench.

Glancing over her shoulder, Maude Ann grinned at her teammates. She wiggled her hips again, took a couple of practice swings—and out of the corner of her eye saw Matt and Gloria disappear through the veranda door into his room.

"Ah, jeez. How's a guy supposed to concentrate?"

"If you're through, could I please pitch now?" Gus asked in a long-suffering growl.

Gritting her teeth, Maude Ann nodded and braced herself for the pitch. When it came she took a vicious swing and smacked the ball with all her might, sending it sailing high over Anna Huttsinger's head in the outfield.

With a grin fixed on her face and pumping her fists high in the air, Maude Ann took her victory trot around the bases while her teammates cheered and shouted, but her throat ached with the unshed tears she held fiercely in check. When she rounded third and saw the blind in Matt's window close, she could almost hear the crack of her heart breaking in two.

* * *

"Mmm. Alone at last." Gloria closed the blind and turned back to Matt. The seductive smile on her face as she sauntered closer left no doubt of what she wanted from him.

No, he corrected. What *they* wanted from *each other*.

"I've been waiting for this all day," Gloria purred, running her palms over his chest. She looked up at him from beneath her lashes and flicked open the top button of his shirt. "I've missed you, lover."

"Have you now?" Matt watched her with a sardonic smile on his lips, making no effort to hide his amusement. He put his hands on her hips and brought her against him. "Seems to me last I heard before I got shot, you were hot and heavy with some lawyer from the DA's office."

"Oh, that. He was a jerk. But then, he's a lawyer, so I should have known better. Anyway, that's been over for a couple of weeks."

"Ah, I see. Now it's all becoming clear. Knowing you, after two weeks you've got a powerful itch that needs scratching. When the lieutenant mentioned this outing, I bet you figured by now I'd be happy to accommodate you."

She grinned, not in the least insulted. "You'd be damn near climbing the walls is what I figured. I mean, sweetie, it's been more than three months, unless Dr. Edwards has been giving you a little 'physical therapy' on the side."

His teasing smile collapsed into a frown, but before he could object, she twined her arms around his neck and brought his head down for a kiss.

Matt tried. For several seconds he held her tightly against him and returned the devouring kiss with something akin to desperation. But it was no use.

The moment he had seen Gloria that morning, he had convinced himself that the raging desire he felt for Maude Ann was merely the result of propinquity. He had been celibate for months, and since she was the only woman around, naturally he had become obsessed with her. He had figured making love to another woman was all he needed to put things into perspective and rid him of this unrelenting longing for Maude Ann, but he was wrong.

It was true that he wanted—hell, he desperately needed—to make love to a woman, but apparently only one woman would do, and his body knew damned well that woman wasn't Gloria. He wanted Maude Ann. Only Maude Ann.

Regretfully, Matt broke off the kiss and grasped her shoulders to ease her back. "I'm sorry." He shook his head and met her surprised expression with a look of genuine regret that he hoped would take the sting out of the rejection. "I'm really sorry, Gloria. But it's just not going to happen."

"But…I don't get it. What's wrong?" Her face suddenly bore a look of mingled pity and disappointment. "Is it your wound? I mean, is it giving you…you know…trouble in that department?"

It took him a moment to catch her drift, and when he did he gave a bark of ironic laughter. "No, it's nothing like that. I'm not impotent."

Far from it. Although he almost wished he was. Then perhaps he wouldn't be tormented nightly with erotic dreams of making love to Maude Ann, which inevitably resulted in his waking up each morning painfully aroused.

"Then what is the problem?"

"I just don't think we should, that's all." Matt wandered over to the window and opened the blind. Immediately his gaze sought out Maude Ann.

The "bench" for both teams consisted of a line of folding lawn chairs behind and to one side of home plate. She and J.T. sat side by side, talking while they watched the game. A suffocating pressure squeezed Matt's chest.

He watched as J.T. propped his elbow on the back of Maude Ann's chair, picked up her long ponytail and absently toyed with the curly mass.

Matt's eyes narrowed. He gritted his teeth so hard a muscle rippled along his jaw.

Gloria's sharp intake of breath caught his attention, and when he turned his head, he found her staring at him with her mouth agape.

"What?"

Her stunned gaze slid from him to Maude Ann and back. "So *that's* it. I wouldn't have believed it if I hadn't seen it with my own eyes."

"Seen what? What're you talking about?"

"You're in love with Dr. Edwards."

"Don't be ridiculous."

"Sweetie, you don't have to lie to spare my feelings. I think it's great. I just never thought I'd see the day when Matt Dolan fell in love, that's all."

"I tell you, you're imagining things."

"Aw, c'mon. Who're you trying to kid? I saw your face when you were looking at her just now. *And* the way you looked at Conway when he touched her. Sugar, you looked ready to commit murder. This from a man who has never before shown so much as a twinge of jealousy over a woman."

Matt opened his mouth to repeat the denial, then closed it again. "All right. So I love her. No need to make a big deal out of it."

"Does she love you?"

"Gloria," he growled, slanting her a warning scowl. She wasn't fazed.

"Well? Does she?"

Matt sighed and gave up. "She says she does."

Gloria threw up her hands. "Then why did you spend the whole day with me, you big dope? Why aren't you out there right now, jerking Conway off her?"

"What would be the point? Just because I love her doesn't mean I'm going to do anything about it." He glanced over his shoulder at her. "No offense, Gloria, but Maude Ann isn't like you. She couldn't handle a casual affair. She would expect wedding bells and happy-ever-after, and I have no intention of ever getting married. You know how I feel about mixing marriage and police work."

The inning ended, and Maude Ann's team took to the field. Matt watched her slip on her glove and stroll to second base with that easy, sexy saunter, and the pressure in his chest eased fractionally. At least J.T. couldn't cozy up to her for a while, he thought with hard satisfaction, watching the reporter trot past her into centerfield.

"Oh, Matt." Gloria's voice held such infinite sadness he shot her a surprised look. "Love is too precious a gift to throw away. Don't you know that?"

"With two marriages behind you, how can you say that?"

Sitting down on the arm of the easy chair by the window, Gloria smiled at his cynical expression and shrugged. "The first time I married for love. Donny was my high-school sweetheart, and we were head over heels." A smile curved her mouth as her eyes took on a misty faraway look. "He was such a sweet boy, my Donny. He died of leukemia at twenty-six. We only had eight years together, but they were the most wonderful years of my life.

"A year after Donny died, I married Nick. I convinced myself I loved him because I was desperate to recapture what I had lost. Within weeks, I knew I'd made a huge mistake. I stuck it out for a year out of guilt, but without love there was no way to make it work."

"I'm sorry, Gloria. I didn't know." Matt, like everyone else, had always assumed she was a two-time divorcee just out for a good time.

"It all happened a long time ago." She straightened her shoulders, shaking off the sadness, and gave him a pointed look. "I made a mistake with Nick, but I learned from it. You better believe, if I ever find love again, I'm going to grab hold of it and never let go." She waited a beat to let that sink in, then added, "And if you don't do the same, you're a fool."

Her eyes dared him to contradict her. Matt stared back at her for several tense moments. Then his gaze went to the window again, and beyond to the woman who haunted his dreams. "Maybe you're right."

"I know I am. At the very least, you owe it to yourself and to Maude Ann to explore your feelings. Who knows, maybe things won't work out for you two. But at least you'll have given it a shot."

Outside, the game ended and everyone headed back toward the lodge. J.T. caught up with Maude Ann and fell into step beside her. Matt watched the other man bend his head toward her and say something, watched the way she smiled in response. Pulling her tightly against his side, J.T. gave her a quick hug.

Matt's hard gaze fixed on the arm that remained draped over Maude Ann's shoulders as the pair strolled along.

His jaw clenched. "You're right. I'll do it."

Gloria laughed as he stalked to the outside door and snatched it open. "Go get her, tiger."

The veranda was full of people when he stepped outside, sweaty softball players and kids digging into the coolers for cold drinks or having another go at the ice cream and watermelon.

"Hey, Matt," Hank called, lifting a frosty bottle from the cooler. "You want a beer?"

"No, thanks. I'll catch you later," he replied absently, searching through the crowd.

At first he didn't see Maude Ann. He frowned, wondering how she had disappeared so fast. Then the group by the cooler shifted and he spotted her heading for the back veranda.

Rather than maneuver through the congestion on the veranda, he decided to take the shorter route and went back inside the way he'd come out.

Gloria wasn't in his room when he stalked through, nor was Maude Ann in the kitchen. Matt went outside again through the back door and nearly bumped into her as she came around the corner.

"Oh." For an instant, she looked dismayed, then her expression turned cool. "Sorry. I didn't see you there," she said, and tried to sidle around him.

Matt sidestepped to block her. "Maude Ann, we have to talk."

Surprise and wariness swam in her eyes when they met his. "Talk? About what?"

"About us."

She caught her breath, flinching as though he'd slapped her. "Us? You want to talk about *us?* I don't believe this." Her face tightened and she darted around him.

"Maude Ann, wait! This is important." He caught up with her at the kitchen door and put his hand on her arm to stop her. The look she shot him was glacial.

"I have nothing to say to you." She shook his hand off and opened the door, but when she stepped inside she turned and snapped, "And there *is* no *us!*"

She slammed the door in his face, and for a moment Matt was so astonished he simply stared at it. Then his temper flared. "Dammit, Maude Ann, what is the matter with you? We're going to talk if I have to…" Disbelieving, he stared down at the doorknob. He tried again to turn it, but it wouldn't budge.

"Looks like she's locked you out."

Matt's head snapped around. A few feet away, J.T. stood with one shoulder propped against the veranda post, his arms folded over his chest. His expression held none of its usual cheerfulness, only censure and a touch of what looked like pity. Matt didn't care for either. Especially not from this guy.

"Butt out, Conway. This is none of your business."

He turned his attention back to the door and rattled the knob. "Maude Ann, open this damned door."

"You're wasting your time. She's not going to let you in."

"How would *you* know?" Matt growled, shooting him a look of pure dislike.

J.T. shrugged. "You don't believe me? Wait and see."

Matt banged on the door. Through the window he could see Maude Ann flouncing around the kitchen, her face set as she banged cabinet doors and slammed drawers. She pulled out more paper cups and napkins and slammed them down on a tray, snatched another pitcher of lemonade out of the refrigerator, then filled a bucket with ice and plopped both onto the tray, as well, but not once did she so much as glance his way.

Matt muttered a curse. "Fine. Don't open the door. There are other ways to get in." She wouldn't lock every door, not when she had a yard full of company.

He stormed down the veranda, intent on reaching his room, but when he drew even with J.T., he stopped and jabbed his finger at him. "And you stay away from Maude Ann. You got that?"

"Oh, I got it all right. And I'll be happy to—just as soon as Maude Ann tells me that's what she wants."

"I'm warning you, Conway."

J.T. chuckled and shook his head. "You know, Dolan, for a smart guy, you can really pull some dumb stuff."

Matt's scowl deepened, turned dangerous. "Meaning?"

"Meaning, from the softball field you have a clear view of your room." His eyes, serious for once, bore into Matt's and as the significance of the statement soaked in, Matt felt sick.

"Aw, hell." Cupping the back of his neck, he let his head fall back and squeezed his eyes shut. She had seen him and Gloria go into his room. He groaned, remembering how Gloria had closed the blinds a few seconds later. He could imagine how Maude Ann must have felt.

His anger and frustration drained away, replaced by guilt and gut-wrenching remorse. That nothing had happened didn't matter. He had gone into his room with Gloria, fully intending to make love to her. He'd been so intent on shaking off his obsession with Maude Ann that he'd never given a thought to how his actions might make her feel.

He muttered a scorching expletive. J.T. was right; he was dumber than dirt.

"I must like you, Dolan," J.T. drawled. "That's the only reason I can figure for why I'm standing here trying to help you. But I gotta tell you, man, after a stunt like that, I'm beginning to think you don't deserve Maude Ann. What the hell were you thinking?"

"That's the trouble, I wasn't." Matt opened his eyes and met J.T.'s accusing gaze head-on. "But for the record, nothing happened between Gloria and me."

"Nothing?"

"Nothing."

"Hmm. Well, chum, you're gonna have one helluva time convincing Maude Ann of that. I'd get started if I were you."

It was on the tip of Matt's tongue to tell J.T. once again to mind his own business, but he bit the words back. J. T. Conway might be a pain-in-the-butt, nosy reporter, but he had at least clued him in on what had Maude Ann so upset.

Matt gave J.T. a level look. "I intend to."

Matt found her sitting on the side veranda in the middle of a group that included John, Tony, Hank, Patty, and Ned and Annie Bledsoe. As he approached the group, Maude Ann glanced up and spotted him, but she merely gave him a withering look and turned her attention back to the discussion.

Matt gritted his teeth. Evidently, she felt confident that he wouldn't make a scene in front of other people. Wrong.

He skirted around the semicircle of porch swing, love seats and loungers and stopped behind Maude Ann's chair. He leaned down and put his hand on her shoulder and gritted his teeth when she flinched at his touch.

"Maude Ann, I need to talk to you. In private."

She barely spared him a sidelong glance over her shoulder. "If you don't mind, I'm talking to my friends."

Conversation stopped and the others watched them curiously.

"This is important."

"Sorry. It will have to wait. I just want to sit here and relax right now."

"Too bad. We're going to talk."

"I said not now," she ground out through clenched teeth.

"Now."

Before she could argue further, he grasped her upper arm

and hauled her up out of the chair. She let out a squeak of surprise, and gasps and startled murmurs went up from the others. Tony came off the porch rail, where he'd been perched, like an uncoiling spring.

"Dammit, Matt, what do you think you're doing?"

Hank stood up, as well, his expression worried. "Hey, Matt, take it easy, ol' buddy."

"Matt, stop it! Have you lost your mind!" Maude Ann protested as he pulled her past John. The lieutenant didn't utter a word, merely cocked one bushy eyebrow and watched them with interest, almost as though he found the whole thing amusing.

"Dammit, Matt, I'm not going to just let you drag the doc off that way."

From behind, Matt heard Tony stomping after them, but the sound abruptly halted, and J.T. drawled, "Let 'em go. They've got things to settle."

Chalk up another point for Conway, Matt thought with grudging gratitude as he frog-marched Maude Ann down the veranda steps. As they started across the yard, she recovered her senses and began to struggle.

"Let me go!"

"Not on your life. And if you don't stop that, I'm going to toss you over my shoulder and carry you."

"You wouldn't *dare.*"

"The hell I wouldn't."

Staring at his set profile, she must have decided he meant it. She gave up trying to pry open his fingers and walked in sullen silence beside him.

They crossed the yard, then the softball field. He didn't stop until they stepped beneath an ancient live oak at the edge of the woods.

Maude Ann jerked her arm free and turned to face him.

"I hope you're satisfied," she snapped. "You've made a complete spectacle of us."

He glanced back at the lodge and saw that all their friends were watching them. Matt shrugged. "If you'd come with me in the first place, like I asked, it wouldn't have aroused their curiosity."

"I don't have anything to say to you," she spat.

Her eyes shot fire, and angry color bloomed in her cheeks. Though he found the display of temper almost unbearably arousing, it was also a barometer of how hurt she was, and that he deeply regretted.

"Well, I have plenty to say to you."

"Go tell it to Gloria. I'm not interested."

"I already have." His voice dropped to a gentle pitch. "That's all Gloria and I did in my room, Maude Ann—was talk. About you. About us."

"Oh, please, do I look stupid to you? Do you honestly expect me to believe that you took her in there and closed the blind just so you could talk?"

Matt raked a hand through his hair and sighed. "I won't lie to you. I had every intention of having sex with Gloria."

He saw the pain flicker across her face and felt rotten. She held her hands up in front of her, palms out. "Please. I don't want to hear this. What you do and who you do it with is your business. All I'm saying is, knowing how I feel about you—*felt* about you," she quickly amended, "you could have at least had the decency and the sensitivity not to flaunt your lover under my nose."

"She not my lover—at least, not anymore."

Maude Ann gave an inelegant snort.

"I couldn't have sex with her, Maude Ann," he said quietly. "I wanted to use her to banish you from my thoughts, but I couldn't. Because she wasn't the one I wanted. She wasn't you."

Maude Ann's head snapped up. She was suddenly still as a wary doe. Caution and a hint of distrust filled her eyes. Her expression turned from angry to guarded, but she remained silent, watching him, waiting.

"I'm in love with you, Maude Ann," Matt said softly.

Other than to flinch, she didn't move or speak for several seconds, merely searched his face for the truth. Finally she shook her head. "I don't believe you."

"Nevertheless, it's true."

"This is rather sudden, isn't it? You certainly didn't seem to feel that way two weeks ago when I told you I was in love with you."

He noted her use of the past tense. It sent a little chill down his spine, but he shook off the sensation. He refused to accept that her feelings could have changed. "I was in love with you even then. Hell, I've been in love with you for months, but I didn't want to admit it—not to you or to myself. That's why I behaved like a jerk with Gloria today. I'd convinced myself that what I felt for you was nothing more than normal desire after a prolonged abstinence. That all I needed was a woman. Any woman. I was wrong."

She stared at him, and he could see the struggle going on inside her. She wanted to believe him, but she wasn't quite there. Not yet.

"I've never felt this way about a woman before, Maude Ann. I've never wanted to. I still don't. But where you're concerned, I don't seem to have any choice."

Some of the doubt faded from her eyes, and her guarded expression relaxed into a sad little smile. "So what you're saying is, you love me, but against your will. My, how romantic."

"Dammit, I'm trying to be honest with you. I've never wanted a serious relationship before. I've never made a secret of that. Even feeling as I do about you, I'm still not sure that it's smart."

She gave a start when he took her hand, but when she made no effort to pull away, he was encouraged. "All I know is that I care for you more than I've ever cared for any woman. I want you in my life, Maude Ann. In my bed. I'm hoping that's what you want, too."

Something flared in her eyes and she opened her mouth to speak, but he silenced her with a shake of his head. "No, don't answer yet. There are some things I have to tell you, because if we do take the next step, I want to be sure that you're going into this relationship with your eyes wide open."

As though bracing herself, Maude Ann pulled her hand from his and crossed her arms over her midriff and nodded. "All right. Go ahead."

"First you have to know that I can't make you any promises. I have no idea where these feelings will lead, or if we'll have a future together." He paused and looked at her with regret, his gaze locking with hers. "I *do* love you, Maude Ann. I've never said those words to any woman before. But I have to be honest with you. I'm not sure I will ever change my mind about mixing police work and marriage. Before we go any further, you need to decide if you can live with that."

"My, my," Maude Ann said with a mirthless little chuckle. "You certainly are a sweet talker, aren't you. You really know how to give a girl hope."

"I'm being open with you, Maude Ann, because I care. I don't want to mislead you. That could only lead to hurt, and that's the last thing I want to do."

Her arms remained folded across her middle. Matt watched her and tried to read which way she was leaning. From her expression, he had the sinking feeling that her decision would not be in his favor. Panic bubbled up inside him, and he wanted to snatch her into his arms and kiss her senseless, sweep her so completely off her feet she had no choice.

But he couldn't do that. Maude Ann meant too much to him to coerce or manipulate her.

She glanced at him and attempted a smile, but it wobbled and didn't quite come off. "I must say, I've had more romantic propositions, but at least you were honest."

"Hey, Maude Ann!"

The call came from the veranda, a jarring reminder that they had an audience. They both jumped and swung around to see John standing at the bottom of the steps, waving at them. Behind him, the others were gathering their children and belongings.

"We're going to hit the road!" John yelled through his cupped hands. "It's a long drive back to Houston!"

"I'll be right there," she called back.

She turned to Matt with another wobbly smile. "Looks like the party is over. We'd better say our goodbyes."

They headed back to the veranda, walking side by side but not touching. Tension hummed between them like a high-voltage wire, but they didn't speak. The only sounds were the crackle of grass stubble beneath their shoes and the faint murmur of voices in the distance. Several times Matt glanced at her out of the corner of his eye, but if she felt his scrutiny, she didn't acknowledge it. She still hugged her arms tightly and stared straight again.

Halfway across the yard, Matt halted. "Maude Ann."

She stopped a few steps ahead of him and looked back. "Yes?"

The sadness he saw in her eyes twisted his gut. She was going to say no.

He was prepared for that, expected it—at least, he

thought he was. He'd even told himself it would probably be for the best. So why did he suddenly feel as though he had an anvil sitting on his chest?

"When you make up your mind, you know where to find me," he said softly.

She stared at him for the space of several heartbeats, then nodded.

Chapter Twelve

She had to refuse Matt. It was the sensible thing to do.

Maude Ann reached the far side of her bedroom and spun around, and the black silk nightgown swirled around her ankles. She paced back toward the other side, twisting her hands together.

What else could she do? she asked herself for the tenth time in as many minutes. No sane, intelligent woman would deliberately enter into a dead-end relationship with a man she loved. That was a sure formula for heartbreak.

But, dear God, how could she refuse even the little bit of happiness he offered when she loved him so?

She made a frustrated sound somewhere between a growl and a scream. Damn Matt for doing this to her! And damn his brutal frankness! She strove for honesty in all areas of her life and admired that quality in others, but did he have to strip her of every illusion? Every shred of hope?

To tell her in one breath that he loved her and in the

next that he didn't know if they could have a future together was unfair. So he didn't believe in marriage for police officers. Big deal, neither did she—at least, not with her. She hadn't bothered to tell him that because there wasn't any point, since he was so adamant on the subject.

For them to have a life together, one of them would have to give in, and she couldn't see that happening. Matt was a police officer right down to the marrow in his bones— and a darned good one. While she appreciated that, she could not bring herself to marry another cop, she thought with a shudder. Not even loving Matt as she did. She simply could not.

If Matt flunked the reentry physical, they might have a chance.

The wayward thought brought a tiny spark of hope, followed instantly by a wave of guilt.

How could she entertain such an idea? The loss of his job would be a crushing blow for Matt. She wasn't sure it would make a difference, anyway. If it came to that, he would either have to leave the force or take a desk job, and he would hate both alternatives. Knowing Matt, he would be so miserable he probably wouldn't consider making a commitment to her.

Which left her right back where she'd started.

No matter how Maude Ann looked at the situation, it seemed her only choices were to break off things now or settle for a brief affair.

Reaching the other end of the room, she swung around and paced back toward the window again. Matt was no help at all. He had left the decision entirely to her. Damn him! Did he really believe that by spelling everything out for her she would not be hurt when their relationship ended?

The spurt of anger faded as quickly as it had come. Sighing, Maude Ann raked her hand through her hair. Yes, of course he did. No doubt he thought he was shielding her, that forewarned was forearmed and therefore she would be able to ward off the blow when it came—or some such skewed male logic.

She shook her head and squeezed the tight muscles in the back of her neck. Men. When it came to love, they hadn't a clue.

The truth was, they were both going to be hurt, no matter what she decided. It was just a matter of when.

She stopped in front of her cheval mirror. The woman in the glass looked back at her with haunted eyes. Against the black nightgown, her skin appeared paler than usual, almost translucent, the freckles across her nose standing out like tiny splatters of paint. She had washed her hair when she showered, but she'd been too distraught to bother with the blow dryer. Now it rioted around her head and shoulders in a mass of untamed curls, which only seemed to make her appear even more fragile.

She looked brittle, ready to shatter, and she hated that. She was a strong, decisive, resilient woman, dammit. Not some dithering little piece of fluff who went to pieces when life dealt her a low blow. She had survived the loss of her beloved husband, hadn't she? One way or another, she would survive this.

Maude Ann went to the window and gazed pensively out at the moonlit waters of the lake. That she was going to be hurt was a given. She was hurting now, for Pete's sake. The question was, she supposed, would it be any more painful to grab a few weeks or months of happiness before she and Matt parted than to make a clean break now—and perhaps always wonder if they could have somehow worked something out.

Sighing, she closed her eyes and leaned forward until her forehead rested against the cool pane of glass. She was rationalizing, looking for an excuse to do what she wanted. She could analyze and pick at the problem all night, but the truth was, deep in her heart, where it counted, she had already made up her mind....

She was going to turn him down. Matt could feel it. What else could her silence mean? It was after eleven, and not a peep out of her.

His stomach clenched. He went to the window and stared out. He had just showered and was naked beneath his robe. Behind him, warm, moist air, laden with the scents of soap and toothpaste and masculine toiletries drifted from the open door of the bathroom. Except for the light spilling through the same door, his room was in darkness, allowing him to see through the gloom beyond the window. Matt stared past the dark shapes of wicker furniture to the stubbled field beyond the side yard, where the white chalk lines of the softball diamond, almost luminescent in the moonlight, glowed.

He'd handled this all wrong. Of course she was going to turn him down. What did he expect after that miserable little speech he'd given her? ''Come be my lover, but don't expect permanence,'' he mimicked.

Oh, yeah, that was going to sweep her right off her feet, all right. What woman could resist such a sweet deal? You're a real silver-tongued devil, Dolan.

Matt groaned. But what else could he do? He couldn't mislead her. He wouldn't do that to any woman. Especially not Maude Ann. He loved her, dammit!

Oh, yeah, he'd definitely made a tactical mistake in the way he'd handled things. Unfair or not, after laying everything on the line, he should have stuck to her like glue, used the feelings they had for each other to his advantage.

He should have wooed her with gentle persuasion, held and kissed her until she couldn't even think of saying no.

Instead, like a noble idiot, he'd left her alone to think things over and come to a decision. Maude Ann was warm and loving and generous to a fault, and he didn't doubt that she loved him. However, she was also an eminently sensible, pragmatic woman. She had to be to run Henley Haven. She loved every child in her care as though he or she was her own, yet when the courts decided one should go elsewhere, she accepted the order without a lot of fuss. A woman who could do that just might decide the risks of being hurt were too great to take a chance on him. So he had a sinking feeling what her decision would be.

The thought brought a gush of panic to his chest. Anger followed close behind. His mouth folded into a grim line. "We'll just see about that," he muttered. Yanking the belt of his robe tighter, he turned on his heel and stomped toward the door. If she thought he was giving up without a fight, she could think again.

With a face like a thundercloud, he snatched open his bedroom door—and came face-to-face with Maude Ann.

She stood just on the other side of the doorway, her hand raised to knock.

"Oh!"

"Maude Ann."

They spoke at the same time, then fell silent, staring at each other.

Matt's chest was suddenly so tight he had difficulty breathing. From the pulse throbbing at the base of Maude Ann's throat, he knew her emotions were running riot, too.

Time seemed to stand still, and for a moment, he couldn't think, couldn't move. Then his gaze lowered from those wide, whiskey-colored eyes to trail down her body, and his heart gave a thump. She had come to him barefoot, wearing a gossamer-thin black negligee over a sexy black nightgown.

His gaze jumped back to her face, and what he saw there made him catch his breath. The glow of love shining from those expressive eyes told him all he needed to know. Twin bursts of joy and relief exploded inside him, one filling his chest to bursting, the other making his knees weak.

"Maude Ann," he said again, but this time his voice came out low and dark, rough with emotion.

Her soft smile pierced his heart, and he felt his insides tremble. Words were not needed and none were spoken. Never taking his gaze from hers, he reached for her, and she walked into his arms.

Maude Ann's arms went around his waist, and as he pulled her close, she sighed and laid her cheek against his chest. For a time they simply stood there without speaking, holding each other, luxuriating in the moment, savoring the taut, trembling pleasure of anticipation, the sense of home-coming. Then Matt grasped her arms and held her slightly away from him. He searched her face, looked into her eyes, his own serious and intent. "Are you sure, Maude Ann?"

She smiled and cupped his face with her palm. "I'm sure. I love you, Matt."

He sucked in his breath. His heart seemed to swell in his chest, and his throat was suddenly so tight he couldn't swallow. Pulling her farther into the room, he shut the door. They stood mere inches apart, gazing at each other. In the semidarkness she looked almost ethereal, as though she was no more than a misty dream his thoughts had somehow conjured up. But this was no dream. This was real. This was Maude Ann, a strong, passionate woman of substance and heart and earthy sensuality.

The very air around them seemed to pulse with aware-ness. The sweet scent of floral bath talc and perfume drifted from her to tantalize him. Matt lifted his hand to her hair, skimmed his palm over it, glorying in its texture, its thickness. Then he dove his fingers into the vibrant cloud, cupped the back of her head and pulled her closer.

"And I love you," he whispered as he lowered his head to her.

The kiss was hungry, full of pent-up passion too long repressed. Matt's lips devoured her. Maude Ann went up on tiptoe, locked her arms around his neck and kissed him back with unabashed need and eager joyfulness.

His hands roamed her back, her waist, her hips. Beneath his palms the negligee glided over the slippery fabric of her nightgown, impeding his hold on her body in a way that was both erotic and frustrating. Finally he gave a soft growl and partially broke off the kiss, lifting his head just far enough to ask in between soft nibbles, "How do you…take this…thing off?"

He heard and felt her husky chuckle an instant before she took a half step back. Watching him with heavy-lidded eyes and a seductive smile on her lips, she pulled on the ribbon tie at the negligee's neckline.

With excruciating slowness, the satin bow collapsed, and the edges of the garment parted an enticing few inches. Her movements languid and deliberately tantalizing, Maude Ann spread the edges wide and shimmied the garment off her shoulders. The black chiffon floated to the floor without a sound and formed a billowy puddle around her feet.

Matt stared. He had never seen a woman so beautiful, so utterly alluring. She stood before him, tall and proud, the black satin gown lovingly skimming her womanly curves, from her breasts to her ankles, her wild mane of auburn curls billowing around creamy shoulders, bare but for the tiny black satin straps. And that face—that magnificent face—with its wide mouth and delicate, freckled nose, those whiskey-colored eyes, direct and honest and filled with love. He had never seen anything so perfect. Matt knew that he could look at that face for the rest of his days and never grow tired of it.

"You're so lovely," he whispered. With an unsteady hand, he reached out and trailed his forefinger over one smooth shoulder and followed the strap downward to trace the low neckline and the pearly flesh that swelled over it.

He felt her tremble, and the delicate reaction sent heat racing through his body to settle, hot and heavy, in his loins. Desire consumed him, urging him to rush, but he clamped down on the need, forcing himself to go slowly.

He cupped her breasts with both hands, flexed his fingers around the soft mounds, stroked, watched the curves plump and almost spill over as he gently lifted. Unable to resist, Matt kissed and nibbled and tasted, leaving a wet line of fire on her skin as his tongue traced the gown's neckline, just as his finger had done mere seconds before.

Then his mouth trailed lower, to where her nipples thrust against the gown. Maude Ann gripped his shoulders, and her head arched back when he took one hard bud into his mouth and suckled her through the slippery satin.

The pleasure was exquisite, drawing a keening moan from her throat. He drew on her with an evocative rhythm, taking her deep into his mouth, wetting the satin cloth. Everything inside Maude Ann quickened and burned as the slow, sweet suction seemed to tug at her womb.

The sensations were too beautiful, too intense, to bear for long, and she took a step back, breaking contact with that tormenting mouth. Breathing hard, her face flushed with desire, she stared into his eyes and raised her hand to the tiny straps and slid first one, then the other, off her shoulders.

The black satin slithered down her body to join the negligee, and she stood before him with her shoulders back and her head high, wearing only earrings, which winked now and then through her cloud of hair.

Matt couldn't have taken his eyes off her if the world was coming to an end around him. His gaze traveled over every inch of her, from the top of her head to the puddle of black satin and chiffon around her ankles. When his gaze rose and locked with hers he had to grit his teeth to control his raging desire.

"You're perfect," he said in a voice rough with passion. "I wanted to take it slow, but—"

"I don't want you to," she said.

"Good, because I can't. I have to have you. Now."

He reached for the belt of his robe. "No, let me," she said, and stepping forward, she took over the task herself. In seconds his robe hit the floor. Her head tipped to one side, Maude Ann studied his body with the same frank interest that he had hers. When her gaze once more returned to his, she smiled.

"You're perfect, too," she said, and closed her hand around him.

Matt sucked in a sharp breath. Arching his head back, he squeezed his eyes shut and bared his teeth. Pleasure surged through him, but he could tolerate the exquisite torture for only a moment. With a sound very like a growl, he swept her up into his arms and carried her to the bed, and Maude Ann's throaty laugh rang out as he fell with her onto the mattress.

Then his mouth was on hers, and the time for laughter had passed. The kiss was deep and ravenous and demanding, and when he nudged her legs apart, she opened to him willingly, eagerly. Raising himself on his forearms, Matt stared into her eyes and drove into her.

The pleasure was so shattering Maude Ann cried out, her body arching.

Their hunger was too huge, their need too great for a slow loving. Still watching her, Matt thrust deep and hard, setting a demanding rhythm. Maude Ann wrapped her legs around him and met each powerful stroke.

Their bodies moved in unison, fitting together as though they had been made for each other. Urgency drove them. Pleasure grew, reaching such immense proportions they could no longer contain it, and the end, when it came, was explosive.

It left them drained and shaken, and so utterly replete neither could move.

Gradually, the thunderous beat of Maude Ann's heart slowed and her breathing returned to something approaching normal. With her eyes still closed, she smiled and ran her palms in slow circles over Matt's back, luxuriating in her right to touch him so intimately. She loved the feel of him, his warmth, the hardness and strength of the muscles banding his back. She loved his smell—a clean musky maleness overlaid with a hint of soap and herbal shampoo. It filled her senses.

Though Matt's body pressed her into the mattress, she felt deliciously weightless, as though she were floating free.

Her eyes fluttered open, and she gazed over his shoulder at the dimly lit ceiling and waited for the regrets to come, but there were none. This felt right.

She loved this man with all heart, and her soul had hungered for this closeness with him. They had not simply had sex. What they had just shared had been the ultimate expression of love. They'd worshiped each other with their bodies, each giving and receiving a pleasure so profound it can only be achieved by those who truly love. How could she regret that?

Maude Ann trailed one hand up his back and neck and winnowed her fingers through his tousled hair, smiling at its thickness, the silky warmth of the dark strands sliding between her fingers. She had made the right decision; she knew that now with absolutely certainty. If she had his love for only a little while, then so be it. Whatever happened, she knew she would never regret this time with him.

When her fingertips tickled the top of his ear, Matt made a contented sound and stirred.

"Am I crushing you?"

She traced the swirls in his ear and shook her head. "No, this feels wonderful."

She felt him grin against the side of her neck. "I'll say," he murmured, rotating his hips against her. He chuckled when she responded in kind, but when he rose and braced on his forearms on either side of her head, his expression turned serious.

"I love you, Maude Ann," he declared in a raspy whisper.

Even in the dim light spilling from the bathroom, she could see the intensity in his eyes. They glittered down at her like blue diamonds from that darkly handsome face.

His fingertips toyed with the wayward curls at her temples, while his thumbs stroked the tender skin along the underside of her jaw. "Dear, God, how I love you. Why didn't I realize that years ago?"

"Because it wasn't time for us," she replied softly. "And I love you, too. More than life itself." So much emotion clogged her throat she barely got the words out. After that, all she could do was gaze lovingly up at him, her eyes slowly banking with tears.

His gaze ran over her face, studying each feature intently, as though committing them to memory. "I never knew that loving someone would be like this. That I could care so much.'' He shook his head in wonder. ''It's like...like I've found a part of me I didn't know was missing.''

''Oh, Matt.'' Too choked up to say more, she cupped her hand around the back of his neck and brought his head down to hers.

Their lips met tenderly, in a slow, rocking kiss that touched the core of her being. It devoured, it worshiped, it burned, and the intensity of it made Maude Ann tremble.

Their bodies were still joined in the most intimate of embraces, and she felt him growing hard again inside her. As impossible as it seemed, passion and need engulfed her, and her hips moved in invitation, one that Matt accepted with enthusiasm.

As desire claimed them again, Maude Ann's heart soared, and with a sigh, she wrapped her arms around him and gave herself up to the spiraling pleasure.

''No! Come back! Don't leave me! Come back!''

Maude Ann awoke with a start. For an instant, she didn't know what had roused her or where she was. Outside, the black sky had taken on a pearly cast, which signaled that dawn was not far away. She squinted through the dimness at her surroundings, and when she spotted her gown and negligee on the floor, it all came rushing back—the passion, the heated words, the incredible pleasure.

She smiled and snuggled her face into the pillow, feeling smug and content. Matt's stamina amazed her. They had made love three times during the night, and each time had been breathtaking.

''No. No, come back! Don't go!''

At the mumbled words, Maude Ann looked over her shoulder at Matt and realized what had jarred her awake. They were lying spoon-fashion, and though he appeared to still be asleep, he was making restless, jerky movements, his body tense against her back. In the dim light she could see that his face wore an anguished expression.

"Matt? Darling, are you all right?" Maude Ann tried to twist around to face him, but instantly the arm encircling her waist tightened, and he held her clamped to him. Reaching over her shoulder, she gave his cheek several brisk pats. "Matt. Matt, wake up. You're having a dream."

He awoke with a start and shot up into a sitting position. "What? What is—"

He looked around, bewildered, disoriented. "I…"

"It's all right." Maude Ann raised herself up on one elbow and stroked his back. "You were just dreaming."

His shoulders slumped. "Yeah. I know."

With a sigh, he flopped back flat on his pillow and draped his forearm over his eyes. Remaining propped above him, Maude Ann put her hand on his chest, stroking her fingers through the silky hair as she watched him try to get his breathing under control. "You've had this dream before, I take it," she said softly, still stroking.

His mouth twisted. "Oh, yeah. Lots of times."

"When did it start?"

"I've had the same dream, off and on, all my life."

She debated for a moment, knowing that with Matt she was on shaky ground when it came to this sort of thing. "Would you like to tell me about it?"

The forearm covering his eyes rolled back a quarter turn. From beneath it he gave her dry look. "Are you asking as a psychiatrist or just out of curiosity?"

"I'm asking as the woman who loves you."

The answer seemed to disarm him, and his eyes softened. He reached out and stroked her cheek. "It's nothing for you to worry about, sweetheart. There's nothing scary or threatening about the dream."

"I'm glad. But why don't you tell me, anyway?"

He gave her an exasperated look, but she merely waited, and finally he sighed and gave in. He told her about the faceless woman in the mist, and how he and other shadowy figures ran after her as she backed away crying.

Maude Ann listened intently, and when he was done she asked, "Do you know who she is?"

"I have a good idea. I'm no psychiatrist, but I'd have to be dense not to have figured out it's probably my birth mother."

"Your *birth mother?*" Maude Ann sat up in the bed. "I didn't know you were adopted!"

Matt grinned at her astonishment and ran his forefinger down her spine, all the way to the shadowy clef at its base. The feathery touch made her shiver. "There's a lot you don't know about me. But you'll learn."

"Matt, stop that." Reaching behind her, she grabbed his wrist. "We're talking about your dream and your being adopted."

"Mmm, I can think of more pleasant things to do."

"You sex maniac. Behave. This is important."

"Spoilsport," he teased, but her look told him she wasn't going to budge,. "Oh, all right. But I warn you, there's not much to tell. For reasons of her own, when I was two years old, my mother put me up for adoption."

"Two? That's unusual. Usually if a woman makes the decision to give up a child, she does so at birth. Do you have any idea why she gave you up?"

"Could be she was bored with motherhood, or she couldn't afford to keep me, or it cramped her style too much to have me around, or she just plain didn't like me. I'll probably never know. Hell, I don't even know her name."

Matt said the words casually, as though the matter was

of no importance to him, but she heard the bitter hurt and anger behind them. "Do you remember her at all?"

"Only in my dreams, and even then, there's no face. But like I said, it doesn't take a genius to figure out who the woman is or why I have the dream. She gave me away, and I didn't understand. Hell, it probably scared the hell out of me."

"Mmm. You may be right. That would be very traumatic for a two-year-old. By then you had bonded with her. And though you say you have no memories of her, they're there, buried somewhere in your subconscious." She thought a moment, then asked, "Do you know anything about her?"

"Not much. She had only two requests of my adoptive parents. First, that I be adopted by an Irish couple, which I assume means I'm of Irish descent, although I don't know that for certain. And she asked that I always wear this medallion piece." The chain that encircled his neck had fallen to one side onto the pillow. He picked it up and held the jagged piece of silver so that she could see it.

"Yes, I remember seeing that before."

Reaching around, Maude Ann turned on the bedside light. Taking the piece of metal from his fingers, she leaned forward to examine it. "There's writing on one side, and it looks like some sort of symbol on the other." She looked at him. "Do you have any idea what they mean?"

"Not a clue. There's not enough there to decipher."

She looked back at the medallion piece again and ran her finger over the uneven edge. "It's looks like it's only a small piece of a disk. Sort of like an uneven wedge out of a pie. I wonder where the rest of it is."

"I assume my birth mother has it, but I don't really know. Or care, for that matter. Hell, I don't know why I even bother to wear the thing."

Maude Ann's heart squeezed and she gazed at him sadly.

Oh, my darling, you wear it because this little piece of silver is your only connection to the woman who gave you life, and whether you want to or not, you do care.

Something of what she was thinking must have shown on her face, because Matt reached out and cupped her cheek. "Hey, sweetheart, don't look so sad."

"I can't help it. It is sad that you never knew her."

"Not really. She probably did me a favor, giving me to the Dolans. I had a great childhood. No kid could have asked for better parents. So don't go wasting all that compassion and motherly concern on me. Save it for the kids upstairs."

A slow smile spread on his face, and his eyes grew heavy-lidded as they zeroed in on her mouth. Maude Ann knew that look, and her body began to tingle. Hooking his hand around her neck, he drew her down to him. "Now that I've satisfied your curiosity about my family," he murmured in a seductive rumble, "it's only fair that you satisfy my curiosity."

Lying half on his chest, she relaxed and luxuriated in the feel of his body against hers. She smiled as his lips nipped and nibbled at hers. "Oh? And just what…could you possibly…still be…curious about?" she asked, between indulging in some nibbling of her own. "After last night…I have no more…secrets."

A wicked chuckle rumbled from Matt's throat. "Sweetheart, I'm just…getting started…exploring your…secrets."

Maude Ann felt as though she were melting from the inside as a languid heat built in the core of her body and spread outward. Responding to the pressure of his hand on her neck, she gave a low moan and surrendered to his kiss, but her lips had barely settled on his when something he'd said jogged her memory.

She jerked back. "The kids!"

"What? Maude Ann, what…" he began, but she was already scrambling off the bed and snatching up her gown and negligee.

He sat up and scowled. "Dammit, Maudie, come back here!"

"I can't. I don't have time. There's too much to do. Oh, how could I have forgotten?" she moaned. She paused just long enough to shoot him a harried look. "Well, don't just lie there. Get up! Get busy!"

"Maude Ann, what the hell is the matter with you?" He glanced at the bedside clock. "It's barely six. The kids won't be downstairs for at least another hour yet. Come back to bed."

She turned with her hand on the doorknob and experienced a flutter of regret. He looked so sexy and so thoroughly male, sitting there in the middle of the rumpled bed glaring at her, hair mussed, jaw shadowed with morning stubble, his naked body bronze and muscled above the white sheet, which lay bunched around the tops of his thighs.

"I can't. Don't you remember? Marshall and Dennis are leaving today. Their cousin is coming for them around ten."

Chapter Thirteen

It was always emotionally devastating when one of the children left the haven, but for the sake of the other kids, Maude Ann tried to present the departure as a joyous event.

She and Jane prepared a special celebration breakfast and did their best to appear happy for the boys. Maude Ann had purchased a small gift for each of the brothers, along with cards, which they all, including Matt, had signed, though some of the smaller kids had needed help printing their names.

To everyone's surprise, Tyrone had a gift of his own for Dennis. The boys had butted heads like two young bulls when Tyrone first came to the haven, but both were scamps, and before long they had been aiding and abetting each other in all kinds of mischief. Now, next to Matt, Dennis was Tyrone's best friend. When he pulled the grubby rabbit's foot, his most prized possession, from the pocket of his jeans and handed it to Dennis, Maude Ann had to look away and blink back tears.

She had been preparing the kids for weeks, ever since she'd received the order from Judge Simpson. She had explained that Marshall and Dennis were going to live with family members who loved and wanted them, and that they were going to have a wonderful life. She had told the other kids that while it was okay to feel sad that their friends were leaving, even to cry if they wanted, they didn't have to worry about them.

She would have given the pep talk, no matter what, simply to allay the children's fears, but after meeting the Hendersons, a pleasant couple in their forties with two apparently well-adjusted and happy boys of their own, she had hopes that this time she was right.

There were tears and a general feeling of gloom as they all said their goodbyes on the front veranda and watched Marshall and Dennis drive away with the Hendersons. That was only to be expected. More troubling was the fear she saw in the children's eyes that they might be the next to be banished from the only safe place they had ever known. Maude Ann wanted more than anything to be able to tell them it would never happen, but she couldn't. And that broke her heart.

She managed to hold on to her composure—just barely— until the car disappeared down the road and the dejected children and Jane and Matt straggled back inside. Maude Ann deliberately dawdled behind the others, and the instant the door closed behind them, she took off at a run.

Before she had taken three steps, she was sobbing and nearly blinded by tears. She would have preferred a private hiding place that no one but her knew about, but there was no such spot. In any case, her grief was too urgent, so the east veranda, which was seldom used this time of day, had to do.

Throwing herself onto the first wicker love seat she encountered, she curled into a ball, buried her face against the blue-and-white canvas cushions and gave in to the wrenching pain.

That was where Matt found her a few minutes later.

He had missed her almost at once. When he'd asked Jane where Maude Ann had disappeared to, she had given him an odd look and muttered a cryptic, "Never you mind. She has to deal with these things in her own way."

He hadn't like the sound of that. Not one bit.

Ignoring Jane's exasperated, "Now, Matt, you come back here!" he had left the kitchen to go look for her.

He had intended to start down at the pier, but the instant he'd stormed out the door, he heard an odd sound from the east veranda and went to investigate.

He came around the corner and stopped in his tracks.

Though Maude Ann's cries were muffled by the love-seat cushions, the sound of her misery and the sight of her shaking shoulders nearly destroyed him.

With an oath, he rushed to her. "Aw, Maudie, come here, baby." Ignoring her weak protest, he scooped her up in his arms and sat down with her in the nearest swing. As she curled against him, he cradled her close and set the swing in motion.

"Sweetheart, what are you doing out here all by yourself," he crooned, nuzzling his jaw against her temple when she burrowed her face into his neck. "No, never mind. Don't answer that. Just let it out, baby. Let it all out. Thatta girl."

It was just as well he retracted the question. He doubted that Maude Ann could have said a word if her life had depended on it. All she could do was huddle in his arms and wail out her grief like a forsaken child.

Her tears soaked his shirt, plastering the cloth to his skin, but he didn't care. As he swung them back and forth, he stroked her back and gazed out at the woods beyond the yard, surprised and bemused. Evidently, she wasn't as stoic as he'd thought.

Normally, crying women sent Matt running for cover, but strangely, with Maude Ann all he wanted to do was give comfort. She was such a strong, self-sufficient woman, that her tears were all the more heartrending, and a measure of how deeply she loved the kids in her charge.

When Maude Ann loved, she loved completely, openly, holding nothing back. He had firsthand experience of that. Her nature was open and giving, and once she accepted the love between them, she welcomed it with a wholehearted joy that both captivated him and scared the wits out of him.

Lord, he didn't ever want to hurt her.

He had no idea how long they sat there, but gradually her sobs subsided.

"Are you all right now?" he asked after a while.

She shook her head. "N-no. But I w-will be." Another little hitching sigh overtook her, and when it was done she sagged against him.

"I—I *hate* to cry," she said with so much vehemence that Matt had to smile.

"I know you do," he agreed solemnly.

"It's just that I h-hate it so much when one of the kids leaves. Today I lost two of them."

"Yeah, that was rough."

She sat up and sniffed, wiping her wet cheek with her fingertips, but she didn't move from his lap.

Stroking her thigh, Matt gave her a curious look. "If it

upsets you so much, sweetheart, why in the name of heaven did you open a foster home?''

Maude Ann looked at him as though she thought that was the most daft question she'd ever heard. ''Because I knew I could help these children. And because they need me.''

And that, Matt thought, said it all.

He knew that her mothering tendencies were part of why he loved her. Each one of these sad-eyed, little lost souls was special to her, and no matter what, she would never voluntarily give any of them away—as his mother had done. Maude Ann's great capacity for love, her unwavering commitment and constancy, were as much a part of her as her auburn curls or the spattering of freckles across her nose, and that made her a woman to prize.

Looking into her eyes, he felt overwhelmed with love for this woman. Her face was streaked with tears, which had all but washed away the small amount of makeup she'd applied that morning to impress the Hendersons. But to Matt she had never been more beautiful. And that beauty went all the way to the bone.

Gazing at her tenderly, he framed her face with both hands and with his thumbs brushed away the lingering moisture. ''You're right, they do need you. So do I.'' Exerting gentle pressure, he slowly brought her face down to his.

He kissed her with all the tenderness he was feeling, savoring her, loving her. She had been through an emotional wringer, and his aim wasn't to arouse, but to comfort and cherish. Nevertheless, the gentle caress packed a wallop, piercing Matt with hot, sweet desire and drawing a last, shuddering sigh from Maude Ann.

''What're you kissin' Miz Maudie for?''

Maude Ann started and would have jumped up, but Matt put his arms around her hips and held her in his lap.

"Tyrone. We, uh…that is…"

"Did you need something, Tyrone?" Matt asked, cutting off Maude Ann's dithering response. To his great amusement, her face turned scarlet and she had trouble meeting the boy's eyes.

"Miz Jane says to tell Miz Maudie she's wanted on the phone."

"Oh, okay. Thank you, Tyrone." Reacting to the statement with the alacrity of a drowning man grabbing a lifeline, she shot off Matt's lap and disappeared around the corner of the porch before the chains on the swing stopped rattling.

Tyrone stayed where he was and eyed Matt with sullen curiosity. "You like that kissin' stuff?"

The disgust in the boy's voice brought a crooked smile to Matt's mouth. "Yeah, I do. You will, too, one day."

"Nuh-uh! I ain't never gonna kiss no yucky girl."

"Yeah, well…" The swing creaked and rocked, rattling the chains again as Matt rose. He put his hand on Tyrone's shoulder and headed for the back door. "The thing is, son, girls don't stay yucky. Round about thirteen or fourteen, they get to be downright tempting."

Tyrone looked up at Matt with an expression that clearly said, "Yeah, right. And pigs fly." A few seconds later, he asked, "Does that mean you gonna kiss Miz Maudie some more?"

Chuckling, Matt gave the boy's shoulder a squeeze. "You got it, pal. Every chance I get."

The following weeks were an eye-opener for Maude Ann. She had not known it was possible to be so happy and so filled with dread, both at the same time, but that was exactly how she felt.

Except for the hours he worked out, Matt spent all his time with her and the kids. He took part in whatever activity she planned for the children, whether work or play, everything from gardening and house-cleaning to doing jigsaw puzzles and playing catch.

After Tyrone caught them kissing, there was no way they could pretend they were not involved, but Maude Ann had not expected Matt to so openly display his affection for her. She had thought, because of the temporary nature of their relationship, that they would behave casually toward each other when they were not alone. Matt, however, was having none of that. He insisted that honesty and loving displays among adults were what the children needed, and she couldn't argue with that.

And loving displays were just what Matt provided. He touched her frequently, putting his arm around her shoulders or her waist, holding her hand, cupping the back of her neck to haul her in for a quick kiss, stroking her hair.

When he felt like kissing her or touching her, he did so, no matter who was watching, whether it was the kids or Jane or J.T. It seemed to Maude Ann that he took special delight in kissing her in front of J.T.

Much to Matt's annoyance, the reporter was a frequent visitor at Henley Haven. He even spent a couple of weekends.

"I just don't see why he keeps hanging around," Matt groused after one such visit. "He knows how we feel about each other." Matt had made sure of that by taking J.T. aside for a talk the very next time he showed up after the picnic.

"Matt! I keep telling you, J.T. and I are just good friends. Friends visit friends. Besides, I'm glad he makes the effort. He's good with the children. He likes them and they like him. These kids need plenty of positive masculine attention.''

''That's another thing. I'm not sure he's a good influence on the kids. Conway tends to be too lenient with them. He's always joking and kidding around, never takes anything seriously. The man's a lightweight.''

Maude Ann's eyes widened. ''Why, Matthew Dolan. It's not just me, is it? You're jealous of J.T.'s relationship with the children, too.''

''Me? Jealous of Conway? Don't be ridiculous. I don't have any reason to be jealous of that jerk.''

Delighted, she went to him and looped her arms around his neck, meeting his scowl with a loving smile. ''That's right. Absolutely none. The kids like J.T., but you're the one they're really crazy about.''

It was true. Matt would always be gruff and intense and at times impatient, but that was just his personality. The children knew that behind that tough exterior was an old softie. And they adored him.

The change in Maude Ann's relationship with Matt brought a halt to Debbie's nightmares, but to be on the safe side, Maude Ann put a baby monitor in the little girl's room. The receiver sat on the bedside table in Matt's room since Maude Ann now spent her nights in his bed.

Matt's condition improved daily, even faster, it seemed to her, than it had before they had become lovers. While she was happy for him, she knew that time was running out, and her sense of dread increased apace with his recovery.

The day of the picnic, his buddies had brought Matt's Jeep to the haven, and a few days later, for the first time, he drove himself to Houston for his checkup. Being able to drive again was liberating for him, and his mood had been buoyant that morning. Maude Ann had smiled at his obvious pleasure and kissed him goodbye, but she'd watched his Jeep disappear down the road with a fist-size knot in her chest. One day soon, she'd thought, Matt would drive away and not return.

For all that they spent each day together, they had almost no time alone until after the children were in bed at night. Late August marked the beginning of the school year for the four oldest children, but even though they were gone from the aven for most of every weekday, Debbie was still there. Crushed that she couldn't go to school with the others, she dogged Matt's and Maude Ann's steps wherever they went.

The school bus did not come down private roads, so each morning and afternoon one of the adults drove the four miles to and from the bus stop out on the highway. On a Friday morning, almost five weeks after the picnic, Maude Ann had no sooner returned from the bus stop and stepped out of the van when Matt grasped her arm and announced that she was coming with him.

At first she was too startled to protest, but when he started marching her toward his Jeep she managed a surprised "Coming with you where?"

"To Houston. We're going to have some time alone together."

"What? Oh, Matt, darling, I'd love to. Really. But I can't go today. I have too much to do." Her protest hadn't the slightest effect on him. Practically trotting along at his side, she cast a desperate look over her shoulder at her assistant. "Tell him, Jane!"

"Don't look at me. I'm on his side." The older woman stood on the front walk, watching the proceedings with interest. "You ask me, it's about time you took a day off. Now you two have a nice time. And don't do anything I wouldn't do,'' she added with a chuckle as Matt gently pulled Maude Ann into the front passenger seat of the Jeep.

In no time at all, he was around the vehicle and behind the wheel. Ignoring her sputtering, he started the engine, punched the accelerator and took off down the road, sending gravel and dust flying. Disbelieving, Maude Ann twisted around and saw Jane standing in the drive, cheerfully waving goodbye.

Twisting around again, she flopped back in the seat. ''Matt, you have to take me back. I can't do this.''

''Sure you can. It's all arranged. I'm having another checkup this afternoon, but we'll have the rest of the time to ourselves. Anyway, you need this. You haven't had a real day off since I came here.''

''But just look at me. I can't go to Houston like this.''

Matt glanced at her T-shirt and jeans. She certainly didn't bear much resemblance to the dignified professional who testified in court on the children's behalf or twisted the arms of corporate bigwigs and Houston's old guard for money. No, she looked like his sweet Maudie, which was a thousand times better. ''You look fine to me. But don't worry, Jane packed you a bag. It's in the back.''

With a sigh, Maude Ann accepted defeat. It was a conspiracy, pure and simple. She hadn't stood a chance. ''At least tell me we'll be back before the kids get home from school.''

''Nope. Sunday afternoon.''

''*Sunday!* Are you *crazy?* Jane can't handle the kids alone all weekend.''

''Relax. It's all taken care of. J.T. called this morning while you were upstairs with the kids. Wanted to know if it was all right if he came out for the weekend.'' Matt glanced at her out of the corner of his eye. For all its brevity, the look oozed hard satisfaction. ''I told him sure.''

"Matt! That's terrible! I'm sure he doesn't expect to be left saddled with the children with only Jane to help."

"The guy claims he wants to help with the kids, so let him."

"Well, it's unfair, and I'm calling him." She snatched up the car phone, only to discover it was dead.

Matt darted her smug look. "Been disconnected ever since I was shot. Relax. J.T. will be fine. He may be a pain in the rear, but like you said, he's good with the kids."

"I'm still calling as soon as we get to a working telephone."

Despite her imperious tone, deep down, Maude Ann was thrilled that Matt had gone to so much trouble to be alone with her. Despite her fierce independence, she had to admit it was kind of exciting to be abducted by the man you loved.

"Fine. You can call from my place," Matt replied, but he didn't seem in the least concerned.

His place turned out to be a charming two-story town house off Dairy Ashford Road in northwest Houston. Along one side at the back, the house was connected to the garage by a utility room, but after parking, they walked through the adjacent small patio and entered through the back door.

Maude Ann was curious to see Matt's home, and as he led her through the surprisingly spacious town house, she was surprised. Not only was the place neat and clean, it was tastefully decorated in a mix of stately antiques and homey modern pieces. The color scheme of subdued pumpkin, rust and silvery gray with touches of navy was masculine without being drab. The overall look was classy. Which, when she thought about it, suited Matt to a T.

The downstairs of the house was made up of a large living/dining-room combination, a kitchen and breakfast nook, a powder room and a den, from which the stairs rose.

Upstairs were three bedrooms, one of which was apparently used as an office/exercise room, and two baths.

It struck her as they were finishing the tour in Matt's bedroom that after being closed up for months, the place should be stuffy and everything covered with a layer of dust, but it wasn't. The air-conditioning hummed, pumping out cool, fresh air, and there wasn't a particle of dust in sight.

"I would have thought you'd have the place closed up while you were at the haven," she said, running her finger along the glossy surface of his Victorian-era chifforobe.

"It was. I called Patty a few days ago. She and Hank have a key to the place. She came over yesterday and gave it a cleaning and brought in some food."

Maude Ann turned and raised an eyebrow at him. "You've been planning this for days, haven't you?"

"That's right." He walked slowly toward her, his gaze never wavering, and her heart began to pound. "I wanted to see you in my home," he said in a low, gravelly voice. "In my bed."

Stopping in front of her, he slipped his arms around her waist and pulled her close, his sizzling gaze searing her. "I wanted to smell you on my sheets."

The words, the intensity with which he uttered them, the dark flush of passion on his face, tugged at her heartstrings, even as something deep in her feminine core quickened and burst into flame. To be desired that much was a glorious thing that no woman could resist. Maude Ann didn't even try.

She wrapped her arms around his neck, and when he lowered his head, she met the kiss with a fiery passion that matched his.

Lips rocked, rubbed, nibbled. Tongues stroked and dueled. Teeth nipped. All the while their hands roamed. Soon, it wasn't enough, and garments dropped to the floor, first Maude Ann's T-shirt and bra, then Matt's shirt.

He bent and kissed and suckled first one nipple, then the other, as Maude Ann moaned and dug her fingernails into his shoulders. He kissed the tender skin between her breasts, drew tiny wet circles there with the tip of his tongue.

Maude Ann retaliated by running her fingers through the hair on his chest until she found his nipples. She toyed with the tiny pebbles, then lightly scraped them with her thumbnail, smiling when Matt shuddered and groaned.

"Dr. Edwards, you're a shameless wanton and a tease," he growled, sweeping her up in his arms and heading for the bed. Maude Ann's husky laugh rang out, then turned to a squeal when he tossed her onto the mattress.

She bounced once, then sank into the softness. Lying there in her faded jeans, bare from the waist up, she stretched luxuriously and gave him a sultry look from beneath half-closed eyelids as he began to peel out of the rest of his clothes. "I know. Aren't you glad?"

Something flared in Matt's eyes, and he paused in the act of unzipping his jeans. Then he flew into action, shucking his clothes and stripping Maude Ann of hers in record time. "Damn right, I am," he growled as he lay down beside her and gathered her close.

"Mmm. How glad?" she murmured, running her hand down his chest, then his flat abdomen, then lower still.

Matt closed his eyes and absorbed the pleasure with a low moan. Slowly he opened them again and glided his hand down her body, mimicking her action. "Why don't I show you…"

Maude Ann's eyes fluttered open, closed, then open again. Finally she focused on the unfamiliar navy-and-rust-striped chair by the window and sat up in bed with a start. Then she remembered.

Matt's side of the bed was rumpled and empty. Hearing no sound from the bathroom, she assumed he had gone downstairs. With a sigh, she lay back on the pillow, put her arms over her head and indulged in a long, sinuous stretch, smiling smugly.

A glance at her watch gave her a shock. It was after one in the afternoon! She couldn't believe she'd slept so long.

Actually, it wasn't like her to fall asleep in the middle of the day at all, even if she *had* just experienced the most beautiful lovemaking of all time. She felt positively decadent. A slow, Cheshire-cat grin curved her mouth, and she stretched again.

Turning her head, she spotted the note propped against the adjacent pillow. She picked it up and read Matt's small, neat handwriting.

Gone for my checkup. Didn't have the heart to wake you. Be back as soon as I can.

Love,
Matt

Smiling, she left the bed and headed for the shower. When she emerged again, wrapped in a towel, she glanced at the small bag Jean had packed for her. Ignoring it, she opted, instead, to wear one of Matt's white dress shirts.

After making the bed, she went downstairs and made herself a sandwich for lunch. When she'd eaten, she spent the next couple of hours wandering from room to room, examining the decor more closely, perusing the framed prints on the walls and the small pieces of Western sculpture scattered throughout the house.

Clouds had begun to roll in shortly after she awoke, and

by midafternoon, when she finished her inspection, the sky had turned so dark the streetlights came on. Lightning flashed almost continuously and thunder rumbled. Then the rains came in typical Gulf-coast fashion, falling fast and heavy. Standing at the patio door in Matt's den looking out was like trying to see through a waterfall.

By four o'clock the storm hadn't abated. Maude Ann was beginning to worry when Matt called.

"This is taking longer than I thought. I probably won't get out of here for another hour. I was going to take you out tonight, but with this storm, that doesn't seem like such a good idea now."

"You're right. This is definitely a night to relax by the fire. I don't mind staying in. I would prefer to, actually."

"Good. I was hoping you'd say that. How about I pick up Chinese food on my way home?"

"Mmm, sounds wonderful."

"Great. I'll be there as soon as I can. But don't worry if it takes me a while. With this storm, there's bound to be some street flooding."

At five after six the lights went out. Matt still hadn't returned, so Maude Ann conducted a groping search in the dark for candles. Knowing Matt's penchant for organization, she knew they had to be either in the kitchen or utility room. She located them in the latter, along with a box of matches.

Thirty minutes later, Matt arrived. "Maude Ann, I'm home. Where are—"

Carrying a rain-spotted sack in each arm, he came to an abrupt halt in the middle of the den and stared. Maude Ann stood at the top of the stairs, wearing only his shirt and a smile. Outside, thunder cracked and rolled. Inside, flickering candlelight cast wavering shadows against the wall and filled the room with a romantic golden glow.

"What are you wearing beneath that shirt?"

Maude's Ann's smile grew sultry, and even in the faint light, she could see his face darken with desire.

Slowly, never taking his eyes from hers, he set the sacks down on the coffee table and started up the stairs.

Later—much later—they ate reheated Chinese food.

The rain continued all weekend, trapping them in the house, but Maude Ann didn't care. As far as she was concerned, the weekend could not have been better, an idyllic three days that she knew would remained etched in her memory forever.

She and Matt made love and talked and made love again. They watched movies, they read the paper together, they shared cooking and cleanup chores. They teased and laughed.

At times, when they told each other about their childhoods, they were nostalgic, even sad when they spoke of their respective deceased parents, whom they had loved dearly.

Matt told her about growing up in a family where police work was a tradition. "I think Dad pinned a badge on my shirt the day they adopted me," he said with a chuckle.

"But what about what *you* wanted? I mean, it seems as though you weren't given a choice, that your career was chosen for you. Didn't you ever have a desire to do something else?" she probed cautiously.

"Not really. When I was about seven, I dreamed of becoming a jet pilot someday, but what kid hasn't? I don't regret making my dad happy. Being a cop is honest work, and it's necessary."

"Yes, but, say, for the sake of argument, you couldn't be a policeman," she said, ignoring his quick frown. "What would you choose to do?" It was touchy territory she was venturing into, but she hoped to open his mind to other possibilities. At the very least, to plant a seed.

''I don't know. Something that would keep me outdoors, I guess.''

No matter how she probed, she couldn't get anything more definitive than that out of him, but it was a start. She hoped.

They talked about politics, philosophy, movies, books and religion. They argued good-naturedly over which team would win the Super Bowl and who was the greatest quarterback of all time. They discussed everything—except the future.

As it turned out, Jane could have saved herself the trouble of packing clothes for Maude Ann. The only thing she wore all weekend were Matt's shirts. Or nothing at all.

It was a magical three days, and Maude Ann felt relaxed and happy as they drove home Sunday afternoon in the drizzling rain. When they stopped in the driveway and the children ran out to meet them, her world seemed complete.

Chapter Fourteen

"C'mon, kids. That's enough swimming for one day."

Tyrone surfaced from a dive and wiped his streaming face. "Aw, Matt, do we gotta quit now? We just got here."

"Yeah, we're having fun," Yolanda chimed in.

"We wanna swim some more," Debbie, Jennifer and Timothy all shouted in unison.

"No arguments. Haul your little butts out of there and let's go. It's half a mile to the lodge. I don't know about you bunch, but I don't want to walk through the woods in the dark."

That got them moving. They grumbled and sent him pouting looks and dawdled as much as they dared, but they waded out of the water. Matt tossed each child a towel and prodded them to gather their things and get moving.

Leading the way down the path, he grimaced, imagining the picture they made. Six months ago, he'd been a hard-boiled detective chasing down thieves and murderers. Now here he was playing baby-sitter and swimming instructor and marching through the woods with a troop of bedraggled kids trudging in his wake like a string of baby ducks following their mother. Some tough cop you are, Dolan.

When they emerged from the woods, he wasn't pleased to see J.T.'s car parked in the drive in front of the lodge.

He scowled. He'd thought, after last weekend, they wouldn't see much of Conway in the future, but there he sat on the front veranda with Maude Ann, sipping lemonade like the lord of the manor.

Making no attempt to hide his annoyance, Matt fixed the reporter with a scowl and climbed the front steps. "You again?"

"Ma-att," Maude Ann scolded.

J.T. grinned. "I thought you might need a baby-sitter."

"We'll call you if we do."

"Pay no attention to him, J.T. The kids and I are glad you're here." The look she shot Matt was meant to be reproving, but the effect was ruined by the laughter in her eyes. That was the trouble with Maude Ann. It didn't do one whit of good to let his jealousy show. She merely laughed at him when he did.

He shot a look at the children. "You kids go take a bath before dinner."

"Why?" Tyrone immediately challenged. "We're not dirty. We've been swimming."

There followed a brief debate about the relative merits of creek water versus soap and water from the tap, but Tyrone remained unconvinced, and in the end Matt pulled rank. "All right, that's it. No more arguing. I'm bigger, stronger and meaner, and I say you're taking a bath. So scoot."

"Now there was a masterful bit of child psychology,"

J.T. drawled as the kids stomped inside. "Why didn't you just get out a whip and a chair?"

"It worked, didn't it?"

Switching his attention to Maude Ann, Matt bent over her until they were eye to eye. "Hi, sweetheart. How'd it go?"

She smiled back at him, her eyes lighting with excitement. "Great. I got the grant."

"Good for you." He gave her a kiss, deliberately lingering over it, mainly because it gave him pleasure, but also to needle the other man.

Matt's swim trunks were still damp, so when the kiss ended, rather than join Maude Ann on the love seat, he sat down on the railing and looked at J.T. again. "I suppose you think you can handle the kids better?"

"I don't suppose, I kno—" J.T. froze. He sat forward and stared at Matt's chest. "Where the hell did you get that?"

"What?" Matt hadn't bothered to button up his shirt when he'd put it on after swimming, and he glanced down and saw the medallion piece nestled in his chest hair. "This?"

"Yes. Where'd you get it?"

Narrowing his eyes, Matt closed his fist around the chunk of silver and fired back, "What business is it of yours where I got it?"

"Because I have one similar to it." J.T. reached inside the collar of his shirt and pulled out a chain. Dangling from it was a piece of a silver disk. "This was left to me by my natural mother when she gave me up for adoption."

"So was mine." Stunned, Matt looked down at the medallion piece in his hand, then at the one dangling from J.T.'s.

J.T. did the same. "When's your birthday?"

"February sixth."

"So is mine. How old are you?"

"Thirty-four."

"Me, too. I was born at St. Joseph's Hospital in Houston at ten after seven in the morning. How about you?"

Matt felt the hair on the back of his neck stand on end. "I was born at 6:45 a.m. at St. Joseph's."

For an interminable time he and J.T. stood unmoving, staring at each other. Matt's chest was so tight it felt as though it was being squeezed in a vice.

Maude Ann looked from one man to the other, her mouth agape. Abruptly, J.T. whipped the chain off over his head and walked up to Matt. "Let me see that."

Too stunned to refuse, Matt took off the piece of silver and handed it to him. J.T. glanced at Matt, then at Maude Ann, then held his own jagged medallion piece up to Matt's.

The silver fragments fit together like two pieces of a puzzle, forming two-thirds of a disk.

Maude Ann sucked in an audible breath. They all stared at the joined pieces of silver, and for the space of several heartbeats no one made a sound. Slowly, the men's gazes rose and met. "Well, I'll be damned," J.T. whispered.

Matt could not have agreed more, but the power of speech had deserted him. He felt as though he'd been pole-axed.

Maude Ann sprang to her feet. "For heaven's sake! Somebody say *something!* Don't you two realize what this means?"

"Yeah, we realize." J.T. aimed a wry smile at Matt. "It appears, Detective Dolan, that you and I are brothers."

"It looks that way."

"Now ain't that a kick in the head?"

Maude Ann glared at first one man then the other, her

expression growing more stupefied and outraged by the second. "That's *it?* That's all you have to say to each other? What is the *matter* with you two? If I had just found out that I had a sister I didn't know existed—a *twin* sister, at that—I'd be so excited I'd be turning cartwheels, for heaven's sake! You two just sit there like a couple of lumps!"

"Triplets."

"What?" She blinked at the nonsequitur.

"My guess is we're two of a set of triplets, not twins." Matt nodded toward the pieces of silver that J.T. still held fitted together. "From the looks of that, I think it's safe to assume that we have another sibling somewhere."

"He's right. There's still a third of the medallion missing. Nice work, Detective."

"Triplets?" Maude Ann said in a dazed voice, and sank back down on the love seat.

"Can you make out what's etched on it?"

J.T. studied first one side of the pieces, then the other. "Nope. Just 'Your' followed by a word that begins with 'h-e-r-i.' Under that are three lines that look like an address. The first line is 'The R-o' something. The next is 'P.O. B-o-' something. Under that is 'C-l-e' something." He turned the two pieces over. "The markings on the other side look like some sort of symbol."

Shaking his head, he handed both pieces to Matt so that he could examine them. "Looks to me like the medallion was deliberately cut so that you couldn't make out the message unless all three pieces were together."

"Could be. The question is, why did our mother do that?"

"Maybe she hoped we'd get curious about the message and try to find the rest someday. Which means she wanted us to find one another."

"If that were the case, why did she give us away to three separate families?"

"She probably didn't have any choice," Maude Ann said.

"Thirty-two years ago, that was common practice of adoption agencies. There was rarely, if ever, any attempt made to keep multiples together. I suppose the thinking at the time was, rather than burden one family with three babies, they would make three families happy with one baby each. Nowadays, we understand the close bond between multiples, even fraternals, which you and J.T. obviously are, and every effort is made to keep them together.

"Maybe you're right, J.T. Maybe she split the medallion among the three of you in the hope that you would find one another again someday. That may have been her only chance of reuniting you."

"Maybe," Matt said, but he had his doubts. He thought over what Maude Ann had just said about him and J.T. having a close bond, but he couldn't imagine it, even if they had shared the same womb and the first two years of life together.

Standing at the railing, J.T. stared out across the lawn at the lake, his face for once pensive. "Do you have any memories of before? When we were still with her?"

Matt didn't have to asked who "her" was. "Only in the form of dreams. How about you?"

"Little flashes now and then. A face. The sound of a voice. Nothing really clear. I do remember sharing a bed with other kids, though. Which, of course, I now know was you and our other sib."

The comment jarred Matt. Suddenly the memory surfaced in his mind's eye, sharp and vivid as a photograph. "A big, iron double bed, right? With railings along the sides that she'd added so we wouldn't fall off. And there was a red-white-and-blue quilt with a big star in the middle.''

"So you remember it, too?"

"Not until just now when you mentioned it."

They were silent for a bit, then J.T. asked, "Well, where do we go from here?"

"I don't know." Matt had been wondering the same thing, but he didn't have an answer. The revelations of the past few minutes had knocked him for a loop. To find out that he had two siblings was mind-boggling. That one of them was J. T. Conway was almost more than he could take in.

"Isn't it obvious?" Maude Ann sent both men a disbelieving look. "You have to get to know each other."

"Sweetheart, we've known each other for over ten years."

"As acquaintances. You don't know each other as family. You need to talk about your childhoods and other life-shaping experiences. Really get to know each other as brothers."

Matt and J.T. exchanged uncomfortable glances.

"And, of course, you need to find your other sibling, also."

Matt frowned. He hadn't gotten as far as thinking about that yet. "Just how are we supposed to do that?"

"I don't know. You're a detective, and J.T. is a reporter. Between the two of you, you ought to be able to think of a way."

"Matt's right." J.T. said. "We don't have much to go on. Just that there's probably a third party out there with the rest of this medallion. We don't even know if it's a brother or a sister. About the only leads we have are our date and place of birth and that he or she was most likely given to an Irish family the same as we were, but we can't even be certain of that. It would be like trying to find the proverbial needle in a haystack.''

"So what? You're just going to do nothing?''

"For now, I think that's probably best.'' Matt cocked an eyebrow at J.T. "What's your opinion?''

"I'm inclined to agree.''

"What! How can you—''

"Maude Ann, don't.'' It was the first time in weeks that Matt had used that harsh tone, and it silenced her instantly. "Look, I know you mean well, but this is something J.T. and I have to work out. Not only am I not sure how we'd go about finding this person, at this point I'm not even sure we should try, or if I even want to try. Hell, it's been enough of a shock to find out that J.T. and I are related. I'm just not ready to further complicate my life.''

"Me, neither,'' J.T. said. "Maybe at some later date, we'll institute a search, but not now. You've got to give us time to absorb this, Maude Ann.''

She was crushed. To her way of thinking, finding a long-lost brother you never knew you had was nothing short of miraculous. Yet these two hadn't even exchanged a handshake. They just continued to eye each other like a couple of wary male wolves.

However, she had no choice but to accept their decision and allow them to work out their relationship in their own way and in their own time.

"Okay, if that's the way you want it. But I still think you're making a mistake.''

As the days passed, Maude Ann became even more convinced of it. The children and Jane were as excited about the turn of events as Maude Ann was, but after the initial shock wore off, Matt and J.T. seemed to retreat from each other.

They exchanged life stories, as she had suggested, but

they were awkward and distant with each other. As she watched them together, it was painfully obvious to Maude Ann that they felt uncomfortable with the change in their relationship and were unsure how to proceed. When she tried to talk to Matt about it, however, he reacted with impatience.

"Dammit, Maude Ann! You expect too much. J.T. and I may have had the same natural parents, but we've led different lives. Besides, the man's been a thorn in my side for over ten years. Now you want us to start acting like brothers? Forget it, Pollyanna. Life just doesn't work that way."

Matt had never spoken to her with such derision, but she tried not to be upset. She told herself that he'd had a shock, that he simply needed time to assimilate and adjust, and he would be fine.

It didn't happen. As the days passed, Matt grew moodier, more remote. He went off by himself for long periods, and when he was with her and the kids, he was preoccupied and abrupt. The children were hurt and disappointed by his behavior, and Maude Ann grew more worried with every passing day.

She could not understand how something that should have been a joyous discovery could cause him so much turmoil. On more than one occasion, she tried to get him to talk about what was bothering him, but he always cut her off, refusing to discuss the matter. One time he was so curt with her she could not overlook his behavior.

That night, for the first time since they had become lovers, Maude Ann did not go to Matt's room. She told herself that they needed a little distance from each other, a cooling-off time. In her heart, though, she was sure that once he realized she wasn't coming, he would storm up the stairs after her and carry her down to his room.

He didn't—not that night, nor the next one, nor the one after that.

On the third day, she didn't see him until late in the afternoon. Jane had just left with Debbie to pick up the children at the bus stop, and for once Maude Ann was alone in the house, or thought she was. She was sitting at her desk in the living room when Matt suddenly appeared in the doorway.

"I need to talk to you, Maude Ann."

His tone and the harsh set of his features sent a chill down her spine, but she put down her pen and smiled. "All right."

He took three steps into the room, then stopped. He looked at her in silence for an unsettlingly long time. "I'm leaving."

The bald announcement felt like a slap, but Maude Ann willed herself to stay calm. "Leaving?"

"Yeah. I talked to Lieutenant Werner this morning. I start back to work in the morning."

Another wave of shock went through her. "But...but you can't. You haven't taken the physical yet."

"Actually, I took it this morning."

"I...I see. You could have told me."

"It wouldn't have changed anything if I had."

"No. I guess not." A terrible trembling started deep inside her. Tears welled up in her eyes, but she blinked furiously to hold them back. "So...you're just going to leave. Just like that. I thought you loved me."

"I do."

"Then how can you leave? How can you just walk away?"

"I don't want to. This is the most difficult thing I've ever done. But dammit, Maudie, I have to get my life back."

"Excuse me? What does that mean?"

"Everything keeps changing. First I got shot, then I came here. Instead of police work, I'm baby-sitting and playing camp counselor."

"I thought you enjoyed that. I thought you cared for the children."

"I did! I do! They're great." He raked a hand through his hair. "Damn, how do I make you understand?"

"Just…say it."

"I don't resent the kids. I love them, and I enjoy spending time with them. That's the trouble—at least, part of it. I enjoy it too much." Too agitated to remain still, he paced to the other side of the room, then swung back. "When Hank and the other guys were here, they filled me in on the status of the cases I'd been working on and what was going on at the precinct. And you know what? I couldn't summon up any interest. None. Zip. Zero." He thumbed his chest and glared at her with something close to panic in his eyes. "*Me!* A guy who lived and breathed police work his whole life. That scared the hell out of me, I can tell you.

"And that's not all. I swore I'd never get serious about a woman. Then I fell in love with you. Hell, I'm so far gone, lately I've started thinking about the future, about commitment, even about adopting these kids. It's crazy!"

Equal parts joy and astonishment shot through Maude Ann. She wanted to rush over and put her arms around him and tell him they could work things out somehow, but she could see how upset he was and that he wasn't finished.

"Then, out of the blue, I get blindsided with this business with J.T. It's too much. Everything is out of control." His eyes pleaded with her to understand. "I have to get my life back, Maude Ann."

She stared at him, her heart slowly breaking. No matter

what she said or did, she was going to lose him. And the
devil of it was, she couldn't even work up much anger,
because now she understood a lot of things.

As a child, Matt had had his secure world snatched away
from him when his mother had given him up, and though
he might not consciously remember the event and he'd had
a good life with the Dolans, the event had left its mark on
him. It explained why he was so orderly and meticulous—
about his work, his personal habits, everything he did.
Those were things he could control.

Maude Ann had only one card left, and she played it.
"Was the life you had really so wonderful? Better than
what you've found here?"

"Maybe not, but it was the life I'd chosen for myself
and I was comfortable in it. It worked for me." He paced
and raked his hand through his hair again. "Look, I don't
know why we're even having this conversation. We both
knew this day was coming. I have to go back. I'm a policeman. It's what I am."

She shot out of the chair and stood shaking uncontrollably, her hands fisted at her sides. "No! It's what you *do*.
What you *choose* to do. Don't you see? You have other
options. Just because you chose one career, one way of life,
doesn't mean you can't change your mind. Life is all about
change, Matt."

"Please, Maude Ann. Don't make this more difficult
than it already is. I've made up my mind."

Her eyes shimmered with reproach. So did her voice.
"You're just going to walk away, then? From me, from
the children, from what we have?"

"I have to."

Defeat weighed on her shoulders like a lead cape. A sob
rose in her tight throat, but she swallowed it down and
fought to control her quivering mouth. She would not beg,

she vowed. She would not. He had made his choice. "I see. When will you go?"

"I've already loaded my things in the car. I just wanted to tell you goodbye."

"You're leaving *now?*" Panic fluttered in her chest. "But what about the children? Aren't you going to tell them goodbye?"

"I think it's better if I don't." He looked at her somberly, his eyes filled with regret. "Goodbye, Maudie."

"No, wait! Matt, come back," she cried, but he left the room and strode out the front door. Maude Ann rushed after him. By the time she reached the veranda he was opening the door of his Jeep. "Matt, please, wait until the children get here."

He looked at her over the top of his car and started to shake his head, but the matter was taken out of his hands when Jane drove up with the children.

They bailed out of the van, Tyrone in the lead, as usual. And, as usual at the end of a schoolday, he was a mess, his shirttail hanging out, tennis shoes untied, a giant splotch of something red on the front of his shirt, papers sticking out of his unzipped backpack.

He spotted Matt and raced over to him, lugging the backpack by a strap. "Hey, Matt, where you goin'?"

"Uh…" Matt looked at Maude Ann, but she wrapped her arms tightly around her middle and lifted her chin.

If he wanted to be a coward and run away just because he couldn't accept change, then let him. But he'd get no help from her.

"I'm going to Houston."

"Can I go, too?"

"I'm afraid not."

"Ah, shoot."

By this time the other children had reached Matt, and the younger ones began clamoring for his attention.

"I got an A on my spelling test today," Jennifer said shyly.

"Hey, Matt, look at the picture I drawed today," Timothy said, waving a crayon drawing in the air.

Debbie tugged insistently on the leg of Matt's jeans. "If you ith goin' thomwhere, you gots to give me a bye-bye kith first."

Not one to be sidelined Tyrone elbowed the others aside and asked, "When you gonna get back?"

Again, Matt glanced at Maude Ann, but except for the tears streaming down her face, her expression remained the same.

"I'm not coming back. I'm going home. Tomorrow morning I go back to work."

Tyrone looked as if Matt had punched him in the face.

"But you *gots* to come back," Debbie wailed, and burst into tears.

Timothy and Jennifer, the most insecure of the group, hung their heads and began to whimper. Refusing to look at Matt, Yolanda took their hands and led them up the steps. When they reached Maude Ann, all three children buried their faces against her and began to cry.

Debbie wrapped her arms around Matt's leg and clung to him like a monkey, pleading, "Don't go! Don't go! Don't go!"

Matt tried to free himself, but the little girl hung on tenaciously. In the end, Jane had to peel the child off him. After aiming a reproachful look at Matt, she carried the little girl to the veranda to join Maude Ann and the others. Every step of the way, Debbie cried pitifully and strained toward Matt with her arms outstretched.

That left only Tyrone. The boy stared at him with accusing eyes. "I shoulda known you'd run out on us."

Matt grimaced. "Look, Tyrone, I *have* to go. It's my job."

"Go on, then! Get outta here, pig!" he shouted furiously. Anger contorted his face, but he couldn't stop his mouth from quivering or hide the hurt in his eyes or staunch the tears that overflowed. He scrubbed at them furiously, but still they streamed down his cheeks in an unending flood. "I don't need you! I *hate* you, you dirty, rotten pig! I *hate* you!"

The last came out on a choked sob, and he whirled around and ran blindly for the veranda and Maude Ann.

Grim-faced, Matt watched him over the top of the car. Briefly, his gaze met Maude Ann's. Then, with a curse, he slammed into the Jeep and took off.

Through her tears, Maude Ann watched the vehicle disappear around the bend in the road and felt her heart cleave in two. Matt was gone. She had lost him.

The children clung to her, wetting her shirt and the top of her jeans with their tears, but she didn't care. She remained where she was, her arms around the huddled group and let them cry out their grief and hurt and confusion while she cried out hers.

Jane stood beside them, alternately patting shaking shoulders and dabbing her own eyes with a tissue.

It was almost five minutes before the children were calm enough to let go of Maude Ann. Forcing her own hurt aside, she dried their tears, administered hugs and kisses and pitifully inadequate words of reassurance. Then, knowing they had to talk about Matt's desertion and work through the pain, she urged everyone inside and into the living room.

They had barely settled when they heard a car coming down the road.

Tyrone's woebegone expression vanished and his eyes lit up. "Maybe Matt changed his mind."

With the resilience of the very young, the other children let out whoops of joy, bolted to their feet and rushed to the window, only to sag with disappointment when the unfamiliar car came around the bend. It was a shabby-looking older vehicle. One fender was missing entirely, and its faded blue paint was now blotched with rust.

"Who's that?" Tyrone asked in a querulous voice as the old wreck screeched to a halt in the drive. The question had barely left his lips when a man jumped out and headed for the front steps with long, furious strides.

Maude Ann recognized him before he gained the veranda. Her heart lurched when she saw he had a gun in his hand. "Oh, my Lord, no!"

Suddenly Timothy started whimpering and backing away from the window. The terror in the boy's eyes was chilling.

"Jane, go lock the back door! I'll get the front! Hurry!" Maude Ann raced from the room with Jane on her heels, but they had barely taken two steps into the entry when the front door crashed open and the wild-eyed man charged inside.

Spotting Maude Ann, he halted, and his eyes narrowed with murderous hatred. "I knew I'd find you, bitch."

Maude Ann's insides were trembling, but she squared her shoulders and stood her ground. "What are you doing here, Mr. Perkins? Aren't you supposed to be in prison?"

Holding one hand behind her, she motioned for Jane to go back into the living room with the kids.

"Whaddaya think? I busted out and came for my son. I seen that story in the newspaper about this place. You sitting there all smug on the porch, coddling my boy, making a little wuss outta him. Didja think just 'cause the picture didn't show his face I wouldn't recognize 'im? I seen the birthmark on his arm. For weeks now, I been searching every lake around this part of the state, looking for this place. And now I found you.''

''That birthmark, as you call it, is a scar from one of many wounds you inflicted on Timothy. Which is why you and your wife no longer have custody of him.''

He advanced a step, his face twisting in a feral snarl. ''If you hadn't'a testified in court, telling the judge all them lies 'bout me'n my old lady, it never woulda happened.''

Maude Ann smelled his whiskey breath and saw that his pupils were so dilated the irises were merely a thin ring of gray around them. The man was not only drunk, he was stoned out of his mind. And dangerous.

Maude Ann's pulse skittered, but she raised her chin another notch. ''I simply told the truth, and you know it, Mr. Perkins.''

''Don't matter none. Ain't you or no snooty judge or nobody else taking my kid away from me. He's mine to do with as I see fit.'' He looked over her shoulder into the living room. ''I hear sniveling. He must be in there. Timmy!''

Maude Ann sidestepped and tried to block the doorway, but he snapped, ''Get outta my way, bitch!'' and shoved her so hard she stumbled back into the room and nearly fell.

All the kids huddled around Jane, their faces white with terror. Timothy sobbed quietly.

''Timmy, shut up that bawlin' and get over here! You're coming with me.''

''No! You're not taking this child!'' Maude Ann stepped in front of the boy, then cried out when Jim Perkins grabbed her hair and jerked her head back. Needles of pain stung her scalp and tears sprang to her eyes.

''You leave her alone!'' Tyrone cried. He launched himself at Perkins, but Jane intercepted him when the man raised his hand to the child.

Clutching Tyrone tightly, Jane glared at the man. "You sorry no-good piece of trash."

"Shut up, old woman, or you'll be sorry."

He stuck his face close to Maude Ann's, and the foulness of his breath made her stomach roil. "I'm taking my boy. But first I'm gonna make sure you never steal nobody's kid again." He shoved the gun into her stomach and grinned maliciously.

"No! Please, not in front of the children," she begged.

He glanced at the kids clinging to Jane and crying hysterically. "You're right. Too many witnesses. We'll take a little walk."

"Everybody, out on the porch," he ordered, motioning with the gun for Jane and the kids to go first. "And no funny business. Remember, I got a gun in her back."

He swung Maude Ann around by her hair and shoved her toward the door so hard she fell to her knees. "Get up, bitch."

He grabbed her hair again, and she cried out when he used it to haul her to her feet.

On the way to the door he spotted the cell phone on the coffee table. Picking it up, he shot her a taunting grin. "I'll just take this. You won't be needing it. Now move."

"Where are you taking her? What're you going to do?" Jane demanded as he pushed Maude Ann past the group on the veranda and down the steps.

"Shut up! And you bunch stay put right there where I can see you."

Yanking on Maude Ann's hair, he kept her neck arched back at a painful angle and shoved and prodded her to his car. Keeping an wary eye on Jane and the kids, he got a roll of duct tape from the car trunk and used it to bind her wrists behind her back. Then, once again, he tugged her along by her hair over to the van and slashed all four tires with the hunting knife he wore in a scabbard on his belt.

Pausing, he eyed the utility wires going into the lodge. He waved his gun at the terrified group on the porch. "Timmy, go get in the car."

The boy whimpered and clung more tightly to Jane, but when his father shouted, "Now, you snivelin' little brat!" he released her and raced to obey, crying every step of the way.

Maude Ann wanted to object, but she knew doing so would only earn her more pain and wouldn't help Timothy at all.

"The rest of you stay right there. I'm warning you, if I have to hunt you down when I get back, you'll regret it. And don't get any ideas about using another phone to call for help, 'cause I'm cutting the wire." He poked the gun barrel into Maude Ann's back and prodded her around the side of the lodge, stopping at the back to cut the phone wire, then shoved her toward the woods.

Tears streamed down Maude Ann's face as they followed the winding path through the trees. Her knees were so wobbly she stumbled several times, earning herself vicious hair pulls and jabs with the gun barrel. She was so scared she barely felt the pain. This filthy, drug-crazed sadist was going to extract his revenge on her. He'd sworn in court when she'd testified at his trial that someday he would find her and kill her, and now he was going to make good his threat.

"Where does this path go?" Jim Perkins demanded, giving her hair another cruel pull.

Maude Ann gasped at the stinging pain in her scalp, and fresh tears stung her eyes, but she would not let herself cry out. "T-to a small cl-clearing."

"Good. That'll do."

The statement sent a chill down her spine.

The clearing was almost half a mile from the lodge, usually a good ten- to fifteen-minute walk, but they seemed to reach it in a fraction of that time.

"Well, now, ain't this nice," Perkins said, prodding her into the middle of the open area.

"Mr. Perkins, stop and think what you're doing. You'll never get away with this. The police will find you and you'll go to jail for the rest of your life. Is that what you want?"

"Shut up! And get down on your knees."

She had no choice. Her wobbly knees gave way beneath her when he pushed down on her shoulder.

"You're making a terrible mistake."

"I said *shut up!*"

Maude Ann yelped, then gagged, when he jerked her head back and stuffed a filthy rag into her mouth.

Her head fell forward and Perkins laughed, and she felt the cold metal of the gun barrel against the back of her head. "Say your prayers, bitch."

Trembling uncontrollably, Maude Ann squeezed her eyes shut and bowed her head. *Oh, Matt. Where are you?*

Chapter Fifteen

Matt drove the two-mile dirt road to the highway like a bat out of hell, sliding around the curves, ignoring the potholes and trailing a plume of dust that looked like a giant rooster tail. He was so upset he barely noticed the rusty old heap that passed him, heading toward the lodge. It was probably just someone going to rent one of John's skiffs for the day.

He knew he should have left before the kids got back. It was bad enough having to tell Maude Ann goodbye without facing all those hurt little faces.

Remembering, he muttered a curse. He hadn't expected the kids to be so upset. There had been no consoling them. He'd had no choice but to just get in his car and go.

Dammit, he hadn't done anything wrong. He'd been honest with Maude Ann. He'd made it clear from the start that he couldn't make any promises. They had no ties on him—

not Maudie, not Tyrone, not any of them. He had nothing to feel guilty about.

He brought the car to a stop at the highway intersection. There were no cars coming from either direction, but he just sat there, gripping the steering wheel so tightly his knuckles showed white. After a moment he rested his forehead on top of the steering wheel and closed his eyes.

But he did feel guilty. He felt like the lowest kind of louse. No matter how hard he tried, he couldn't erase from his mind the picture of Maude Ann and the kids clinging to one another, staring after him with tears streaming down their cheeks. The scene would stay with him for the rest of his days.

The hell of it was, he was going to miss them as much as they missed him. He missed them already.

Matt thought about his life before he'd been shot, the long hours, the violence and unspeakable horrors he'd seen, coming home to his empty town house. There had been women, but at most those times had amounted to the appeasement of a physical need and a few hours of companionship. So maybe he hadn't been happy, exactly, but he'd been content. Surely he would be again.

Then he thought about Maude Ann and her warmth, her giving spirit, that earthy sexiness she exuded, the love she lavished on him, and on everyone who mattered to her. He thought about the kids who were slowly blossoming under her care, about the laughter and the noisy chaos, about the skinned knees and the tears, the happiness, the affection, the sense of belonging, and the sheer joy of being alive that Maude Ann brought to everything she did, everything she touched. And he thought about how much he loved her, how she filled his heart and all the empty places in his soul.

Matt raised his head. He stared straight ahead at the pine

forest on the other side of the highway and tried to imagine his life without Maude Ann.

After a moment, his mouth folded into a firm line, and he turned the Jeep around and floored the accelerator.

He drove back to the lodge with even more urgency than when he'd left, all the while going over in his mind what he'd say to Maude Ann. He had hurt her deeply. He wouldn't blame her if she refused to take him back, but he intended to do everything he could to convince her. Hell, he'd get down on his knees and beg, if he had to.

When he drove around the last curve, pandemonium greeted him. "What the devil?"

Jane, Jennifer, Yolanda and Debbie stood in the road, jumping up and down and frantically waving their arms at him. He barely had time to screech to a stop before hitting them. When he got a good look at their faces, his gut clenched.

He was out of the Jeep in a flash. "What is it? What's wrong?" His gaze shot past Jane to the piece of junk in the drive. "What's Timothy doing in that car?"

"Matt! Thank God you came back!" Jane cried, grabbing his hands. He could feel her trembling. "Timothy's father burst in on us right after you left. He's going to take the boy," she sobbed.

Matt's gaze darted again to the old car. "Like hell he is. Where is he?"

"He took Maude Ann into the woods. Oh, Lordy, Matt, he has a gun! He means to kill her!"

Icy fear shot through Matt, but the red-hot rage that followed galvanized him into action. "Have you called 911?" he demanded, climbing back into the Jeep.

"We couldn't. He took the cell phone and cut the telephone line to the lodge."

Damn. And his car phone was still out of operation. Matt

quickly unlocked the glove box and removed his service revolver and a pair of handcuffs, hooking the latter on a belt loop of his jeans. "Which trail did he take?"

"The one to the clearing. But wait, Matt, that's not all!" Jane cried, trotting along beside him. The children scrambled after them. "As soon as Perkins disappeared into the woods with Maude Ann, Tyrone took off after them."

Matt halted. *"What?"*

Jane wrung her hands. "I couldn't stop him, Matt. I swear, I don't know what that child thinks he can do. He's going to get himself killed, too. That Perkins is a mean one, and I think he's high on something. He'd just as soon kill a child and a woman as step on an ant."

"All right, listen to me. You and the kids go get on the houseboat. Take it out of the cove as quickly as you can. When you get out into the lake, head for Brown's Marina and call the sheriff."

"The houseboat?" Jane paled. "Y-you want me to go out on the lake in a boat? I…I can't."

"Yes, you can. I know you're afraid of water, but it's up to you to keep these kids safe. A boat is the only way to get away from here, other than my car, but if Perkins hurts Maude Ann or Tyrone before I get to them, I'm going to need it."

"But…I don't know anything about boats."

"I do!" Yolanda said. "I can handle it, Matt. You showed me how."

"Good girl. Now get Timothy and hightail it down to the pier. Hurry!"

Before he'd finished speaking, Matt took off running. He raced around the lodge and across the backyard, skirting around the toolshed and garden, dodging trees and leaping over the kids' toys. Driven by fear, he ran flat-out, straining for all he was worth, his feet pounding the narrow path in rhythm with his thudding heart. Dear God, please let them be all right, he prayed. Don't let that slimeball hurt them. Please.

He was almost to the clearing when he heard the shot.

Matt's heart leapt into his throat. Then he heard Tyrone's shouted taunt and his panic eased fractionally.

It took every ounce of self-discipline he possessed not to charge into the clearing. Instead, he left the trail and crept through the woods to the perimeter. Flattening his back against a tree, Matt held his gun pointed skyward at his right shoulder and cautiously peered around the trunk.

The sight of Maude Ann on her knees in the middle of the clearing filled him with rage. Her hands were taped behind her back, and a cloth of some kind filled her mouth. But what tore at Matt's heart most was her defeated posture. She knelt with her shoulders slumped, her head hung as though all hope was gone. Her glorious hair had fallen forward around her face, leaving her tender nape exposed. That someone had brought this strong, valiant spirit to this was obscene.

Perkins stood a few feet away from her, spinning this way and that and screaming obscenities while trying to get a bead on Tyrone, who, from the shelter of the woods, pelted him with clods and sticks and a few colorful expletives of his own.

"Atta boy, Tyrone," Matt whispered. The kid darted from one tree to another, keeping up the barrage, never giving the gunman an opportunity to turn his attention on Maude Ann. Matt wanted to kiss him.

Tyrone popped out from behind a tree at the two-o'clock position from where Matt crouched. "Hey, stupid!" he hollered at Perkins, and threw a fist-size clod with the accuracy of a major-league pitcher, hitting the creep in the temple as he spun toward him. Perkins cursed and fired, and the bullet splintered a branch just inches above Tyrone's head.

Matt saw red and tore out into the clearing. "Drop the gun, Perkins!"

The man spun and fired, and Matt fell to the ground with a searing pain in his right leg.

"Matt! Matt!" Oblivious to the crazed gunman, Tyrone came screaming out of the woods just as Matt went down.

Perkins turned back and took aim at the boy.

"Go back! Go back!"

In the fall, Matt had dropped his gun, but he hadn't time to find it. He lurched to his feet and threw himself at the man, catching him with a shoulder butt to his kidneys as he fired.

The shot went wild, and Perkins screamed and went down flat on his face. Matt's momentum carried him down with him, and Perkins breath left his lungs in a loud *whoosh* as Matt landed on his back. While the man writhed and wheezed and struggled to suck air into his lungs, Matt pushed up to his knees and cuffed Perkins hands behind his back.

Tyrone skidded to a halt beside Matt. His eyes nearly popped out of his head when he spotted the blood pumping out of Matt's leg. "Oh, *man!* You're hit *bad.*"

"Yeah." Matt rolled off Perkins and pressed his hand to the wound, but blood continued to flow around his fingers. "I need something to tie around this."

"Here, use this!" Without hesitation, Tyrone whipped off the precious Dallas Cowboys T-shirt Matt had given him and handed it over. Tyrone loved that shirt, and his willingness to sacrifice it spoke volumes.

The instant Matt had the shirt tied over his wound he held his arm out to the boy. "Here, help me up. We have to see about Maudie."

Tyrone looked doubtful, but for once he obeyed without arguing. Agony streaked through Matt, but he clenched his jaw and struggled to his feet. Leaning on the boy, he reached down and relieved Perkins of his gun and knife, then hobbled over to Maude Ann.

She had struggled to her feet when Matt went down, but she was so shaken she could barely stand. As soon as he reached her, Matt jerked the filthy rag out of her mouth, hooked his free arm around her and pulled her tightly against his chest. Tyrone held on to both of them.

"Matt, oh, Matt," she sobbed.

"Are you all right?"

Too overcome to speak, she nodded against his chest.

"Thank God. Thank God." With his cheek against the top of her head, he squeezed his eyes shut and repeated the litany over and over.

For a while the three of them stood together in the middle of the clearing, as though isolated in their own world, Matt holding her close with one arm and Tyrone with the other. The boy had his arms wrapped around both adults. After a while, though, Maude Ann stirred and mumbled. "Please. My hands."

"Oh, sweetheart, I'm sorry. Here, Tyrone, take the creep's knife and cut that tape off. And be careful not to cut Miss Maudie."

As soon as she was free, Maude Ann put her arms around Matt's waist. Matt tried to hug her back, but the adrenaline rush that had carried him that far had faded, and loss of blood and shock were catching up with him. He was shaking so hard he could barely stay upright. "S-sorry, love, I..."

"Matt! *Matt!*" Maude Ann screamed and clutched him as he sagged in her arms, but she couldn't support his weight, and she sank to the ground with him.

Tyrone stood over them, his face ashen. "Is he dead?" he asked in a small, frightened voice.

"No!" Maude Ann snapped, but she wasn't sure until she pressed her finger to the side of his neck and felt a faint pulse. "No, he's just passed out."

Across the way, Perkins moaned and tried to sit up. Maude Ann and the boy jumped. She quickly pulled the pistol Matt had taken from him from the waistband of Matt's jeans and aimed it at the man.

"Tyrone, I want you to run as fast as you can to the lodge and tell Jane to take Matt's car and go find a telephone and call 911." She made a mental note to herself to locate Matt's gun when reinforcements arrived.

"Yes ma'am."

J.T. nearly rear-ended the Jeep when he came around the last bend. He slammed on the brakes, cursing. Why on earth was Matt's car sitting in the middle of the road with the driver's door open? He looked beyond the Jeep to the car in the driveway. "Jeez, what a wreck," he murmured. He'd never seen the car at the lodge before, and he wondered who owned it. And why were both driver-side doors standing open on it, too?

J.T. climbed from his car and looked around. Usually the kids came running out whenever he drove up. Where was everybody?

The question had no sooner gone through his mind when Tyrone burst out of the woods near the back corner of the property and came streaking across the side yard toward him, yelling and waving his arms. J.T. ran to meet the boy.

"Mr. Conway! Mr. Conway! M-Matt's been shot!"

"*What!*" J.T. dropped down on one knee before the boy and grasped his shoulders. Winded, Tyrone's chest heaved as he gasped for breath, and he had difficulty speaking. "Matt's been…sh-shot! He's bleedin' real ba-bad."

J.T.'s heart began to club against his ribs. Unconsciously, his hands tightened on the boy's shoulders. "Where is he? Who shot him?"

"T-Timothy's dad. He was gonna…gonna shoot Miz Maudie. They're in…in the c-clearing."

"Timothy's father, too?"

Tyrone nodded. "Matt cuffed 'im 'fore he passed out. Miz Maude, she's h-holding a…gun on him and tryin' to help Matt, too, but that…that Perkins, he's a real bad dude."

J.T. shot to his feet. "Okay, you go in and call 911 and I'll go help Matt and Maude."

"No, wait! We ain't got no phone. Tim's dad cut the wire."

"My cell phone." J.T. plucked the slim phone out of his shirt pocket and flipped it open. "You wait here for the sheriff and the paramedics and take them to the clearing," he instructed, punching in the number as he headed for the woods.

Relaying the information to the 911 operator as he ran down the path, J.T. silently prayed that they would be in time. It seemed to take him forever to reach the clearing, and all the while, a dozen horrifying thoughts ran through his mind. What if he was too late? What if Matt died? What if this Perkins guy somehow slipped out of the cuffs and overpowered Maude Ann? What if he'd already killed them both?

He had almost reached the clearing when he heard the first faint wail of sirens in the distance. Relief poured through him, but it turned to fear again when he heard Maude Ann shout, "Stay down and don't move! I'm warning you, I'll shoot!"

J.T. cursed and turned on more speed. He reached the clearing in time to see the handcuffed man awkwardly climb to his feet. He stood there for a second, sneering at Maude Ann. She was on her knees beside Matt, applying pressure to his wound with one hand and aiming a gun at Perkins with the other.

"You ain't got the guts to shoot me, bitch."

J.T. reached Maude Ann in three long strides and took the gun from her hand.

"Oh, J.T. Thank God you're here," she gasped, before turning all her attention to Matt.

Facing Perkins, J.T. fixed him with a narrow-eyed look and aimed the gun at his chest. "Maudie may be too soft-hearted to shoot you, Perkins, but I'm not. C'mon. Give me an excuse to pull this trigger."

"Who the hell are you?" Perkins blustered.

"I'm the brother of the man you just shot, the guy who is going to blow a hole through your sorry hide if you so much as twitch. Now lie down on your stomach and stay there."

Perkins had sense enough to know he meant business, and obeyed. J.T. dropped to his knees beside Matt, taking a position that kept the prone man in view. "How's he doing?"

"I don't know. He's lost a lot of blood."

He could see that. The cloth she was using to apply pressure was soaked through and blood covered her hands.

Maude Ann's gaze lifted to meet his, and the fear swimming in her eyes made his gut clench. "Oh, J.T., I can't lose him now," she said.

"You won't," he vowed. "We won't. I didn't wait all these years to find out I have brother just to have him die on me. Here, let me do that." J.T. took over from her and applied pressure to the wound in Matt's leg.

The sirens, which had been growing steadily louder, stopped abruptly, and he and Maude Ann exchanged a look of profound relief.

"You hang in there, Matt," J.T. urged in a fierce voice. "Help is on the way."

It was almost nine that evening before Matt was pronounced out of danger. It was later still before all the explanations were made, all the statements were taken and the children reassured and driven back to the lodge by Jane.

After Jane had called the sheriff, the marina owner had given her and the children a ride back to the lodge. They had arrived just as the paramedics emerged from the woods with Matt. Quickly commandeering his Jeep, Jane had loaded the frightened children and followed the ambulance to the hospital.

Now, only Maude Ann and J.T. were left. They stood, one on each side of Matt's bed, waiting for him to wake up. Maude Ann held his hand and stroked it over and over, unable to take her eyes off his beloved face even for an instant.

Finally Matt's eyes fluttered open. His gaze immediately zeroed in on Maude Ann. "Maudie. Are you all right?"

She squeezed his hand and smiled. "I'm fine, thanks to you and Tyrone."

"Perkins?"

"The slimeball's in jail."

At the sound of J.T.'s voice, Matt turned his head and looked at him. "What're you doing here?"

"Where else would I be when my brother has been shot?"

"If it hadn't been for J.T., we might none of us be here. He called for the ambulance, then arrived in the clearing just in time to stop Jim Perkins from getting away,'' Maude Ann informed Matt.

"I was more concerned that he would attack you again,'' J.T. said.

Matt looked at him for a long time, then nodded. "Thanks. I'm indebted to you.''

"Damned right, you are,'' J.T. said, grinning. "And I've figured out how you're going to repay me. I've already filed my story about Perkins's rampage, including my firsthand account of what happened during the time I was there, but when you feel up to it, I want an exclusive interview with you, Maudie, and Jane to get the details of the whole story. Plus, this time, I want follow-up interviews to chronicle your recovery.''

"I might have known.'' Matt shot him a disgruntled look, but after a moment he sighed and said grudgingly, "All right, Conway. I guess I owe you that much.''

Shortly after that, J.T. left, and Maude Ann and Matt were alone for the first time since he had driven away earlier that afternoon. Had it really been only six hours? It seemed to her they had lived a lifetime in those few hours.

They gazed at each other in silence, both profoundly aware of how close they had come to disaster. Maude Ann stroked his hand and said softly, "You came back.''

"Yeah. I had to.''

"If you hadn't…'' She closed her eyes and shuddered.

"Shh.'' He brought her hand to his mouth and placed a warm kiss against her palm. "I did come back. That's all that matters.''

She nodded. "Yes. You're right. Except that you were shot. Matt, I'm so sorry. If you hadn't come to my rescue…''

"I would have lost you, and I couldn't have survived that.'' He looked down at his bandaged leg. "Can you believe it? Perkins's bullet hit just a inch from the first wound. The doctor told me when I woke up in ICU briefly that I can forget about going back to the street."

"Don't listen to him. The doctors said that six months ago and you proved them wrong. You will again."

"Honey, the first bullet did major damage. Sure, I got back enough mobility to pass the physical, but not a hundred percent. There's no way those mangled muscles and tendons are going to come back after a second assault."

"Oh, Matt. I'm so sorry. I feel terrible."

"Don't. I doesn't matter."

"How can you say that after that scene this afternoon? We both know that your job means more to you than anything in the world."

"Not anymore." He smiled at her skeptical expression. "Don't you want to know why I came back?"

"Why?"

"Because when it came down to the wire, I couldn't imagine living without you. I could imagine living without my job, but not you. So you see, I'd already decided to give it up before I took that bullet out in the clearing."

"Oh, Matt."

"I'm not much of a bargain, sweetheart. I don't have a job, and I'll probably have a limp for the rest of my life, and if it's possible, I want to adopt all the kids. But if you'll have me, I promise that I'll love you, and them, until the day I die."

Maude Ann stared at him, not quite able to believe what she was hearing. "Are...are you saying...?"

"I'm asking. Will you marry me, Maude Ann?"

Tears welled up in her eyes and spilled over, one by one. "Oh, Matt," she said in a quavering voice. Too choked up to speak, she leaned forward and touched her mouth to his in a soft, lingering kiss, ripe with promise of love everlasting. When at last she raised her head, she looked deep into his eyes, and her lips curved in a misty smile. "Of course I'll marry you, my darling."

*   *   *   *   *

This August, watch out for the next riveting installment in A FAMILY BOND, *when Ginna Gray's new book,* IN SEARCH OF DREAMS, *comes your way from Silhouette Special Edition.*

Then in September, be on the lookout for this gifted author's exciting debut in MIRA Books with the gripping family saga, THE PRODIGAL DAUGHTER.

You have just read a

Silhouette

Special Edition
book.

Silhouette Special Edition always features incredible authors like Nora Roberts, Sherryl Woods, Christine Rimmer, Lindsay McKenna, Joan Elliott Pickart—and many more!

For compelling romances packed with emotion always choose Silhouette Special Edition.

Silhouette®
Where love comes alive™

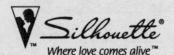

Silhouette®

where love comes alive—online...

Visit the *Author's Alcove*

➢ Find the most complete information anywhere on your favorite Silhouette author.

➢ Try your hand in the Writing Round Robin— contribute a chapter to an online book in the making.

Enter the *Reading Room*

➢ Experience an interactive novel—help determine the fate of a story being created now by one of your favorite authors.

➢ Join one of our reading groups and discuss your favorite book.

Drop into *Shop eHarlequin*

➢ Find the latest releases—read an excerpt or write a review for this month's Silhouette top sellers.

➢ Try out our amazing search feature—tell us your favorite theme, setting or time period and we'll find a book that's perfect for you.

All this and more available at

www.eHarlequin.com
on Women.com Networks

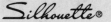

ATTENTION
LINDSAY McKENNA FANS!

Coming in April 2000 from Silhouette Books:

**This special 3-in-1 volume contains the
three exhilarating novels that began the popular
MORGAN'S MERCENARIES series!**

Coming in **July 2000** *from Silhouette Special Edition:*
MAN OF PASSION

Coming in **August 2000** *from Silhouette Books:*
MORGAN'S MERCENARIES:
HEART OF THE WARRIOR
A brand-new, longer-length book!

**Only from Lindsay McKenna and
Silhouette Books.**

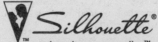

Where love comes alive™